They didn't speak a word. The look in their eyes, the smiles on their faces, and the gentleness of their touch expressed all that was in their hearts. Damien lowered his mouth to Lacey's waiting lips and bestowed a kiss that rocked them both to the depth of their souls. And when they parted, both knew that their relationship would never be the same. Their thoughts once singular, were now plural, to include the other. And their hearts once empty were filled with the possibility of a new love.

LACE

GISELLE CARMICHAEL

Genesis Press Inc.

Indigo Love Stories

An imprint Genesis Press Publishing

Genesis Press, Inc.
P.O. Box 101
Columbus, MS 39703

ISBN: 1-58571-134-9
Manufactured in the United States of America

First Edition

Visit us at www.genesis-press.com
or call at 1-888-Indigo-1

DEDICATION

Lace is dedicated to Eastlake Fire Station #19 in Birmingham, Alabama and Chief I. Brooks for making the community proud. A special dedication is also extended to the men of the Louisiana Native Guard whose story deserves to be told.

CHAPTER 1

The car came out of nowhere. The sound of squealing tires and crunching metal drowned out all other sounds as the world spun out of control through the shattered windshield. Lacey Avery fought with the steering wheel to bring the car under control, but the careening vehicle headed toward the telephone pole on the opposite corner. She braced as the loud crushing blow reverberated throughout the vehicle and down her spine. The airbag exploded on impact. A burning snap from shoulder to hip forced her back as a piercing scream ripped from her throat and filled the air. Finally, the car came to rest partially on the sidewalk, as all inside was quiet.

"Engine 24, accident at the intersection of Highway 49 and Pass Road. Injured woman trapped inside vehicle. Police are on scene," dispatch notified the rushing men as they climbed into the fully equipped fire truck.

The driver hit the siren as he roared out of the firehouse driveway with lights flashing. He wove in and out of traffic skillfully and headed to the scene. The other men donned their gear, not sure of what they would find. Captain Damien Christoval was in constant contact with dispatch reporting their estimated time of arrival. Calls like these always brought back memories of another call three years ago. The accident site could be seen just up ahead as they hooked a right. He inhaled a deep breath and prepared to go to work. When the truck pulled into the intersection, debris from the small sports car crushed into the side of the pole littered the street. *This was going to be bad*, Damien thought to himself. He forced down the sickening feeling rising in his stomach. He quickly gave out orders and sprung into action.

"What happened here?" Damien asked the police officer closest to the vehicle as he headed toward the victim.

"A Memorial Day drunk in a Suburban struck this lady in the driver's door and sent her spinning into that pole. We found him a block away on the side of the road passed out, unharmed."

"Isn't that the way it goes?" Damien asked as he approached the vehicle and assessed the scene. "We're going to have to cut her out," he yelled to his men, not sure if the woman in the car was alive or dead. It really didn't matter because either way, she had to be removed. He climbed onto the hood of the car where he could see the woman's head resting against the steering wheel. The airbag had deployed properly and hopefully cushioned the blow. The broken out windshield provided him with access to the victim. He reached in, located a pulse, and yelled back to his men to hurry up with the equipment. "We have a live one here and I want to keep it that way."

Someone was with her. She tried to force her eyes open, but something got into them making her close them. As she heard the voice again, she managed to speak. "Help me."

The small desperate voice drew their attention and heightened the sense of urgency. Captain Damien's men began working feverishly. He yelled over the sound of the equipment prying and cutting through metal. "Help is here. Just remain still and we'll have you out in a little while." Damien made himself as comfortable as possible on the hood of the car.

"My arm hurts," the woman whispered barely loud enough to be heard. Immediately she felt large hands scanning the length of her arms.

"Your left arm is broken," Damien replied in a deep authoritative voice. He continued to run his hands down her body from his position on the hood. When he touched the area just under her left breast, she winced and cried out in pain. "I think you may have a cracked rib as well, so stay still." He backed out of the window to relay the information to the arriving emergency medical technicians.

"Don't leave me! Please don't leave me here," the woman pleaded frantically as she raised her head, panicked at his leaving.

Damien immediately returned to the broken out window and froze. *It couldn't be,* he thought as he stared into the familiar face. Sara was dead. Three years now. He closed his eyes as the pain of that night nearly choked him. When he opened his eyes again and looked at the woman pleading for his help, he realized that it wasn't Sara, just a woman who could very easily be her twin. She possessed the same thin brown face, small round nose, and sculptured cheekbones as Sara. Her lips were thin and slightly wide like Sara's as well. Both women had pointy little chins that hinted of stubbornness. Even the texture and length of their hair was identical. Long auburn glossy strands fanned out around the woman's back and shoulders as she reached blindly for him. He quickly pushed the fog away and climbed back into the window. He hadn't been able to help his wife, but he would do everything he could for this woman.

"Calm down. I'm right here. I'm not going anywhere without you," he crooned in a soothing voice as he took the right hand extended in his direction. Just then her eyes fluttered open and he gazed into their warm sherry brown depth. Damien felt something inside of him stir to life. Her eyes were mesmerizing and intoxicating in their rich color and for a moment only the two of them existed.

"I want you to listen to me closely. You're injured pretty badly. My men need to check you out and gather vital information, so I need you to calm down and stop moving around."

"Okay," she responded and closed her eyes. "But, don't let go of my hand."

A small smile crept across Damien's face. "I won't," he replied, threading their fingers together.

"Captain, you know the information we need," the EMT whispered into Damien's ear as he passed him a neck brace.

Damien nodded, understanding that he and the lady had formed a connection. "I need some information from you. But before I begin, I need to slip a neck brace on you." Working quickly, he fitted the cushioned brace around her neck and secured it. "Okay, are you up to talking?"

"Yes," she answered, and tried to open her eyes as a drop of blood blinded her.

"I need something to stop the bleeding here," Damien called to the EMT as he saw the problem. With a gauze swab in hand, he gently cleaned the stream of blood and applied pressure to the open wound. "What's your name and address?"

"Lacey Avery, 340 Marsh Lake Road, Ocean Springs."

Damien repeated the name inside his head, liking it, then relayed the information. "I'm Damien Christoval and my men are going to have you out of this wreck shortly. How old are you, Lacey?"

"Thirty-two."

"Thirty-two?" Damien responded, surprised. "I thought you would say twenty-five." His voice held laughter. Lacey Avery possessed a youthful appearance just like Sara.

She forced a smile as she finally opened her eyes to look at Damien Christoval. She liked his deep voice with just a hint of a Southern accent. It was comforting. "I wouldn't be twenty-five again for anything."

Damien understood exactly where she was coming from. He laughed. "I agree with you. So Lacey, who should we notify about your accident?"

"Daniel Overstreet, 872-5555. He'll notify my parents."

Damien relayed the information to the EMT while trying to ignore the unreasonable feeling of disappointment which came over him.

"Your boyfriend will be notified immediately and told to meet us at the hospital."

Was it her imagination or did she hear disappointment in his voice? Lacey tried to roll her head to the side so that she could get a better look at Damien Christoval, but the brace hampered her actions. Using only her eyes, she managed the task. Damien Christoval was near black in complexion, with smooth clear skin. His hair was cut close and revealed deep waves against the shape of his well-proportioned head. His eyes were a hazel brown, despite his skin tone, and framed with curling lashes. His narrow nose seemed odd in such a dark face, yet not unappealing. But it was his mouth, wide with a fuller bottom lip and thin top lip, that fascinated her. It looked tempting and promising. And his smile was a brilliant white as he noticed her watching him.

"Is something wrong, Lacey?" Damien asked. The lady had been examining him with great interest.

"Not a thing," she whispered more to herself than him. "Daniel is my best friend, not my boyfriend." She watched his face for a reaction. Seeing none, she dismissed the thought.

Damien tried to hide his relief in her explanation as he met her sherry eyes. He wondered if the lady had picked up on his disappointment. Had his men? He chanced a glance around and noticed everyone busy at work trying to free Lacey from the vehicle. He reprimanded himself for losing focus on the job.

"What's taking them so long to get me out?" Lacey inquired anxiously. She wanted to glance in the direction of the action to gauge the status, but knew that she couldn't. But she wanted out. The space was closing in on her. "Please make them hurry," she whined fretfully.

"It won't be long," Damien tried to reassure her. He went back to asking questions as a way to distract her. "You come from a large family, Lacey?"

"No. I'm an only child."

"Oh man, I couldn't imagine being an only child. It's five of us—

three boys and two girls. I'm the oldest. We gave our parents headaches. If we weren't into one thing, it was something else. Now the grandkids are following in our footsteps."

Lacey listened to the love in his voice as he spoke of his family. She had always wanted to belong to a large family and had even planned on one of her own, but life had other ideas and so she moved forward.

"Do you have children?" she asked.

Damien turned his head to glance out toward the street. Yes, he had wanted children – a large family to be exact. "No."

Lacey didn't catch the forlorn expression on his face, so she had no way of knowing how desperately he wanted children of his own. "I bet you're the uncle who buys all the noisy toys for the nieces and nephews to take home," she remarked in a faint voice.

"That's me; the noisier the better." He laughed deeply. "So, Lacey, what do you do for a living?"

Lacey smiled, despite the pain in her arm. "I'm a writer."

"A writer? What do you write?" Damien asked curiously.

"Books for women."

Damien's eyes came to life with amusement. "You mean romance don't you?" He laughed deeply. "My mother and sisters read those things religiously."

Lacey listened to his laugh, enjoying the sound. This man was a great distraction from the pain in her left side.

"Do you use a pen name?" Damien continued with the questions.

"Yes. 'Lace'."

Damien's eyes immediately came up to lock with hers. An unnamed force passed between them. *Lace*—delicate, beautiful, and seductive. The name fit her. "I'll have to ask them if they've read any of your books."

She responded by smiling. Her head hurt and she felt nauseous. Lacey sucked in a quick breath in an attempt to alleviate the symptoms.

"We're ready, Captain."

"Okay," Damien responded to a member of his team. He focused back on Lacey. "How are you doing?"

"I don't feel so good," she whispered back.

Alarmed, Damien called an EMT over. "Something is wrong."

The young man quickly set about taking her vital signs once more. The readings were in the normal range. After asking Lacey a series of questions, he diagnosed her symptoms as the affects of a concussion.

Satisfied with the diagnosis, Damien ordered his men to proceed, and turned to Lacey. "Okay, sweetheart, we're about to remove that door. Keep your head still."

Lacey did as instructed. She could hear the men prying at the door and their relief when it removed easily. With no choice, she reluctantly released Damien's hand as the EMTs went to work stabilizing her injured arm. Gingerly she was removed from the wreckage and placed on a stretcher. She was quickly strapped in and loaded in the back of the ambulance. Everything happened so quickly that she didn't get to say good-bye to Damien. The sirens wailed as she was whisked away to the hospital. She was immediately rolled into the trauma room where a staff of people quickly went to work on her injuries.

Two hours later, after a series of tests and x-rays, Lacey was finally settled into a room. Her arm was in a cast and her ribs bandaged tightly. Daniel and her family were in the room with her. She could hear their light chatter about how lucky she was, but her mind was on Captain Damien Christoval and how comforting he had been in her hour of need. Her eyes drooped closed as an image of the man flashed in her mind.

Damien Christoval sat behind the desk in his office. He was documenting the traffic accident from which they had returned. As he logged off the computer, a knock sounded at the door. "Come in," Damien called out.

Kenneth Gordon, a driver and long time friend, walked into the office. A tall man in his mid-thirties and solidly built, Kenneth collapsed into the chair opposite Damien's desk. "How are you doing, man?" He watched Damien closely.

Hazel eyes met darker orbs. Damien sensed that his friend knew. "I'm okay."

Kenneth wasn't convinced. "The lady gave me pause as well."

"You saw her?" Damien asked excited.

"Yeah man, and I thought I was looking at Sara."

Damien stood from behind his desk and walked to the window on the left. It was dark outside now. "For a moment I couldn't move. Then, I looked closely at Lacey and realized it wasn't Sara." He came back to the desk and sat on the corner. "But I tell you, I felt like she was back and I had a chance to save her."

Kenneth reached out and laid a comforting hand on Damien's shoulder. "I'm sorry you had to go through that. I know how much you loved Sara and how you mourned her death."

Damien couldn't reply, so he merely nodded his head.

"You know I'm here for you."

"Yes, I do." He changed the subject. "I called the hospital to check on Lacey. It appears she'll be there for a couple of days, but the outlook is good."

Kenneth watched Damien closely. His friend appeared casual; however, the glint in his eyes and the modulation of his voice said otherwise. "Make sure your interest in this woman is about her and not Sara."

Damien's eyes narrowed as he faced his friend. "I'm not interested in this woman. I inquired about our rescue. End of story."

"If you say so."

"I say so, man." Damien rose from the desk to pace the floor. "I don't have time for a woman. With Pop recovering from surgery and Holly back at home with the kids, where would I find time for a woman? Anyway, Lacey Avery is capable of holding a man's attention on her own." Damien suddenly realized that he was rambling and that Kenneth looked amused.

"Maybe you should make time, my brother." Kenneth rose from the chair. He walked to the doorway and paused. "Give Miss Avery my regards when you see her."

"I am not interested in that woman," Damien yelled to Kenneth's retreating laughter. But the moment the words left his lips, he knew that he lied. Lacey Avery had piqued his male curiosity and the impulse to act upon it was strong. However, the arguments he had presented to Kenneth were valid ones. He retrieved the keys to his truck from the desk drawer. He tossed them into the air and caught them on the descent down. Turning off the lights in his office, he called it a day.

The memories of those last days with Sara came flooding back to mind on the drive over to his parent's home. They were painful memories. Ones he would rather forget. However, every time someone mentioned children, or he approached an accident scene, they were back with a vengeance. But he couldn't change the past, and so he had learned to bury the memories as well as the pain. He hooked a right onto his parents' street and took a deep breath. By the time he turned off the engine, he was back to being, "Good old Damien."

CHAPTER 2

He unlocked the front door of his parents' home. Each child of Melinda and John Christoval still had a key to the front door and knew that they were free to use it at any time. Damien called out as he locked the door behind him. "Hey, where is everybody?"

Melinda Christoval appeared through the swinging door of the kitchen. She was a tall woman with large hips after five children, but solidly built and strikingly attractive. Her coloring matched her son's, as well as her nose and eyes. She opened her arms to greet her eldest child. "Hi, baby. How did your shift go?"

"Busy as usual," he answered quickly. At the moment he didn't want to think about the woman they had pulled from the wrecked vehicle. Lacey Avery had been on his mind during the drive over. Her sherry eyes kept coming to him. He walked past his mother and entered the kitchen. Just as he thought, the Christoval clan was seated around the table.

As always, his Dad sat at the head of the table, and his oldest sister, Holly, sat on his right, with his two-year-old niece, Raye, balanced on her lap. Little DeMarcus, the four year old was under the table playing with action figures, while Gabriel, the oldest at six, sat at the other end of the table, brooding.

Melinda followed her son knowing that something had happened today. Damien had never been able to hide his emotions from her. Maybe it was due to his being her first born, or possibly, Damien's loving gentle nature, but whatever it was, she knew something was on his mind. She shook her short silver-layered locks with concern as she followed him into the kitchen. She would refrain from prying because eventually Damien would come to her with his thoughts.

"How are you feeling, Pop?" Damien asked his Dad as he took the chair to his left.

"I'm doing fine, son." John Christoval patted his son on the knee. "Your mother had me up walking the neighborhood early this morning and right after lunch. I had a check-up with the doctor yesterday and everything looks good."

"I'm glad to hear it and I'm glad to hear you're following your exercise plan. After open heart surgery, exercise is extremely important."

"As well as eating properly," Melinda threw in.

"Ah, Linda, it was just a pat of butter on toast," John defended himself, knowing where his watchful wife was headed.

Melinda strolled to the table with her hands planted on her hips. "It was butter and all the rest of that artery clogging food that put you in the hospital. You know you should be using the recommended margarine."

"That stuff doesn't have any taste. If I had wanted plain toast, I would have had it."

"Well, I tell you what," Melinda narrowed her eyes in warning. "From now on, there will be no butter in this house for you to sneak, old man."

"Who you calling old, woman?" John took offense. He pushed his chair back and captured his wife in his arms. Pulling her close, he planted a kiss on her that silenced the room. He released her with an exaggerated smacking noise and licked his lips as he walked out of the room. His step was high and lively. "And there's more where that came from," he tossed out from the other side of the door.

Damien and Holly sat at the table, blushing. This wasn't the first time they had seen their parents be passionate and playful. They had grown up on it and searched for it in their own relationships. However, this was the first time since their father's surgery that he had behaved like his old self. Their attention turned to their mother whose eyes had darkened with passion and love. It was obvious that she was thrilled to see her husband returning to normal.

"What y'all looking at?" Melinda returned to her pots on the stove. However, her mind was on the love of her life.

Damien and Holly broke out into laughter as the kids went back to their activities. Their parents' love always gave them comfort.

"Dang, I'm the one who feels old," Holly managed to say through her laughter. "My mother is getting more romance than me."

At the mention of romance, Lacey Avery came to mind. An image of him planting one on her as his father had just done, rocked him to the core. He sucked in a startled breath. The action caught his sister's attention.

"Are you all right, Damien?"

Melinda turned back toward the table. She noticed the stunned expression on her son's face.

"Yeah, fine," Damien managed to get himself under control. He could feel his mother's all knowing eyes on him. "It was just your mention of romance that jogged my memory."

"A woman, dear brother?"

Damien rolled his eyes as a smile swept across his face. "Yes, a woman, but not like you mean. We responded to a vehicle accident today and I met this woman who writes romance novels. She writes under the name of 'Lace', and I..." Damien didn't get to finish because Holly and Melinda both broke out squealing. "I take it you've heard of her?"

"Heard of her!" Holly slapped her hands on the tabletop. "I've read every book she has written. She writes the most heartwarming love stories. The men in her books are down-to-earth, everyday men who know how to treat their women."

"And the love scenes," Melinda drooled.

Damien stared at his mother in shock. "What exactly is this woman writing?"

Holly removed her daughter from her lap and ordered the children into the family room. After they were gone, she dug into her purse on the floor and removed a book. "This is her latest, *Brush Strokes*. It's about a widow who hires a house painter," she commented as she searched for a page to read. She located the passage she was looking for and dramatically cleared her throat before reading.

Lawrence placed Jenny in the middle of the clean drop cloth and pulled his shirt over his head to reveal a brown wall of glistening muscle. He reached for Jenny and methodically removed each item of clothing hiding her sensuous body. As each item was peeled away, he placed a feather soft kiss upon the exposed flesh. Her breasts, her stomach, a hip, thigh, and the valley of her desire were all blessed with a kiss.

Damien sat up straighter trying to imagine the woman he had met writing such words.

When Jenny was bare before him, Lawrence retrieved the instruments of his profession. Brushes in all sizes and textures were made ready. At the base of Jenny's foot, he teased her arch up to the bend of her knee with a silky brush. She trembled from the sensation. All the while, he held her eyes and whispered naughty promises. Across her abdomen, a soft bristled brush was used to tantalize her senses and heighten her desire. Another more coarse, bristled brush taunted her nipples into hardened peaks. Jenny trembled. Finally he parted her thighs and applied the whispery edges of another brush. Jenny bolted as the sensual taunting escalated and she lost the strength to resist the pleasure awaiting her. With one final stroke, she arched her back and painted his brush with love.

"Damn!" Damien exclaimed, then immediately apologized. "I'm sorry, Mama. But is it legal to write something like that? Do those books come in brown wrapping?"

Both women laughed devilishly. "I tell you, Damien, after a night of reading her books, sleep is hard to come by," Holly replied exuberantly.

"Mama, I can't believe you read those," Damien looked shocked, and pointed at the book in Holly's hand.

"Now, Damien, just how do you think all you children got here? Your father and I could write a couple of books of our own," Melinda teased her son. She enjoyed the embarrassment on his handsome face.

"That's all right, Mama, we don't want to know," he quickly replied, while making eyes at his sister.

Holly laughed, then grew quiet as she thought about her marital status. "Maybe I need to hear your secret, Mama, because at least you've been able to keep your man at home."

The playful mood suddenly died, and Holly wished that she had kept her mouth closed. She didn't need everyone feeling sorry for her. So her husband had left her for another woman. It wasn't the end of the world. She had three healthy, beautiful children and a family who loved her. Poor Damien had lost his love and the chance for that big family he always wanted. But instead of complaining, he was always giving of himself to others. The mentoring program at church benefited from his compassion. Her own children relied heavily on Damien. Since their father's departure, her big brother had been stepping into the vacant shoes and helping to ease her children's pain. No, she didn't have anything to whine about and so she attempted to lighten the mood.

"So Damien, what is Lace like? She doesn't place her picture on her books which adds to her mystery. There was even a rumor that she was really a man," Holly told him.

"Well, Lace is definitely a woman," Damien supplied with enthusiasm. "I simply can't place the woman I met with those words. She's tall and willowy with beautiful sherry brown eyes and a thin face. Her smile and her eyes are special." He went on to describe Lacey and the nature of her accident. By the time he finished speaking, both women were looking at him oddly.

His mother covered his hand with her own. "You like this woman." It wasn't a question, but fact.

"Yes, I do."

"Then ask her out," Holly chimed in.

Damien shook his head in doubt. He wasn't sure if he was ready for a serious relationship and he knew if he pursued Lacey Avery, his intentions would be serious. "It's not that easy."

"Damien, sweetheart, no one is asking you to forget Sara or the life the two of you shared, but you are thirty-eight years old and way too young to simply allow life to pass you by. If this woman interests you and she feels the same way about you, then I think you deserve a little happiness," Melinda counseled her son lovingly.

"I'll think about it," he promised. Damien thought to mention Lacey's resemblance to Sara, but decided against it. He didn't need his mother and sister questioning his interest in Lacey like Kenneth had. He knew that Sara was gone and that Lacey Avery was the woman who kept flickering in his memory. He decided to give it a couple of days. Maybe it *was* her likeness to Sara which stirred him. He had loved his wife dearly. If the feeling remained after a couple of days, then maybe he would test the water. But until then, he had no plans of moving in her direction.

"I've got to go." Damien abruptly put an end to their conversation. He knew without asking, that his mother sensed that there was something more about Lacey Avery.

"Damien, do you think you'll be seeing Lace again?" Holly asked.

"Her name is Lacey Avery and no, I don't think that I will be."

Holly and her mother glanced at each other. They both heard the unspoken something in Damien's voice that said he wasn't so sure. Holly looked at her big brother and prayed that this Lacey Avery was the woman for him. It was time that he got back to living and loving. "Oh well, if you should, I really would like to have my books autographed."

"Sure," Damien responded with a frown. He leaned over and planted a kiss on his mother's cheek. "I'll see you both tomorrow."

"You're not eating with us?" Melinda asked, concerned.

"No ma'am. I've got some errands to run before heading home." He waved and headed toward the front door. He could be heard saying goodnight to his father; then the door closed behind him.

"So what do you think?" Holly asked her mother.

Melinda's hazel eyes twinkled. "I think I'd better dig out my own books for autographing."

Damien sat in bed and reached over on the nightstand. He pulled the book out of the plastic bag and stared at the cover. A scantily dressed African-American couple was in a sensual clench. His fingers traced over the raised lettering of "Lace." In the privacy of his room, he began to read *Brush Strokes*. He was nearly finished when he closed the book several hours later. There was so much more to this story than the titillating love scenes. The complex characters were interesting and real. Lacey made you care about them and their love affair. He actually found himself giving the male character advice. As he turned out the bedside lamp and slid down in bed, one particular love scene popped into his head. He could feel himself become aroused, and cursed. He tried to think of something else, anything that would ease the ache, but all that came to mind was Lacey Avery and the mysteries she must hold. After a while of counting sheep, he was finally able to find peace in sleep.

The next shift was relatively quiet. A small trash dumpster fire and an elderly fall victim were the only runs. Firehouse chores filled the otherwise quiet hours. Damien was in his office working on monthly reports when a commotion in the common area drew his attention. It was near the dinner hour. He logged off the computer and pushed away from his desk. He headed for the common area. When he arrived, he noticed all his men gathered at the entrance of the kitchen. As he approached, they parted the way for him to enter. Styrofoam containers from a popular local eatery lined the countertops.

"Where did all this come from?" he asked.

Kenneth retrieved a card from the countertop and passed it to Damien with a broad smile. "See for yourself."

Damien glanced at his friend curiously. It was obvious that Kenneth was enjoying the moment and waiting for a response from him. He accepted the card. The inside note read:

A small expression of my appreciation.

Lacey Avery

Damien folded the little white card. He could feel Kenneth's eyes on him waiting for a response. "That was nice of the lady," he finally said as he met Kenneth's smiling face. He turned to his men, "Dig in guys." Damien pocketed the card, then stepped out of the way as the men filed in helping themselves to the mouthwatering dishes.

"Aren't you eating?" Kenneth asked.

"Sure I am." Damien grabbed a plate off the counter, then passed one to Kenneth. The two men fell in line with the others and grabbed the last two chairs around the long dining room table. As they ate the delicious meal, the men made small talk while referencing Lacey's thoughtfulness. *And it was quite thoughtful,* Damien admitted. Most people took their daily responses to their crisis for granted, but Lacey hadn't done that. Her actions said a great deal about the type of woman that she was.

"Someone should personally thank the lady," Kenneth nudged his buddy.

Damien rolled his eyes. Despite his desire to ignore Kenneth's meddling, he had to admit that he was right. Lacey's thoughtfulness deserved a face-to-face thank you, and as captain of the station that responsibility fell upon him. He pushed away from the table and went to the sink to rinse his plate.

"Where are you going?" Kenneth asked, following behind Damien. His brown eyes were filled with mischief.

Damien didn't bother to supply an answer. Instead, he passed his plate to Kenneth and said his good-byes. Exiting the side door to the parking lot, Kenneth called out to him, halting his departure. He swung around to face him. "What's up?"

Kenneth walked up to Damien a little unsure about what he was about to say. He knew that he had been teasing his buddy unmercifully about this woman, but something in Damien's eyes hinted of a true interest in the lady and that concerned him. "Hey, look. I know I've been riding you pretty hard about this woman, but if you're really interested in her, you need to examine the reason."

"I know."

Kenneth halted Damien's reply with a raised hand. "I'm only saying this because I love you like a brother and every woman deserves to be pursued because of who she is and not who she may remind a person of."

Damien folded his arms across his massive chest as he rocked back on his heels. "Look, I admit that the woman interests me and yes, initially it was because she resembled Sara. However, as I told you before, Lacey Avery can hold a man's attention on her own."

Kenneth nodded his head as he listened and understood what Damien was saying. "All right, just as long as you know who you're pursuing."

"Now I didn't say I was pursuing the lady. I'm going to say thanks for the meal, remember?"

"You tell yourself that when those big brown eyes land on you," Kenneth returned to his good-natured ribbing.

"Later man," Damien tossed out as he opened the door to his truck. Within minutes he pulled out of the parking lot headed for the hospital.

CHAPTER 3

Lacey Avery awakened in her hospital room to discover herself alone. She was thirsty and searched for the pitcher of water and cup the nurse had provided earlier in the day. It sat on the far corner of the bedside table. To get it, however, would be a stretch and potential hazard for someone with an arm in a cast, so she waited patiently for her mother to return. After several parched minutes when it appeared her mother would be gone longer than she had anticipated, Lacey pressed the call button to the nurses' station and waited. Finally, someone responded with a promise to be there shortly. And so she waited again. She dragged her tongue across her parched lips. The action did nothing to ease her thirst. She eyed the sweating plastic water pitcher and decided that it wasn't that far after all. She perched on the edge of the bed and stretched as far as she could.

"I wouldn't do that if I were you."

Lacey turned in the direction of the male voice and lost her delicate balance. She let out a helpless yelp as she started to fall.

Damien tossed the bouquet of flowers he carried onto the bed as he dove for her falling body.

Lacey cried out in agony as her bruised ribs revolted against her stupidity and the pair of strong hands preventing her fall. Tears instantly filled her eyes and spilled down her cheeks.

Damien pressed her delicate body against his as he held her mere inches from the hard tile floor. He breathed in deeply as he collapsed onto the floor in a sitting position. He pulled Lacey down across his lap.

"Breathe slow and steady. Let the pain out." Damien kept a watchful eye as she followed his advice. Without thinking he swiped away her tears with his thumbs. "Better?"

Lacey's watery eyes held his as she nodded yes, in response. The feel of his hands resting familiarly on her hip and across her exposed thigh rendered her temporarily mute.

"Now, what where you trying to do? Break that other arm of yours?"

Lacey searched his hazel eyes feeling utterly ridiculous. She could see the humor twinkling in them and couldn't help the sheepish smile which blossomed across her face. Nor could she help the flush of warmth overtaking her as she remembered she wore a thin nylon gown, courtesy of her mother.

"Of course not. I was thirsty and trying to reach the water pitcher," she answered softly and glanced at the pitcher.

Damien's eyes followed hers. He grabbed it and the cup from where he sat. He poured a little into the cup and passed it to Lacey.

"Thanks," Lacey whispered as she accepted the cup and took a long drink. She kept her eyes focused on Damien. She couldn't believe that he was there with her. Lowering her empty cup, she passed it back to him and watched as he returned it back to the bedside table. "It seems you've come to my rescue once again."

"It's my pleasure," Damien said, his eyes roaming over her face. He remembered the flowers and craned his head to locate them on the bed. "These are for you. My men send their thanks for that wonderful meal you had sent over."

Lacey buried her nose into the summer bouquet. "They're beautiful, thanks."

"You're welcome." Damien and Lacey continued to look at each other without speaking. It was Damien who broke the silence. "My mother and sister are huge fans of yours."

Lacey's face brightened. "You remembered to ask about me. I'm flattered."

"I'm a man of my word, Lacey." Damien swept a strand of hair off her forehead. "I thought I would go deaf from their screams when I told them that I had met you."

She laughed. "You exaggerate."

"I swear to you I'm not. My sister was so excited that she grabbed your latest book and read me a passage from a love scene."

Embarrassed, Lacey rolled her eyes. "Please tell me you're kidding." She tugged on the hem of her pink nightgown.

"Brushes in all sizes and textures were made ready," Damien recited.

Lacey gasped with shock and covered her face with her hand. "I can't believe she read that to you."

Damien laughed heartily. "I can't believe someone so innocent looking could write such sensual words. What secrets do you hide, Lacey Avery?" Damien arched a brow.

"Look, don't get any ideas about me," she warned as she tried to crawl off his lap. "It's all imagination."

Damien effortlessly hauled her back across his lap. "I wasn't getting any ideas, Lacey. I was teasing. *Brush Strokes* was surprisingly far more than I imagined. It was painfully realistic and touched me deeply. You're quite talented."

"Thank you. You actually read it?" She looked at him, surprised by his words.

"I did and I enjoyed it." He smiled honestly. "By the way, my sister would like an autograph from you."

Lacey returned his smile. She liked this man probably more than she should, but at the moment, sitting there with him was one of the best moments in recent memory. "As soon as I'm released, I'll make sure you receive an autographed copy."

"I'm going to hold you to that. Remember, I know where you live," he teased. His hazel eyes mapped the soft curves of her face while struggling not to venture below the neck. He could feel the heat from her thin body radiating through the fabric of her gown.

Just at that moment, Laura Avery entered her daughter's room and stopped dead in her tracks. There, on the floor, Lacey sat in the lap of some man she didn't know and in her gown, no less.

"Lacey Rebecca Avery, what in the world is going on in here?"

Lacey and Damien hadn't heard the door open. They had been too busy staring into each other's eyes. At the sound of her mother's voice, Lacey tried to scramble to her feet, but fell back into Damien's lap in pain. "Help me get up," Lacey pleaded while grimacing from the pain.

"Hang on, you're going to hurt yourself," Damien instructed Lacey as he placed her arm around his neck. "Give me your weight."

"I can't do that."

"Lacey, I'm trained for this. Trust me." Their eyes connected.

"Okay." Lacey did as instructed and was surprised at how easy Damien made it look to rise from the floor with her additional weight weighing him down. He swung her effortlessly into his arms and back into bed. Her nightgown hiked up on her right thigh as he positioned her in bed. Without thinking he reached for the hem.

"Stop that." Lacey swatted Damien's hand and yanked the covers up to her chin. The bouquet of flowers tumbled out of her hand onto the floor. Absently glancing at them, she turned to face her mother. "Mama, we didn't hear you come in."

"Obviously." Laura Avery came completely into the room. Her purse landed in the vacant chair. She retrieved the bouquet from the floor and returned it to her daughter. Then she turned her curious eyes onto the man now sitting on her daughter's bed. "And who might you be?" she asked Damien when it became obvious that her daughter had forgotten her manners.

"I'm sorry, Mama."

"Too late," Laura said to her daughter, cutting off her explanation, and waiting instead for Damien to respond.

Damien gave the petite woman his best smile. In the capacity of his job, he was always coming into contact with protective parents and a friendly smile usually helped to alleviate the tension. "Damien Christoval," Damien introduced himself and extended his hand.

Laura Avery immediately recognized the name. Lacey hadn't been able to stop talking about the fire captain who pulled her through the accident. "It's a pleasure to meet you, Captain Christoval. I can't thank you enough for what you did for my daughter. Please express my thanks to your men as well." She drew Damien into her arms for a hug.

"I sure will do that." Damien separated from the woman's embrace and flashed a smile at Lacey.

Laura took a peek at her daughter and noticed the bright twinkle in her eyes. It had been a long time since Lacey has shown interest in a man, and the undercurrent flowing between the two hinted that the feelings were mutual. Well, she needed to know a little more about this man and his intentions. "Your parents must be mighty proud of you."

Damien smiled. "Yes ma'am, they are."

"And do they live here in the area?" Laura continued to delve.

"Yes, they live in Orange Grove."

Laura pondered his answer for a moment, then continued. "Well, I assume you're not married considering my daughter was sitting in your lap when I entered the room."

"Mom!" Lacey warned.

Laura didn't bat an eye or miss a beat. She pressed further. "I doubt you asked him whether he was married while you were trapped in that car and considering I found you all comfy in his lap, I think you should know whether or not he has a wife at home."

A little smile turned up the corners of Damien's mouth. He glanced at Lacey and noticed that she looked as though she wanted to disappear. He winked at her.

"Actually, Mrs. Avery, I'm a widower."

"Oh, Damien, I'm sorry," Lacey whispered taking his hand.

He met her eyes and tightened his hold on her hand. He could tell that she was genuinely sorry for his loss and not simply spouting platitudes. "My wife died three years ago in a traffic accident."

Laura Avery could have kicked herself, but after all this was her child and she was simply being a good mother. "Forgive me, Damien, I didn't mean to open old wounds."

"It's quite all right. It's easier to talk about these days."

"Well, I'm sorry for your loss, and since I've put my foot in my mouth, I'm going to leave you two alone. I'll be on the fourth floor visiting with Mrs. Vickers from church." With that said, she quickly left the room.

There was silence for several minutes following her departure. Lacey finally spoke, apologizing for her mother. "She can't help her busybody ways."

Damien's hazel eyes studied her for a moment. He glanced down and realized that they still held hands. "I have one at home just like her." They shared a smile. "Have you ever been married?" Damien watched something flicker in her eyes.

"No."

Short and sweet, Damien thought. He was a little rattled to be speaking with Sara's look-alike about marriage and thought now was a good time to leave. "Well, I just wanted to come by and say thanks for the meal and see how you were doing."

Lacey was slightly disappointed that Damien was rushing off so soon. She had enjoyed their brief conversation. "Thank you once again for all that you've done." She glanced around the room searching for something to write with. A pad and pen sat near the telephone, just out her reach. "Could you write down your sister's number and address so that I can give her a call or mail her an autographed book?" Lacey asked, pointing to the pad and pen.

Damien picked the items up and began to write. He paused with a thought. "When you're feeling better, would you mind doing this in person? My sister has gone through an ugly divorce and I think meeting you would go a long way in cheering her up."

Lacey liked this kind and considerate man. "I would love to. Why don't you write down a number where you can be reached, and I'll call you when I'm back on my feet."

"You're good people, Lacey Avery," Damien remarked. He quickly wrote down his number. Then, as an afterthought, he leaned into Lacey and planted a kiss on her cheek.

"So are you, Damien Christoval. Have a good evening."

"You, too."

Lacey watched, feeling dejected as Damien left her room. She had been enjoying their time together and had hoped he would stay a little bit longer. But obviously, the mention of his deceased wife had changed the mood in the room. She wondered if he was still in love with her and if this would be the last time she saw him. Glancing at the notepad containing his phone number, she had to ask herself how serious he was about her contacting him. The woman in her hoped he was very serious because she had enjoyed sitting in his lap. The inappropriateness hadn't changed the desire to do it again, or affected how safe she felt being with him.

Laura Avery returned to her daughter's room a little after Damien left. Her friend had been asleep, so she had tiptoed back out of the room. Now she stood in the doorway watching her daughter holding a notepad, lost in thought. An uncharacteristic dreamy expression brightened her face. The look concerned Laura because she knew that Lacey was vulnerable. The last man she had given her heart to had nearly crushed her daughter with his cruel and thoughtless words. Their effect had been lasting. Though giving the appearance of being outgoing, Lacey was cautious not to allow a relationship to become serious. She described every relationship as a "friendship," and tried desperately to keep them on that level. But life and love were controlled by no one, as Lacey sometimes discovered. Unfortunately, when she perceived a man's interest had gone past friendship and was heading into the love and future phase, she found a reason to break it off. In the last two years, she had actually stopped going out altogether. Daniel had become her ever-willing escort to functions and though his intentions were good, Laura sometimes felt that he aided her daughter in hiding out from the world. But now, seeing Lacey with that little smile on her face and wonder in her eyes, Laura thought maybe things were about to change.

"Captain Christoval, gone so soon?" Laura asked, coming into the room.

Lacey turned her head in her mother's direction. She carefully laid the note pad containing Damien's telephone number down on the bedside table. "Yes. He simply wanted to stop by and thank me for the catered meal I had delivered to the station house."

"He could have picked up a telephone to do that," Laura remarked as she eased down on the bed.

Lacey knew her mother and wouldn't be baited.

Laura watched her daughter as she pretended not to be interested. She glanced in the direction of the bedside table. "Is that a telephone number over there?" she asked, feigning innocence while pointing at the pad.

Lacey laughed and rolled her eyes. Her mother was hopeless. "Yes, it's a telephone number."

"Captain Christoval's?" she asked, with obvious hope.

"Yes." Lacey didn't give her any more than that.

"Lacey Rebecca Avery, are we going to play twenty questions? Now tell me why that man left his telephone number behind."

Lacey burst out laughing until the pain in her ribs reminded her that they were injured. She held her middle as she continued to laugh. Eventually she got around to answering. "Damien asked me to meet his sister who's a fan of Lace. He left his phone number so that I could call him when I'm released from the hospital to make arrangements to meet her. Now, are you satisfied?"

"Watch your mouth, young lady," Laura jokingly replied. Well, it wasn't what she was hoping for, but it was a start. One phone call and one get together could definitely lead to many more.

CHAPTER 4

Lacey removed the note pad containing Damien's telephone number from her purse. It had been there for nearly a month. Running her fingers over it for the hundredth time, she debated about placing the call. She wasn't certain if he had been sincere about the request, or simply making small talk. Finally, deciding that she would never know unless she called, Lacey dialed the number. The answering machine in Damien's home picked up after the third ring and she began to leave her message.

Damien returned to his bedroom with a towel tied low on his hip. He was headed over to his parents' home to take care of some minor chores for his father. Since the open-heart surgery, he had taken care of the yard work and any other task requiring attention. He had just entered his bedroom when Lacey's unmistakable voice came to him over the answering machine. He had waited several weeks to receive this call and he wasn't about to miss it now. He quickly ran across the room and snatched up the telephone.

"Lacey, I'm here," Damien shouted into the phone over her recording. He punched a series of buttons to deactivate the answering machine. "Sorry about that. I was just getting out of the shower."

Lacey groaned to herself. She could have done without his explanation. For weeks now she had been dealing with her own secret fantasies of the man and now a shower scene would no doubt, take center stage in her next fantasy. She knew that it was foolish of her to think of him in such terms. Damien had never shown her anything but friendliness; however, somewhere in the back of her mind she desired far more. Maybe it was his gentle caring of her during the accident, or possibly the strong arms which prevented her disastrous fall in the hospital. Whatever the reason, Damien Christoval was never far from her mind.

"Sorry to interrupt."

"Don't apologize. I was hoping to hear from you."

Lacey allowed his words to settle over her. His deep masculine voice was music to her ears. She didn't try to analyze their meaning or decide upon a proper response. She simply went with the truth. "I've been debating whether or not to call you for several days now. I wasn't sure if your request for me to meet your sister was sincere or if you were just being polite."

Damien sat on the side of the bed realizing that he wasn't the only one apprehensive about this budding friendship. He knew for himself that it had the potential to be something far greater and listening to Lacey, he would venture that her thoughts were similar. "I was very sincere. Are you up to a meeting?"

Lacey exhaled her nervous breath. It was going to be all right. "Most definitely."

"How about today? I'm headed over to my folks' place in about an hour. I can swing by and pick you up."

She was going to see Damien. "Today is perfect except I'm not at home. I'm at Daniel's gallery in the Crossroads."

"Of course, your friend is Daniel Overstreet, the sculptor. No problem. I'll be there within the hour to collect you." Damien returned the phone to the nightstand with a little pep in his step. After weeks of debating the wisdom of befriending Lacey Avery, Damien was now convinced that his interest in Lacey had nothing to do with Sara. When he had thought of her, it had been of her beautiful sherry eyes and her sweet smile. The feel of her nestled in his lap was also difficult to forget. But before he could move on with this relationship, he had to come clean with Lacey about her resemblance to Sara and pray that the news wouldn't drive her away.

Lacey returned the receiver to its cradle as Daniel walked back into the office space in the rear of the gallery. She wore a little smile as she gave her attention to her friend.

"Hey, who was that on the telephone?" Daniel Overstreet asked. He carried his latest piece to the desk and gently sat it down.

"Captain Christoval," Lacey answered while admiring his new creation. "This is so beautiful."

Daniel smiled, pleased with the compliment. The piece had been a labor of love and a gift for his father. It captured the image of a father and son. The piece would be perfect for a retirement gift.

"That's the fireman who helped you?" Daniel questioned further.

"They all helped, but Damien was the person who kept me calm while I was being cut out of the wreckage."

Damien, was it? "So you called him? I didn't realize that you kept in touch with him."

Lacey made a face. She could always count on Daniel to pick an innocent remark to pieces. "If you must know, Damien's mother and sister are fans of Lace. He said his sister's spirits were down due to a really bad divorce and had hoped meeting me would be a boost. So he asked if I would be willing to meet her and autograph her books."

"And of course you agreed."

"Yes, I did," Lacey answered with a nod of her head. She walked out onto the gallery floor. There were several new pieces by other local artists on display.

"He sounds like the thoughtful type," Daniel continued to probe.

"He's a nice man," Lacey remarked without looking at him.

Daniel silently observed his best friend. He was very familiar with Lacey's moods, but this one he hadn't seen in quite some time. "You like this man."

Lacey didn't answer right away. Instead, she continued to wander around. Finally, unable to avoid the subject any longer, she returned to the office area. She didn't sit down. Her thoughts and nerves were too jumbled for that. Meeting Daniel's concerned gaze, she finally answered. "Yes I do, but it's utterly ridiculous considering I know very little about the man. Maybe this attraction stems from his being a lifeline while I was trapped. I don't know what it is, but I can't seem to get him off my mind." Her good hand was planted on her hip with her left leg slightly extended. She rocked to a nervous rhythm.

Daniel knew how afraid she was of involvement. In the past it had brought her nothing but heartache. It was understandable that this newfound attraction was a little frightening.

"Stop thinking so far into the future. Step back and simply let it happen at its own pace." For the next several minutes Daniel gave Lacey some heartfelt advice. He could only pray that she would consider it.

Lacey nodded her head as she mulled over his words. "You're right, as usual."

"So, when are you going to see this guy again?"

A little smile spread across her face. "He's actually headed over here now. He's picking me up for the meeting I told you about."

"Great. I get to check your little friend out," Daniel remarked with smugness. He reared back in his chair and propped his feet up on the desk.

"You're my best friend, not my father. Besides, there is nothing to check out. You can't really say that Damien and I are friends."

"I beg to differ with you, Ms. Avery." Damien stood bigger than life in the gallery entrance.

Lacey spun around stunned. "Damien!" She watched spellbound as he walked toward her like an apparition.

As he stopped in front of her, his eyes swept her slim body appreciatively. She was tall for a woman, about five-nine and willowy thin, but not in an unattractive way. White linen slacks paired with a silk lilac blouse complemented her brown complexion and sleek figure. Lilac toenails winked at him from white sandals. Her left arm was still in a cast and supported by a silk scarf tied into a sling.

"I don't allow just anyone to sit in my lap," Damien purred in a deep masculine voice. The look he gave Lacey was hot and triggered the memory of his touch.

Damien glanced at the man in the rear of the room for the first time. He was what he and his friends would call a pretty boy. His golden skin tone and curly *good hair* would have the women flocking to his side. His refined features were accentuated by a close cut beard that, coupled with his long-lashed eyes, could make women swoon. He wondered if Lacey was attracted to the look.

"You must be Daniel," Damien said, extending his hand.

Daniel immediately stood to accept the offered handshake. Damien Christoval had about two inches on him and mountains of muscles, not that he wasn't physically fit himself. Obviously, the physical aspects of Damien's profession kept him in tip-top shape.

"Yes, I am. Good to meet you, Damien." Daniel responded warmly. "What is this about Lace sitting in your lap?" Daniel wore a big smile.

Both men glanced at Lacey only to receive stony glares. "Do you want to tell the story or should I?" Damien asked.

Lacey dramatically rolled her sherry eyes up to meet his. "By all means, go right ahead."

Daniel listened intently as Damien recounted the events, including when Mrs. Avery walked in on them. By the time Damien concluded, Daniel was laughing hysterically. He tweaked Lacey's nose and laughed even harder when she swatted his hand away. "After that story, you two are definitely friends. Actually, very good friends. I haven't seen you in your jammies since we were kids."

Lacey glared at Damien as if to say *look what you've started.* Eventually her glare gave way to a smile. "Are we going to meet your sister or not?"

Damien chuckled. "Yes, ma'am we are. Ready to go?"

"I was ready before you told that story." Lacey returned to the desk and picked up her purse.

Daniel followed her and flung an arm around her neck. "Come on, Lace. Don't be like that."

"I'll deal with you later," she promised Daniel with a pointed look.

The men started laughing once more as Lacey turned and headed for the door with her head held high. Damien tossed out a "good to meet you" to Daniel as he hustled to catch up to Lacey. She walked in front of him. Her gait was confident and purely feminine. He remembered the narrow span of her waist and the feel of her derriere, but in those slacks he got his first view of what he only knew by sensory. It was perfectly shaped and just enough for a woman of her size. Glancing up as they approached his Ford F-150, Damien realized that Lacey had caught him in the act of checking her out.

"That's a nice shade of purple on you," he remarked, then opened the door for her.

"Right," Lacey tossed out as she climbed inside. She watched Damien close her door, then walk around to the driver's side door. When he climbed in and closed the door, she faced him. "How could you do that to me? Daniel will be teasing me about that for years."

Damien met her big pretty eyes and nearly drowned in their beauty. The light was angled just right, and it intensified their color. "Come on, he seems like a good guy." He placed his arm on the back of her seat as his eyes studied her lovely face.

"He is a good guy, but he is also a relentless tease." Her body warmed as she realized she was being appraised. "How about when we get to your parents' home, I tell this little story and see how you feel?" A wicked gleam danced in her eyes.

Damien flashed his beautiful smile. Waving a hand before her, he pleaded, "Please don't. My mother and sisters live on your romance novels and will have us engaged and married before we leave the house."

This time Lacey laughed. "All right, as long as you never mention this story again."

"Deal." Damien stuck his hand out.

Lacey glanced at the large masculine hand that had held her, now stuck out to seal a deal. Cautiously, she placed her hand inside his and became aware of the rapid beat of her heart. *One day at a time, Lacey.* "Deal."

Damien pulled into the sprawling driveway of his parents' home. He spotted Holly's minivan and his younger sister Patrice's Mustang. It appeared that Lacey would have the full attention of all the Christoval women. Knowing that he couldn't put off his confession any longer, Damien rolled down the windows, then switched off the engine. He turned facing Lacey with an uneasy smile.

"I've thought about you a great deal since that night in the hospital." He reached over taking her hand.

"I've thought about you as well." Lacey squeezed his hand affectionately.

Damien smiled at those words. "There's something I have to tell you before we go inside. The night of your accident...when I saw you...for the briefest moment I thought..."

"Damien!" the high-pitched feminine voice pierced the air. "Why are you sitting in the truck?" Melinda Christoval shouted from the front porch, halting the conversation inside the vehicle. She craned her neck to see the woman inside.

"I believe you've been discovered." Lacey smiled over at Damien with amusement.

"It appears so," Damien whispered nervously. A couple more minutes and the truth would have been revealed. Now, he could only pray no one would say anything. *Fat chance!* He opened his door and walked around to assist Lacey down.

"I'm nervous," she whispered and accepted the offered hand.

"Hey, I thought you would be accustomed to meeting new people." He smiled reassuringly.

Lacey returned his smile as she tightened her hold on his grip. "I am in a bookstore, book convention, or library, but this is different. This is your family and you know how families can grill you."

Damien laughed nervously because he did know. "And mine are professional interrogators."

"You're not helping, Damien." Lacey cut her eyes at him.

"Stop worrying. They're going to love you," he said threading their fingers together.

"Do I look okay?" Lacey glanced down at the wrinkles in her linen slacks.

Damien swept her with an appreciative glance. "You look beautiful," he whispered with more emotion than he had intended.

Lacey glanced up quickly to search his eyes. What she saw was a man suddenly uncomfortable with his disclosure. "Thank you." She squeezed his hand.

"You're welcome. Come on." He tugged on her hand and led them up the walkway.

Melinda Christoval stared disbelievingly at the woman standing beside her son. *Sweet Jesus!*

Alarmed by the expression on his mother's face, Damien rushed to head off disaster. "Mama, this is Lacey 'Lace' Avery. She came by to meet everyone and to autograph your books." The words rushed from his mouth as his eyes pleaded for her to remain silent.

Melinda didn't miss her son's silent request. She slid her disapproving gaze from Damien to the lovely young woman timidly standing before her waiting to be acknowledged. It was obvious she had no idea that she resembled Sara. It wasn't her place to set matters straight. She focused instead on putting Lacey at ease. "Lacey, we don't stand on formality around here," she said taking a step forward. She greeted Lacey with open arms. "A friend of Damien's is a friend of this family. Welcome to the Christoval clan."

Lacey returned the embrace. She was relieved to find Damien's mother so warm and friendly. "Thank you, Mrs. Christoval."

"Come on in and meet the girls," Melinda said, leading them inside.

Lacey followed. She glanced around the spotless living room as they went along, feeling the love in the home. Pictures in all sizes and frames littered the tabletops. Diplomas of each of the Christoval children sat on the mantle. She stopped in front of Damien's diploma from Tulane University and noted that he held a Masters Degree in Business Administration. Raised voices from the kitchen drew her attention. She glanced around for Damien and his mother and noticed them standing in the swinging door of the kitchen.

Lacey followed into the bright yellow kitchen. A white stove with double ovens to the right held several simmering pots and the aroma in the room was delicious. To the left, a solid oak oval table with seating for six was positioned in front of a large window which offered plenty of natural light. The refrigerator was also to the left, just inside the doorway.

"Girls, this is Damien's friend, Lacey Avery." Melinda made quick introductions. Utilizing her mother's ability to communicate only with her eyes, she warned her daughters to remain silent about the obvious. Their acquiescence came in the form of slight nods.

To Lacey, their silence was interpreted as shock and surprise. She glanced at Damien, feeling a little uncomfortable by the prolonged silence. Finally she broke the mood by speaking. "It's a pleasure to meet you both. Damien tells me that you're fans of Lace." She clenched her hand tightly in nervousness.

Holly and Patrice greeted her in true Christoval fashion. She was swept up into two welcoming embraces. Soon the kitchen was filled with excitement as the women began to chatter.

"Where's Pop?" Damien asked his mother.

"He's out back on the patio."

Damien held out his hand to Lacey. "Come with me; I want to introduce you to my father."

Lacey took Damien's hand and excused herself from the women. Mrs. Christoval joined them and silently prayed that her husband wouldn't have another heart attack when he saw Lacey.

"Dad," Damien called to his father as they stepped out onto the patio. "I've got someone I want you to meet."

John Christoval looked up from his newspaper to stare at the woman beside his son. For a moment there, he thought he was looking at Sara, but this woman was much taller. His eyes swung to Melinda who stood behind Damien with her finger pressed to her lips. He understood the meaning and held on to his comment. Pushing to his full height, equal to his son's, John smiled broadly as he greeted their guest. "How do you do, young lady?"

Lacey studied John Christoval closely. He was tall like his son and handsome, but still showed signs of his recent illness. His face was gaunt and thin, as was his body. Only the loose fit of his clothes indicated that he had once been a large man. But his eyes were bright and assessing, and his smile warm and genuine. "Well, sir. It's a pleasure to meet you."

"Dad, this is Lacey Avery," Damien made introductions.

"You're that writer my wife and daughters have been buzzing about for the past month."

Lacey smiled up at Damien. "Yes sir, I am."

After a moment of small talk, the three returned to the house, leaving Mr. Christoval to his newspaper. The women cleared a place for Lacey at the table. Holly jumped up and headed to her bedroom as she remembered the books that she wanted autographed. She was back in a flash, excited and slightly out of breath. Lacey quickly set about signing each one. The women began firing questions at her while she did so. Damien briefly interrupted to ask Lacey if she would be all right while he mowed the lawn.

"Sure, I'll be fine." She waved him away and returned to her conversation.

"All right then, I'll leave you in their capable hands," Damien said, then focused on his mother. " I'm going to change into some work clothes, then I'll be back so you can show me what you need done in your flower beds."

"Sounds good, son," Melinda replied dicing potatoes.

Damien took one last look at Lacey surrounded by the Christoval women and smiled at how easily she had settled in. His sisters returned to asking one question after the other and Lacey, good-naturedly, tried to answer each and every one. Leaving the kitchen behind as he headed to the bedroom he had once shared with his brothers, Damien's ears were sensitive to Lacey's distinctive alto voice. As he climbed the stairs, she laughed. The sound of her voice stirred feelings inside that stopped him cold. Not yet ready to analyze those feelings, he forced himself to continue upstairs.

CHAPTER 5

Lacey was enjoying herself immensely. The sisters wanted to know all there was to know about Lace. Which book was her favorite? What she was writing next? Would there be a sequel to *Brush Strokes*? All were easy questions for Lacey to answer. She had heard and answered them all before.

"Lacey," Mrs. Christoval interrupted her daughters' barrage of questions. "Tell me a little about yourself."

"I was born and raised here on the coast. My mother teaches at Biloxi High. She'll be retiring next year. Dad retired last year from the telephone company," Lacey answered.

"Did you always want to write?"

A tiny smile touched Lacey's lips as she recalled her first love. "No. My dream was to coach collegiate women's gymnastics. I took gymnastics from the age of three through my days at the University of Alabama."

"Did you try out for the Olympic team?" Patrice asked.

"No. From an early age it was obvious that I was too tall to compete on a national or international level."

"So why aren't you teaching?" Mrs. Christoval asked.

"I suffered an injury that ended my gymnastic career and after that, it wasn't the same for me. I guess I lost the desire to coach."

"That's awful, baby." Melinda patted Lacey's hand with motherly affection. "But when life throws us a curve, we make new dreams."

"You're right and that's what I did. While I was hospitalized, I began writing. I wasn't sure I would succeed, but I kept reading and learning about the publishing industry and decided that I could do it."

"Well you have in a big way," Melinda commented. "Women all over America wait in anticipation for your next book."

Lacey laughed, still not quite believing how successful she had become as a writer.

"Tell us the truth, Lacey," Patrice, the youngest, entered the conversation. She was a striking beauty with reddish-brown complexion and the same hazel eyes as her mother and brother. A head of thick hair that women would kill for, was styled carefree and youthful. "Who is your hero? Surely there's a man who keeps you inspired and awake at night."

A vision of Damien immediately flashed before her eyes. Then, as luck would have it, Damien picked that exact moment to return to the kitchen. He was dressed in black denim shorts which showcased his muscular hairy legs. The T-shirt he wore was old and conformed to his solid chest and bulging biceps like a second skin. Lacey lost the ability to form a complete sentence. He was masculine and had a commanding presence. Her eyes slowly traveled up the length of his body to connect with his seductive hazel eyes.

Damien had heard the question and now stood rooted in place as his eyes met Lacey's. The intensity of the look she gave surprised and excited him. It told him that he wasn't alone in his feelings.

Lacey finally managed to pull her eyes away and faced the three women at the table, but not before Mrs. Christoval and her daughters had exchanged knowing glances. Lacey sucked in a breath and answered the question. "Your brother and his men are the heroes in my life. They rescued me from the twisted metal of my car and for that I will be forever grateful." She prayed no one would call her on her response.

"Excuse me ladies," Damien interrupted. He was quite pleased with Lacey's response. "Mama, if you'll show me what you want cut out in the garden, I'll get right on it."

"Sure, son."

"Lacey," Damien called getting her attention. "I shouldn't be any longer than a couple of hours."

"Don't worry about it," Lacey said dismissively. "Your mother invited me to stay for dinner." Her eyes held his for a reaction. She hoped he didn't mind his mother asking, or her accepting the invitation.

Damien's brows rose at the news. He could feel four pairs of eyes on him, but the only pair that held him fascinated at the moment, were sherry brown and questioning. "Great. Well, I better get started on this yard." Damien hiked a thumb over his shoulder in the direction of the back yard. He left the kitchen without another word.

Outside Melinda found her husband napping. She motioned for Damien to speak quietly, then set out into the yard pointing out the shrubs and trees requiring pruning. But before returning inside the house, she asked Damien about Lacey.

"Son, are you interested in that girl?"

Damien laughed. His mother didn't beat around the bush. If she really wanted to know something, she asked. "I've been asking myself that question for several weeks now."

"And the answer?" Melinda watched the play of emotion on her son's face.

"Yes ma'am, I'm very interested in Lacey Avery."

Melinda wore a worried expression on her face. "Damien, I'm not going to ask whether you noticed the uncanny resemblance between Sara and Lacey because I already know the answer. You aren't with this girl because she looks like Sara are you?"

Damien glanced down into his mother's concerned face. He had asked himself that question too and wanted to answer his mother honestly. "Yes, Lacey could be Sara's twin, but no, Mama, I'm not interested in Lacey because of Sara. Lacey Avery holds her own interest for me. She's completely different from Sara, so when I look at her, it's Lacey that I see."

"It would have been nice if you had told us about the resemblance. I nearly fainted when Lacey stepped out the truck, and I thought the girls were going to pass out on the kitchen floor when they saw her. But then the differences kick in and you realize she's a different person. She's tall."

"Five-nine, to be exact. I like the height. It saves on the back," Damien laughed.

Mrs. Christoval agreed with him. "I never did understand what tall men see in short women, but all you boys married little bitty things."

Damien laughed deeply because he and his brothers had heard this complaint from his mother before. She herself was five-nine and their father six feet. "Not everyone can be tall, Mom."

"Maybe not; so leave the short women for short men," she said laughing, as she winked at him. "Lacey's different in others ways from Sara," Melinda voiced and captured his complete attention.

"You noticed."

"Yes, I did. Lacey's soft-spoken and despite her height, delicate."

Damien walked toward the shaded swing in the rear of the yard and sat down. He watched as his mother approached. When she was close enough to hear him, he began to relieve himself of his thoughts.

"You're right; nothing like Sara." Damien felt bad for saying that, but knew that it was true. "Sara was passionate about her career and aggressive to the point of being cut-throat at times. But I loved that fire inside of her because in my line of work, I knew that she would be all right if something were to happen to me. However, I didn't feel needed by Sara. I sometimes felt as though I was just another item on her "things to do list" that she had accomplished."

Melinda Christoval had never heard Damien speak about Sara this way. Though she agreed with everything he said, she had been under the impression that Damien's marriage was a happy one. Today she had doubts. "What does Lacey make you feel?" she asked watching him closely.

Damien glanced away, then returned his eyes to his mother. "She makes me feel like a man and the decisions I make are okay. At the scene of the accident, while the guys were cutting her out of the wreckage, I told her about the kids." He smiled remembering her remark. "She said I was the type of uncle who bought the noisy toys." He laughed.

Melinda laughed too, because Lacey had pegged him correctly. She had also managed to put a smile back on her son's face and the light back into his eyes.

"She didn't try to tell me that I was spoiling them or that they needed educational toys. She understood in that brief conversation that I simply loved them." He looked at his mother to see her reaction.

Melinda sat down beside him in the swing and took his hand. "Lacey sounds like a wonderful girl."

"From what I've seen of her, I believe that she is."

"Then she doesn't deserve to be hurt. You have to tell her about her resemblance to Sara before someone else does. You know how children are. The first time they see Lacey, one of them is going to blab."

Damien smiled thoughtfully. His mother was right. He was just thankful that they weren't here today to rat him out. They were with his brother Phillip's family, spending the night. "I'll tell her when I take her home this evening."

"Good. Now, I'm going back inside to finish dinner."

Damien watched his mother return to the house. He rose from the swing and began mowing the backyard. While his body took care of the physical task, his mind was mentally working out what he would say to Lacey later.

"Thank you for everything Mrs. Christoval." Lacey hugged Damien's mother.

"It was my pleasure. I'm sure I'll see you again." She looked at Lacey, then Damien.

"Night, Mama." Damien stepped from behind Lacey to hug his mother.

"Good night, baby. Drive carefully," she whispered back.

Damien and Lacey waved as they pulled out of the driveway. At the corner he turned right and headed for Interstate 10. Five minutes passed with no conversation between them. Lacey broke the silence unable to stand the quiet any longer.

"I like your family." She could tell that Damien was deep in thought, but had no idea what was going on inside his head. Over dinner he had been fun and attentive. He had included her in their numerous family debates and shared stories of their childhood, but now he was silent and distant.

Damien glanced over at Lacey. He could see the curiosity in her eyes and knew what he should do, but for the life of him, he couldn't tell her about Sara. "They really like you, too."

"Is everything all right?" Lacey stared at him. When he glanced at her, she continued. "Did I overstay my welcome?"

"No, of course not." Damien reached out taking Lacey's right hand which lay in her lap. He knew he had to provide her with some type of explanation for his odd behavior and so he said, "I'm just a little tired."

Lacey accepted the explanation. She had watched Damien with his family, and knew that they relied on him heavily. He had taken care of the lawn, then washed his parents' vehicles, as well as his sister's. When he returned inside, Holly had asked him to look at her computer, which he did without hesitation. Before they left he had repaired a malfunctioning toilet. Lacey could indeed imagine that he was exhausted.

"You should have told me. Daniel doesn't live too far from your parents. You could have dropped me over at his place."

Damien cut his eyes at her in disbelief. "Lacey, there is no way in hell, that I would take you to spend the night at some other man's house. Be it friend or otherwise. I'm not that tired," he replied looking at her directly. He still held her hand and squeezed it a little tighter. It was soft and warm in his larger hand, but felt somehow familiar.

Lacey stared at their joined hands as she mulled over the meaning of his statement. She liked the way they looked together and had to fight hard not to think too far into the future. "You work too hard," she heard herself say.

"They're my family and I have to take care of them."

Lacey glanced over at him. "And who takes care of you?"

Damien was silent for quite some time. He didn't have a ready answer. Eventually he replied by blowing off the question. "I don't need to be taken care of, Lacey. I'm a grown man."

"Everyone needs someone, Damien."

"Are you applying?" he asked watching her.

Lacey didn't hesitate to respond. "Of course. Everyone needs a friend."

Damien listened and nodded his head. "Is that what you're offering—friendship?"

"That's all I have to give," Lacey whispered and glanced out the side window. Damien was too much man to mess around with. She had to let it be known up front what she was offering. There was no room for confusion, because with his large family and his obvious love for them, there was no doubt in her mind that he wanted a family just like it. She prayed he would drop the subject.

But Damien couldn't do that. In that moment he knew that he desired far more from Lacey Avery than mere friendship. "You're wrong, Lacey," Damien said as he pulled into her driveway and turned off the engine. He grasped her chin and forced her to look at him. "You have so much more to give and I've decided that I want it all." His eyes searched hers for a moment before he leaned over and lightly brushed his lips against hers. "Do you have plans for next Friday?" he asked when he pulled away.

Lacey sucked in a quick breath to steady her nerves. The feel and heat of Damien's mouth made her stomach flutter. Only now did her dazed brain process his question. "No." She finally met his hazel eyes. They were darker and a little dreamy.

"Good. The guys are giving me a little birthday party over at the Voodoo Groove Nightclub. I was hoping you would join me."

Lacey's eyes fluttered with excitement and a little doubt. She really liked Damien, but his comment about wanting it all had her worried. However, it was only a birthday party with some of his friends. "I would love to join you."

"Great. I'll pick you up here about eight-thirty."

Lacey mentally went down her calendar and remembered that she was flying back that day from a book signing. "I'm doing a signing in Atlanta on Friday and my flight isn't due in until seven. I'll have to run home and change. Why don't I meet you there?"

Damien was suddenly afraid that she was trying to back out of their date. He didn't want that. "Lacey, you aren't planning on standing me up are you?" His lips were curved into a smile, but his eyes were assessing and serious.

Lacey was humbled by the look of seriousness in Damien's eyes. It was quite clear that he really wanted her with him Friday night. "No, Damien, I'm not planning on standing you up. I'll be there." She met his probing eyes, allowing him to see that she was being completely honest with him.

Convinced, Damien exited his side of the vehicle and came around to assist Lacey. He took her hand in his as he led her to the front porch of her house. It was a two-story tan brick home with green trim and a fireplace. It sat on a spacious corner lot. Hanging baskets lined the covered porch and perfumed the night air. Damien stuck his hand out for the key when she removed it from her purse. He unlocked the door,

47

stepping aside when the alarm beeped its warning. He waited patiently for Lacey to enter the code to deactivate the system. Then returning her keys back into her hand, he kissed her lightly once more and said good night.

Lacey stood in the doorway until he drove out of sight. Closing the door and activating the alarm, she headed into her bedroom to analyze the day. But Daniel's words came back to her and he was right. She would take it one day at a time.

Damien pulled up in front of his brother Phillip's home. He knew that it was late, but Phillip was a night owl and he wouldn't be disturbing him. He needed to talk to someone and Phillip, though two years younger, was mature and a dedicated family man. As he stepped on the porch, the door swung open, and Phillip waved him in.

"Mom told you I would probably be by?" Damien asked knowingly.

"Yeah, she did." Phillip went to the kitchen, grabbed a couple of beers, and headed back toward the den and the big screen television. He returned to his recliner, and Damien sat on the brown leather sofa. "So does this woman really look like Sara?"

Damien accepted the offered beer and popped the tab. Not looking at his brother he answered. "Like her twin, but taller." He took a long drink.

Phillip, who took his looks from his father, was of a fair complexion, but possessed that same commanding height and build. "Man, you're playing with fire. You need to let this woman go."

"I can't do that." Damien looked over at him. "This woman is special."

Phillip could hear the intensity in the reply. "Well then, you have no choice but to tell her about her resemblance to Sara. If you don't, someone else will and she'll be hurt."

"I know and I was going to tell her tonight, but couldn't bring myself to do it. Something about Lacey tells me that she's been hurt and I don't want to hurt her again."

"Damien, finding out that she looks like your dead wife is going to hurt her. She's going to feel like a substitute for the real thing."

Damien drained the can of beer, crushing it in his palm before glancing at his brother. "I'll tell her Friday when I see her."

CHAPTER 6

"Thanks for picking me up at the airport," Lacey said to Daniel as she dashed around his guest bedroom, dressing for her evening out with Damien. She wore a navy blue haltered jumpsuit with a keyhole in the bosom and sash that tied around her waist. The halter consisted of a metal choker around the neck to hold the front of the jumpsuit in place. The pants were slightly blousy, allowing just enough movement to be sexy and easy to dance in. On her feet she wore heeled sandals in the same identical shade of navy. Her toenails were painted a lighter shade of blue in a chrome polish. Her make-up was natural looking and flawless, the only added touch had been to her eyes. The shading of colors really set off the hue of her sherry eyes. Lacey had thought to sweep her hair up, but Daniel had encouraged her to wear it down. It was now a body of waves.

"Damn you look good," Daniel said from his perch on the bed. "Is it too late to stop being your friend?"

Lacey smiled through the mirror at him. His words gave her confidence to see the evening through. "Stop it, you're making me laugh." She attempted to insert the large gold hoop into her ear a second time.

Daniel rose from the bed to stand behind Lacey. He wrapped his arms around her and held her tight. Their eyes connected in the mirror. "Relax. You're going to knock Damien's socks off when he sees you."

Lacey smiled wistfully into the mirror. "I really like this man."

"I know, honey."

"But I'm afraid to get too close to him, Daniel."

"There's plenty of time to worry about that later. Tonight, simply enjoy yourself."

"Okay, but his family is close and so big. What am I doing?" Her eyes conveyed her confusion.

Daniel held Lacey a little tighter. He loved her so much, but he refused to be her crutch any longer. "Lacey, you are a successful writer, an adult. It's time you take control of your life. Stop being a victim to the past. If you want this man, go get him, and should the issue arise, just make sure that his love for you is greater than any desire he may have."

Lacey stiffened in Daniel's arms. He had never talked to her like that before and she was hurt. She pulled away from him and walked across the room. The callousness of his words hurt her deeply. She couldn't even face him as she spoke. "I'm sorry for dumping my problems on you. It won't happen again." She quickly began packing up her things. She wanted to get out of Daniel's place as quickly as possible.

Daniel rolled his eyes heavenward. Lacey wasn't going to make him feel guilty for telling her what she needed to hear. "Lace, you know that's not what I meant, but if you want to storm out of here in some childish tantrum, then go right ahead. But you know that I'm right. You've allowed one man to make you feel inadequate, so you've run from the rest. Well let me tell you something," Daniel advanced on her and snatched the clothes that she had been gathering out of her hand. He grabbed her by both arms forcing her to look at him. "From first impression, Damien Christoval is not going to be a push over. If he sets his sights on you, he'll stop at nothing to have you. And I mean all of you, Lace. Not what you dole out to satisfy the poor fool of the hour. This man will want you body and soul."

Lacey glared at the man she had called her friend for most of her life. She didn't understand why he was saying these things to her. "For how long, Daniel? Until he finds out that I can't have children," she practically screamed at him.

"See, that's what I'm talking about. You've already played out the scenario. You know what Damien is going to say and do before he does. You can't control people."

"I'm not trying to control Damien."

"Yes, you are. Just like you have controlled every other man since Calvin. You want to be with Damien and have him desire you, yet you want to keep the relationship friendly. Well, in case you haven't noticed, sweetheart, Damien is a man in every sense of the meaning. He's going to want you in his life and in his bed."

Lacey bit her lip as she thought about what he was saying. She made it to the bed and sat down. Daniel was right and she knew it, but what did she want to do about it? It would be so easy to simply go with the flow and see where it led, but for too long now, she had steered her own course. But isn't that what Daniel was warning her about? Damien wouldn't allow her to lead him around. He would make demands of his own and she would be faced with some hard choices.

"Lace," Daniel called her name softly as he kneeled in front of her. "You like Damien very much. I can see it in your eyes."

Lacey smiled down at her friend, now accepting that what he said wasn't meant to hurt but to help. "Yes, I do, but he also frightens me because I know with him, I won't be in complete control of the relationship."

"That can be a good thing."

"Maybe. Daniel, I want to find love and happiness like the next person, but my happiness doesn't include children."

"First of all, Lace," Daniel said taking her hands. "If a man really loves *you*, then having your love will be enough. But you'll never find him if you're always keeping men at bay. Now finish dressing and I'll drive you over to the club."

It was approaching nine thirty and Damien was getting worried. He had called Lacey's home twice with no answer. She had promised to be there tonight and he had believed her, but now he wasn't so sure.

"Man, if you check that watch one more time I'll scream," Kenneth joked.

"I don't know where she could be," Damien said glancing at the entrance to the club once more. Disappointed, he turned his back on the door and missed Lacey's entrance.

Kenneth glanced at the doorway and smiled. "Take a look," he said to Damien.

Lacey stood in the doorway of the club. She searched the main floor. Bodies swayed to the latest dance tune, while others occupied tables around the floor or sat at the bar. She didn't know exactly where to find Damien and his friends. She clutched the gift she had for him a little tighter as she was bumped by a group rushing to the dance floor. Just as she was getting worried that she would never find him in this madhouse, there he was before her. He was dressed in a navy blue suit with gold shirt and coordinated silk tie. Damien looked good. His beautiful eyes were aglow with appreciation for her efforts; his smile intoxicating. Lacey couldn't help but return the smile.

"I thought you weren't coming," Damien finally said. "I see the cast is gone."

"Yes, it is." Lacey flexed her arm. "I told you that I would be here. I always keep my word, Damien." Lacey stared into his eyes as she spoke.

"As do I, Lacey. I hope you remembered what I said to you the last time we saw each other."

Lacey blinked rapidly as his words came flooding back to her. *You have so much more to give and I've decided that I want it all.* "I do."

Damien smiled and took her hand. He was leading her over to their table when Lacey heard him say, "Good. Now you know where I stand."

Lacey followed silently behind Damien as they dodged tables and bodies. But all that was a blur to her as she recalled the conversation with Daniel. He was right, and so taking a fortifying breath, Lacey decided to sit back and let nature do its thing.

Damien stopped at a group of tables pushed together in the far corner of the club. He didn't worry that someone would notice the resemblance between Lacey and Sara because all the guys, except Kenneth, were new to the station. Kenneth's wife, Mia, had already been informed by her husband of the sticky situation and asked not to mention anything to Lacey. She had given Damien an earful and gotten his word that after the evening was over, he would tell Lacey about the resemblance. So as they arrived, he freely made introductions all the way around. Damien pulled out a chair for Lacey next to Mia since they were closer in age than some of the other women around the table.

"What would you like to drink?" Damien whispered close to Lacey's ear. His hands rested on her shoulders and he felt a slight tremor race through her body.

"A glass of white wine," she whispered back and tried to hide the effect of his warm breath against her ear. However, the intense look Damien gave her before parting told her that she hadn't suceeded. She watched him walk away to the bar.

"Damien is a good man," Mia said to Lacey, drawing her attention. She had to struggle not to stare. It was amazing how much she looked liked Sara. The only thing that gave her away was the obvious height and her odd eye color. "Here, let me take that gift from you." Mia took Lacey's package and placed it at the end of the table with the other gifts.

Lacey faced the woman. "I'm beginning to discover that. How long have you known Damien?" Lacey talked over the music.

"I met Damien when he and Kenneth decided to be firemen," Mia replied just as loud.

"So, you knew his wife?"

"Yes, the three of them attended high school together. Damien is the godfather of our two boys."

Lacey nodded. She realized that Mia hadn't elaborated.

"Do you have children?" Mia asked.

"No."

Mia laughed. "The Christovals have adopted us all."

Lacey laughed with her. "It seems they welcome everyone."

"You've met them I take it?" Mia looked a little surprised.

"Yes, I have, and Damien's family was warm and welcoming," Lacey was saying as Damien returned. "Thanks," she said accepting the glass of wine. Damien sat beside her with his arm stretched along the back of her chair.

"Damien tells me that you're a writer," Mia picked up their conversation.

"Damien talks too much," Lacey said shyly as she bumped Damien with her shoulder.

"I'm proud of you. Is that so wrong?" Damien said smiling at her. They were nose to nose.

"No, it isn't." Lacey flashed him a pleased smile.

"May we have everyone's attention," the guy named Howard was saying. He had his arm around his pretty blonde wife. "I know this is Damien's night, but Katie and I have a reason to celebrate tonight as well. We're having a baby," he proudly announced and received a round of congratulations. Everyone began rushing the couple with hugs and kisses.

Lacey smiled broadly at the young couple's blessed news. The look in the father-to-be's eyes as he looked down on his wife was one of love and adoration. Lacey's eyes misted from the depth of his love and the knowledge that no man would ever look at her in that way. She glanced

LACE

away from the touching scene and collided eyes with Damien who was waiting to congratulate his friends. He smiled and she returned it. When he beckoned her to his side, she didn't hesitate to join him. He gathered her in the circle of his arms.

"It's wonderful news, isn't it?"

"Yes, it is," Lacey answered, looking over her shoulder at him. She could tell that he was geninuely happy for his friends.

They moved forward and eventually were able to add their well wishes to the many others. Damien led Lacey out onto the dance floor before returning her to the table. He had an overwhelming urge to hold her close. A slow tune was just beginning to play and so he drew her into his arms. They fit perfectly together. Lacey was just the right height to complement his own. She smelled wonderful as well, and so he buried his nose into her wave of auburn hair.

"You look incredible, Lacey," Damien whispered close to her ear as he pulled her closer. His hand caressed the bare flesh of her back. The skin there was smooth and baby soft.

"Thank you," Lacey whispered as she rested her head on his shoulder. She closed her eyes as the music played and Damien held her closer. She inhaled his spicy cologne and felt a sense of peace. When the song ended, Damien returned them to the table. He and the men crowded around one end of the table, while the women sat at the other. Lacey listened to the conversations around her. She was actually having a wonderful time and liked Mia greatly.

"You must be important to Damien for him to bring you here," a feminine voice said over Lacey's left shoulder. She turned around to see the striking young black woman named Trina standing there. "I don't mean to be rude, but Damien hasn't brought a woman to any of these functions since his wife died."

"Did you know Sara?" Lacey asked.

"Not personally," the woman said taking a seat. "But I've heard repeatedly how much he loved her."

Lacey sensed an underlying resentment. "I'm sure he did. She was, after all, his wife."

"Well, of course, but from what I've heard, they shared a special, one-of-a-kind love. And according to the rumors she was this dynamic lawyer going places and Damien was devastated when she died." What Trina didn't say was that she had thrown herself shamelessly at Damien numerous times before finally giving up and settling for one of the other guys.

Lacey nodded, not sure how to respond.

"I'm making you uncomfortable." The woman reached out touching Lacey's hand. "That wasn't my intention," she lied. "I just thought you should know the kind of competition you're up against. Beauty and intelligence. Not that Damien isn't worth a good fight mind you." The woman allowed the words to settle around them. "Evidently something about you caught his interest for you to be invited here tonight."

Lacey managed a smile. She glanced toward the end of the table to where Damien sat with the other men. He sensed her eyes on him and looked dead at her. He winked before focusing back on the conversation around him.

Kenneth caught the exchange and smiled. Lacey Avery could indeed hold a man's attention. "She's lovely, Damien," he leaned over saying.

"I know."

"Come on everybody," Mia called, gathering everyone around as the waitress brought a birthday cake over to the table. The group automatically began to sing Happy Birthday as Damien came to stand beside Lacey. After the song, and a wish, Damien blew out the blazing candles. Presents were opened promptly after the cake was served.

"This one's from Lacey," Mia said handing Damien another gift.

Damien glanced over at Lacey as he took the rather large package from Mia. "You didn't have to do this," he said to her.

Lacey smiled. "Sure I did. It's your birthday."

Damien ripped open the wrapping then raised the lid on the exposed white box. Inside he found a Daniel Overstreet original creation. It was a sculpture of a fireman in full gear with an ax thrown over his shoulder. The facial features of the fireman were distinctively African-American. The number on his helmet was twenty-four.

"Oh, baby, it's wonderful," Damien said without thought to the endearment. He held the gift up for everyone to see. There was a round of oohs as the figure was passed around. Damien was so moved by her gift that he leaned over and kissed Lacey deeply. His tongue swept into her mouth before she had a chance to protest. The taste and warmth of her mouth created such a firestorm of passion inside of Damien that he temporarily forgot that they had an audience. When they finally drew apart, it was to find the whole table wearing smiles.

Lacey was a little embarrassed and a great deal shaken by the kiss. It had been intense and demanding and much too brief. To lighten the moment she quipped, "I think he likes it."

"You think?" Mia replied. Then the entire table broke out into laughter. Damien glanced back at Lacey apologetically before pulling her to his side.

"Sorry," he whispered.

"Don't be," Lacey whispered back and smiled. They continued to stare at each other for a moment longer as their relationship took a change.

The party finally broke up around one in the morning. Everyone had had a good time and made their final good-byes. Kenneth and Mia helped Damien and Lacey carry his gifts out to his vehicle. Once they were secured, the couples talked for several minutes more. Mia and Lacey exchanged business cards with the promise to get together for lunch one day next week while the guys made plans to play basketball Sunday evening. After another round of hugs, they finally said their good-byes.

Damien and Lacey kept up a steady stream of conversation inside the vehicle on the drive to Lacey's home. It was the first time that they had really talked at length. They discussed what was taking place in the news, in their local community, as well as the evening. An intimacy was born. At the traffic light just before her home, Damien looked over at Lacey and felt his heart fill with something new. She had gone from being just a friend tonight to the woman of his desire. He reached over taking her hand and didn't let go until they were at Lacey's home.

"Aren't you coming in?" Lacey asked Damien as she walked into the foyer and realized that he wasn't following. He remained in the door-way.

"Not tonight," he said, reaching for her hands. He drew her close so that he could look into her eyes. "Did you have a good time tonight?"

Lacey smiled as she nodded her head. "I had a wonderful time."

"I'm sorry if I embarrassed you with that little kiss."

Lacey's eyes sparkled with laughter. "That kiss wasn't so little, Damien."

He laughed, and proceeded to wrap his arms around her waist. "You're right it wasn't, but it was an expression of my feelings, as is this." Damien lowered his mouth to Lacey's in another scorching kiss, all the while very aware of the rapid thumping in his chest. Lacey part-ed her lips to receive him and moaned deep in the back of her throat. Damien responded to her sound of pleasure by increasing the pressure of his lips. In them he expressed his pleasure and joy to be with her. Slowly, he tempered the kiss as he separated their mouths. The look in his hazel eyes was one of yearning. But it was much too soon for he and Lacey to contemplate being intimate. They were still in the getting-to-know-you stage and he had every intention of doing things properly. This relationship was worth the wait and held potential that he wasn't willing to risk on lust.

"I should be going."

Lacey smiled, with passion reflected in her eyes. She was well aware of the yearning in his kiss and knew that she herself felt the flicker of desire. But when she was with Damien she thought of a forever kind of love and after hearing about his marriage to Sara, Lacey knew that he was a forever-type of guy.

"Perhaps that's best."

"Before I do though, I wanted to invite you to spend the day with me tomorrow."

"What did you have in mind?"

"I participate in the Louisiana Native Guard reenactments out on Ship Island and I was hoping you would come with me tomorrow. We could have breakfast before boarding the ferry, unless you get seasick." He gave her a questioning glance.

She smiled. "Breakfast will be fine."

"Good. At nine we'll take the ferry out to the island. We can take one of the tours through Ft. Massachusetts or, if you've done that before, we can just kick back on the beach and relax until the reenactment."

"It all sounds fabulous. But I'm ashamed to say that I have never been out to the fort. It was only recently that I actually heard about the black troops who served at the fort during the Civil War, so I can't wait to see it."

Damien had felt that same excitement when he first learned of the Native Guard. He had done extensive research on the Second Regiment and joined the local reenactment group. Now he could proudly share his passion with Lacey.

"And I can't wait to show it to you," Damien whispered." He paused knowing now was the time to be honest with Lacey. He held her hands loosely in his while working up the courage to approach the subject of her resemblance to Sara. Just as he opened his mouth to speak, the pager on his hip vibrated. Damien ignored it.

"The other day at my parent's home I was trying to tell you something."

"I remember."

The pager vibrated once more and this time Damien couldn't ignore it. He released Lacey's hands to check the readout.

Lacey knew from the intensity of his eyes that the message was serious and that their night was officially over. "Is it work?"

"Interstate pile-up. We're being recalled." Damien finally glanced back to her. "I'm sorry, honey, but I've got to report in." He kissed her quickly, then backed out the door, their conversation forgotten. "I'll see you in the morning."

CHAPTER 7

Lacey was dressed and waiting for Damien by the time he arrived the next morning. She met him eagerly at the door with a smile followed by a kiss that went from sweet to a continuation of the passion they had found last night. Reluctantly, she broke away and headed toward the living room.

"Good morning," she said over her shoulder.

"It is, after that kiss," Damien replied with enthusiasm. He took in the layout of Lacey's home as he followed her through. From the foyer the house was laid out going to the rear. To the left, just off the front door, was a spacious and very neat kitchen in blue. Directly ahead but to the right, a staircase led to the second floor and off to the right, a room with a closed door. Following her on back, they passed the dining room on the left as well, then further back into the living room located at the rear of the house. It was large and spacious, decorated in a contemporary style. A fireplace was positioned in the corner to the right of the room. Just inside the doorway was a small computer workstation. From the many papers stacked on the surface, Damien surmised this was Lacey's place to write.

"So this is where the great masterpieces are created?" he asked pointing to the slightly cluttered station.

"I know it's not much, but it serves the purpose." She smiled. "I keep promising myself that I'll do something with my spare bedroom, but you know how it is, you never seem to get around to it."

She stood in the middle of the hardwood floor with a shy smile on her face. It was clear to him that she was a little uncomfortable. She balled her hands into tight fists down beside her thighs in what he was becoming to recognize as a sign of nervousness.

"I'm ready to leave when you are, unless you would prefer I cook breakfast here."

Damien took in Lacey's appearance. She looked way too good to be cooking. Her slim body was dressed in orange and yellow floral capri pants, yellow tube top, and a sheer orange blouse. Her feet were bare and she had never looked more appealing to him. He felt like a man returning home after a long trip away. The feeling stunned and slightly frightened him. But as he admired the woman standing before him, he knew there was nothing to fear because Lacey was just as vulnerable as he was.

However, the heat in Damien's eyes gave no indication of his vulnerability. They perused her body with a male familiarity that spoke of long sweaty nights of lovemaking. Lacey licked her lips just remembering the feel of his muscled arms around her and the taste of his mouth mating with hers. Her sherry eyes were extremely expressive and Damien knew that her thoughts were of a sensual nature.

"We better get out of here before I say the hell with that reenactment," Damien voice was thick with barely contained emotion. His eyes followed Lacey's shapely hips as she spun around and retrieved her orange braided sandals by the desk. When she was ready, he extended his hand in her direction and received simple satisfaction when her flesh came into contact with his.

At nine o'clock sharp the ferry pulled away from the dock. A light breeze helped to curtail the effect of the hot Mississippi sun. Lacey stood within the circle of Damien's arms on the top deck near the railing taking in the view. The coastline from east to west was an array of summertime colors. Sea gulls flew overhead, while a pair of dolphins off the side of the ferry entertained the passengers with their beauty. She was glad that she had agreed to come today.

"Aren't they beautiful?" Damien said to Lacey.

"Magnificent." Lacey turned around inside his arms so that she could see his face. They both wore sunglasses and so she pushed hers on top of her head, then reached for Damien's. She smiled impishly when he looked at her questioningly.

"I can't stand talking into reflective sunglasses. I like to see people's eyes."

"Well, Ms. Avery, you're welcome to look into my eyes anytime you desire," Damien teased before kissing her on the cheek. "Now what did you want to talk about?"

"I was wondering if your family has been out to the fort for the reenactments. I just thought it would be a wonderful learning experience for your nieces and nephews."

At the mention of the kids and the knowledge that she was thinking about them, Damien's heart was fast becoming Lacey's. "Yes, they've been out a couple of times, but maybe the two of us can bring the children again."

"I'd like that. Things are always so much more fascinating through a child's eyes."

"Why aren't you married with children, Lacey?" Damien surprised himself by asking the question that had been on his mind since meeting her. She possessed all the qualities a man could desire in a wife.

For a serious moment Lacey considered telling Damien the truth. But as she glanced around the crowded ferry, she knew that this wasn't the right place for such a personal and maybe volatile conversation, so instead she simply told him that she had once been engaged.

"How old were you?" Damien asked.

"Twenty-one."

"What happened?"

Lacey sighed as the memories came rolling back, but she refused to allow them to ruin the day. "I had a terrible accident that placed me in the hospital for several weeks and while I was in the hospital, my fiancée came to visit me one day and told me that he had changed his mind." She glanced off to the left of Damien not focusing on anything in particular.

"Just like that? There was no explanation?"

"Sure there was, but in the final analysis, it boiled down to he didn't love me."

Damien knew that he had been given the condensed version. He could also tell by Lacey's stiff expression that whatever the cause for the breakup, it had had a permanent effect on her. Not for a second did he believe she still loved the guy, but he did believe her actions today where in direct response to that event. He secured her chin in his hand and forced her to look back at him.

"I'm sorry that he hurt you." He brushed his lips against hers. "However, I'm very glad he didn't marry you." He gave her his high wattage smile.

Lacey's heart was near overflowing with emotion. She studied Damien's dark face, loving the way the sun made his hazel eyes appear golden. And his beautiful smile had the power to make her knees weak. She traced his lips with her fingers while her eyes caressed his handsome face. "Not half as much as me."

Damien drew her into his arms for a hug. When he released her, he asked about her accident. "Holly was telling me that you did gymnastics in college."

"Actually since the age of three, but yes, the accident took place in college."

"I'm sorry you lost your dream."

"Some dreams aren't meant to be. And then others can lead you to places and people you never imagined. Like the day of my car accident. I was leaving a book signing when that drunk hit me, and guess who came to my rescue?"

Damien laughed as his eyes took in her subtle beauty. Although Lacey was a knockout, her gentle, feminine nature toned down her beauty. It was there just waiting to be revealed in the quiet moments when she didn't know she was being watched. But he had been quite aware of the male stares as she walked past on his arm.

"Tell me about Sara," Lacey asked. The question brought Damien out of his daydream fast. His eyes searched hers. The interest was honest and filled with curiosity about the other woman he had loved.

"I guess you've heard plenty about Sara?"

"Quite a bit, but not from you. How long were the two of you married?"

"Ten years."

Ten years. Lacey felt the foundation of her new confidence wobble.

Damien hadn't noticed the look of concern on Lacey's face because his mind was weighing what to say. He let his hands fall to the side as he stepped around Lacey to lean forward on the railing. He glanced out into the middle of the Gulf thinking about his wife. Slowly he found the proper words to describe her, but not once did he dare think to mention their resemblance. Damien knew that he couldn't hurt Lacey further by dropping that news on her now. Not after hearing about her broken engagement and seeing the hurt in her eyes.

"She was a beautiful fireball of energy. Sara was always on the go. People loved her outgoing nature. You know she was one of those people who never met a stranger."

"I heard she was a lawyer."

"Sara's career was very important to her. She was a young black lawyer on her way to the top, and she wasn't going to allow anyone to stand in her way of achieving that goal. She would drag me from one social function to another. Networking was the word she used."

"I bet you two made a beautiful couple; both of you going places in your careers."

Damien glanced over at Lacey with a peculiar expression that she would wonder about later. "We were an odd couple. I'm tall and Sara stood an even five feet. She was a social butterfly and I was simply the fly. But together, with no outside interferences, we were a beautiful couple."

For different reasons they both fell silent. Damien watched Lacey from the periphery and wondered what she was thinking. Had he said too much or maybe not enough?

"Sara never came to one of the reenactments with me. She felt it was a waste of both our times."

Lacey turned to face him. She covered his hand gripping the rail with her own. Privately she thought the great Sara was a little self-centered.

"Teaching others about our history is never a waste and I'm extremely proud of you." The words flew from her mouth before she could call them back. Damien's eyes swung to her and studied her with a critical observance. She hadn't meant to infer anything bad against Sara. It was just her mouth running before her brain could kick in. "I shouldn't have said that."

"Why?" Damien asked while threading his fingers through hers.

"Because it sounds like I was criticizing your wife." Lacey's eyes danced nervously.

"My wife is gone, Lacey." Damien looked her in the eyes. "And I didn't take your words as criticism. I thought you were giving me a pat on the back." He smiled to lighten the moment.

Lacey was relieved. "I was." She laughed nervously.

"Come here," Damien said, pulling her into his arms. He held Lacey to his heart knowing that he was a goner. It had never taken him long to decide upon what he wanted. Usually when he saw it, he knew instantly that it was to be his. The same had happened with Sara in high school and the day of the accident with Lacey, he had known then, that she was the woman for him.

The ferry captain announced they would be docking soon and to gather all carry-on items. The twelve-mile ride out into the Gulf of Mexico had gone by quickly while they talked. Damien wished they had more time because they were finally sharing the important events in their lives.

The two disembarked. Damien held Lacey's hand as they walked down the wooden pier to the white sandy shores of Ship Island. Beach goers were racing for the ideal positions on the beach. Others were headed to the snack bar, with many more, like Lacey and Damien making their way to Fort Massachusetts. At the entrance, the tour was just beginning.

Construction of the circular masonry fort, named after the Union blockade ship by the same name, began in 1859 and continued over a seven-year period. During that time it was under British, Confederate, and Union control. The structure roughly contained a million red bricks and featured beautiful arched or vaulted passageways. There were originally forty or so buildings constructed at the fort. The hospital, barracks, mess hall and bakery were just a few. And, during the Civil War, the fort was used as a prison camp for captured Confederate troops. The Second Louisiana Native Guard was an all-black regiment, responsible for guarding Confederate prisoners, making sure the fort was in fighting condition, and monitoring gulf shipping activity while the North blockaded the South. The Second Louisiana Native Guard was also the first black regiment to see military action in the Battle of Pascagoula on April 9, 1863. After the war, many in the Guard went on to fight for their civil rights during Reconstruction.

After the tour, Lacey and Damien purchased drinks at the snack bar, then located two chairs on the beach to await the reenactment. They discussed the tour information and the pride they had found in the men of the Native Guard. At two o'clock, Damien excused himself to get dressed. Before leaving he gave Lacey an arousing kiss with promises of more later. She had watched him leave with a smile on her face. Then promptly at three o'clock, the cannons fired and the men of the Second Louisiana Native Guard rushed out into position. Their many black officers called out orders in defense of Fort Massachusetts.

Damien portrayed one of the seventy-six Native Guard officers who served. Dressed in Union blue, his muscular physique did wonders for the uniform, and his natural authoritative voice commanded attention as he recited *A Black Soldier's Creed,* written in 1863 by Joseph E. Williams, a black man from Pennsylvania who recruited freed slaves in North Carolina to serve in the Union Army. By the time he finished, many eyes were bright with tears. The African-Americans witnessing his portrayal nodded their heads in affirmation. Lacey beamed with pride.

"That is one fine man," a woman from behind Lacey whispered to her girlfriend.

"I wonder if he's taken?" the friend whispered back.

"One hundred percent taken," Lacey said over her shoulder.

The two women glanced at each other and laughed. "All right now, but you can't blame a sister for trying."

Lacey joined in their laughter because she did understand the appeal of an intelligent black man. Not to mention Damien's handsomeness.

The reenactment ended and the actors began mingling amongst the crowd. Damien made a beeline for Lacey. He had seen some of the glances in her direction from the males in the audience. He wasn't giving any of these guys a chance at his woman.

"So, what did you think?" Damien asked as he drew Lacey into his arms. His smile was bright and just for her.

Lacey noticed the two women watching them. They gave the thumb ups and disappeared into the interior of the fort. She gave Damien her attention. "I thought it was quite impressive, and Damien, I have never been as proud of anyone before as I am of you right now. This is a part of our history that has been lost, left out of the history books, and men like you bring it to life for our children. You were wonderful," she whispered as the emotion that she was feeling clogged her throat. She threw her arms around Damien's neck in an embrace that he would never forget.

"Baby, you sure know how to make a man feel good about himself." Damien returned her embrace. He was consumed with pride, for himself and for what he had discovered in Lacey. "Let me go change and then we can take the next ferry back to port."

"Okay," Lacey agreed as she released him. She searched around for somewhere to wait. Spying a bench near the lone entrance to the fort, she told Damien she would wait for him there.

"I won't be long."

The trip back was just as eventful as the ride over. The only difference in their conversation now was that they talked of each other and left the past in the past. Today they had created a new memory that only they would share and a bond based in heartfelt emotion and not mere desire.

Damien purchased a cup of ice cream that the two of them shared. A spoonful for her—a spoonful for him. There were smoldering glances and lots of silly giggles as they whispered back and forth. Several older couples exchanged knowing glances as they watched the young couple nurturing a new love.

CHAPTER 8

In August things were beginning to pick up for Lacey. Her first mainstream novel, *Rescue of the Heart* was generating a great deal of interest. There were national book tours and signings. Women's groups were clamoring to have her speak at their charity functions. And more hours were spent on airplanes than at home. However, always mindful of their new relationship, Lacey mapped out her schedule so that she was at home on Damien's days off. By day, he was free to take care of any family obligations that came up, but the evenings were theirs. They took turns cooking or shared the task. Occasionally they had dinner out, but Lacey wasn't a big fan of restaurants. The movies, however, were a favorite of theirs. And then some evenings they simply did nothing more than talk and lay intertwined on the sofa.

That's where her thoughts were as she drove home from yet another trip away. She had started leaving her vehicle parked in the long-term parking at the airport so that she wouldn't have to inconvenience someone with picking her up. As she drove out of the parking lot, her thoughts were of Damien. She had missed him intensely while on this trip. She didn't analyze the meaning, only accepted that it was true. At the traffic light on Highway 49, she debated about going right toward the interstate and home, or left to the fire station and Damien. When the light turned green she turned left and headed to the man she had missed. The drive to the station wasn't long. It was actually a straight shot. Less than ten minutes later, she was pulling into the driveway of the fire station. She immediately spotted Damien's truck and pulled in beside it. She didn't know the proper etiquette for visiting a fire station. Did one simply walk up to the front door and knock like at someone's home? Then a thought occurred to her. She searched in her purse for her cell phone. Locating it, she selected the code for Damien's preprogrammed office number. The phone rang. As she waited, she noted the time was a little after nine in the evening. She hadn't given consideration to the time when she drove over, but as Damien's voice came to her over the phone line, she dismissed her concern.

"Captain Christoval."

"Hi sweetheart."

"Lacey baby, where are you? Are you at home?"

"No, I'm not."

"Please tell me you're not still in Atlanta."

"You sound as though you've missed me." Lacey laughed.

"I have and when I see you, I'll show you just how much."

"Well come on out here and show me," Lacey stated boldly while trying not to laugh.

"Where are you?" Damien's voice rose with excitement.

"Standing beside your truck with a big smile on my face."

"Woman, why didn't you say so?" Damien nearly shouted.

The phone line went dead as he slammed down the phone in her ear. Then the front door swung open and Damien walked through. His eyes quickly sought her out. They lit with joy. Then his face blossomed with a smile that set Lacey's heart racing with excitement. She couldn't believe how much she had missed this man. But as Damien stopped in front of her and opened his arms, Lacey eagerly stepped into them and knew that she was where she had always wanted to be.

They didn't speak a word. The look in their eyes, the smiles on their faces, and the gentleness of their touch expressed all that was in their hearts. Damien lowered his mouth to Lacey's waiting lips and bestowed a kiss that rocked them both to the depth of their souls. And when they parted, both knew that their relationship would never be the same. Their thoughts once singular, were now plural, to include the other. And their hearts once empty were filled with the possibility of a new love.

Damien let the tailgate down on his truck and lifted Lacey inside. It was a warm night with a pleasant breeze. They sat arm in arm in back of the truck looking up at the stars. For several minutes they sat silently savoring the closeness. Then Damien glanced over at Lacey and realized that she wore a dreamy smile on her face. His curiosity got the better of him.

"What are you thinking about?"

Lacey sighed as she rested her head on his shoulder. "How happy I am. It's been a long time."

Damien knew where Lacey was coming from. "I feel the same way," he replied, kissing the top of her head.

"Daniel convinced me to see you that second time. My confidence with men had been shaken and according to him I have been running from serious involvements for the last several years."

"I've sort of been hiding out myself," Damien confided.

Lacey laughed dryly. "Aren't we a pair?"

"Yes we are, Lacey. A pretty good pair," Damien said as he raised her face to his. "And remind me to tell Daniel thanks."

"I'll do that."

Damien suddenly grew serious. Here was the opportunity to come clean with Lacey about Sara. He stroked the side of her face while silently praying that she would forgive him.

"I've been trying to tell you something for a while now," Damien started speaking.

Lacey could visibly see the change in him. Whatever he had to say was stressful; painful even. The evening was too perfect for such seriousness. She raised her hand to cover his lips. Looking into his worried eyes, she spoke. "What you have to tell me, does it affect your feelings for me?"

"No. But..."

She covered his mouth once more. "No buts, I don't want to know.

This moment is too perfect to ruin and we're both happy. That's all that matters."

Reluctantly, Damien agreed. He settled back with Lacey in his arms knowing that this secret wouldn't keep much longer.

"Now, isn't this better?" Lacey commented as she placed her head onto his chest.

With his thoughts troubled, Damien leaned forward kissing the top of her head. "Life is better with you by my side."

Lacey smiled in remembrance a week later. She and Damien had snuggled for several minutes more in the back of his truck before she had finally said goodnight. And oh, what a goodnight it had been.

Now, she moved around the living room of her home lighting candles. She wanted everything perfect when Damien arrived. Tonight was the end of his shift and she knew that this week in particular had been extremely difficult for him. Holly's ex-husband had returned to town and was causing problems over at the Christoval home. Knowing that his father wasn't in any physical condition to handle Steven Porter, Damien had been forced to take off from work to confront the man. There had been several more run-ins before Steven disappeared just as fast as he had appeared. The toll of worrying about his father, and now his sister, was weighing heavily on him and tonight Lacey wanted to do something special for him to help ease the tension.

The dining room was set with her best china and crystal. The meal was right on schedule. In the living room, her surprise waited. A body pillow lay on the floor. Scented oils and lotions sat in a tray on the coffee table. A believer in aromatherapy, she had selected candles in a fragrance conducive to relaxation. And soft jazz was cued and ready. Now all she required was Damien.

She had taken particular care with her appearance tonight. She wore a white satin lounger with haltered top and wide-legged pants, cut low on the hips. A thin belly chain accentuated the look. She had selected the outfit because it was comfortable, casual, and seductive. Not that seduction was really on the agenda for tonight, but there wasn't any harm in keeping Damien interested. Her long hair had been twisted on top of her head and held with a jeweled clip. Small gold hoops dangled from her ears.

She had thrown caution to the wind and gone where her heart led and so far it hadn't steered her wrong where Damien was concerned. He was kind and gentle and always thinking of her needs first. His loving spirit had gone a long way in helping her to heal her battered heart and tonight was an expression of her appreciation.

Damien was mentally and physically exhausted. He seriously considered going straight home, but knew Lacey was waiting for him and he wouldn't disappoint her. However, he wasn't sure he would be very good company. But, as he pulled into Lacey's driveway, he gained a burst of energy just thinking about the woman who was fast making a place inside his heart. He didn't have to pretend to be someone he wasn't with Lacey and he appreciated that. She accepted the closeness of his family and his sense of duty where they were concerned. The quiet times together were the best, and enough. They didn't need outside people, events, or things to keep the bond between them strong. It just was.

"Hi," Lacey greeted Damien at the door. She stepped back into the foyer as he entered. She could see the exhaustion in his walk and in the slowness of his smile.

"Hi, baby." Damien dropped a kiss on her lips, and stood back examining her appearance. "Lacey, girl, you're about to make me forget how tired I am." He reached for her and she dodged him.

"Dinner is ready."

"What if I want dessert?" Damien said following behind her. His eyes were fixed on her fine swaying hips

"Then you have to eat your dinner," Lacey tossed over her shoulder as she gave him a saucy glance.

"Then let's eat fast."

Lacey escorted Damien back into the living room once dinner was complete. She lit a match and systematically began lighting the candles in the room. When the room became washed in candlelight, she blew out the match and laid it on the tray. With the stereo remote, soft jazz soon filled the air.

Damien stood where she had left him in the doorway. He wore blue pleated slacks and a lighter shade of a blue button down shirt. He glanced around at her handiwork, suddenly not as exhausted as he had been a moment ago. Lacey was up to something and he eagerly anticipated her next move.

She didn't keep him waiting long. Lacey returned to him standing in the doorway and led him over to the pillow sprawled in the middle of the floor. She stopped and met Damien's curious gaze. She kissed him lightly, as she reached for the buttons on the front of his shirt.

"You do so much for everyone else," she said as the first button gave way, "that tonight I wanted to do something for you."

"And what might that be?" Damien asked with a voice suddenly laced with tension. His hazel eyes watched closely as Lacey released yet another button.

She glanced at him briefly. "A massage." She undid another button and pulled the tail of his shirt free from his pants.

Damien swore under his breath as the sheer magnitude of her words registered inside his head. A desirable woman was removing his shirt to give him a massage. He didn't think he was strong enough to handle Lacey caressing his body.

"Baby, maybe this isn't a good idea."

Lacey laughed. "It will help you to relax. I know you've been under a great deal of pressure lately."

The only pressure that was concerning Damien at the moment was below his waist. "I'm fine, Lacey." Damien tried to convince her, but it was too late. The last button gave way and Lacey stood before him examining her find. She ran her delicate looking hands across the hardness of his chest and lower over his washboard abdomen. After what seemed like hours of pleasurable torture, she planted a kiss in the middle of his chest, and proceeded to remove his shirt. Lacey pushed the folds of the shirt back off his muscled chest and over wide shoulders, down bulging biceps, and further down strong arms. When his hands were free of the shirt, she ceremoniously draped it across the table and ordered Damien to lie down.

He took a deep breath as he complied and tried to ignore the rising bulge in the front of his pants. Stretching out on the body pillow, he had to admit it felt pretty good. The music, candles, and the softness of the pillow had Damien rethinking this idea of Lacey's. But the moment her hands touched his back, slick and warm with oil, he asked himself what the hell he had been thinking to agree to this.

Lacey skillfully went to work releasing the tension in Damien's upper body. She worked the oils into his wide shoulders with strong sure strokes. With the pads of her fingers, she kneaded down the length of his back before applying slight pressure in the bend. Working her way back up, his arms and hands were next, followed by the neck area. The muscles there were extremely tight under her fingers. But as she rubbed and worked the oil into his flesh, the muscles slowly began to ease. Damien purred when she touched a particular spot and Lacey knew that he had stopped fighting her touch and given himself over to the skill in her hands.

She admired the beauty of his dark body under her fingertips. The skin was clear and smooth despite the hard toned muscles underneath. His body gave off natural heat that she found sensually disturbing.

Damien hadn't realized how tense and tight his body was until Lacey began to work her magic. The muscles rioted under her manipulation at the beginning, but slowly eased and became pliable. He was surprised by the skill and strength in her small delicate hands, but she had been a gymnast he reminded himself. That skill required strength, endurance, and grace. But the feel of her straddling his body and the sweep of her pants against his lower back as she occasionally raised up to reach his neck area was beginning to cause a different type of tension to stir inside of him again. Closing his eyes, he tried to concentrate on the feel of Lacey's hands on his flesh and not the fantasy trying to take dominance inside his head.

Damien's breathing was slow and shallow. His eyes were closed as he lay quietly beneath her. Lacey could tell that she had achieved her goal in relaxing him. He had fought her like she knew that he would, but in the end, his body had taken over and responded to her touch.

Lacey took the opportunity to study Damien. He looked beautiful and peaceful sprawled on the floor. Her heart filled with a powerful emotion that she didn't dare acknowledge; however, the desire to be close to him was gnawing at her. She tried to resist the temptation pulsing through her body, but soon lost the fight. Defeated she leaned forward covering Damien's upper body with her own. The heat from his body caused her to sigh with pleasure as the dormant womanly need inside of her awakened with a vengeance.

Lacey closed her eyes and moaned as the flames of desire burned hotly in the pit of her belly. She eased over Damien and rolled to the side to stretch out beside him. Her eyes mapped a course over his unique face. He was all male, yet no less beautiful. His near-black skin enhanced his masculine appeal. Lacey had to touch him. Her hand smoothed his dark brows and caressed his narrow nose. Next, it grazed his lean cheek as her eyes hungrily studied his mouth. She knew the feel and taste of it. Just thinking about the pleasure it could give her caused another wave of desire to wash over her. Lacey sighed with a growing frustration.

"Oh, Damien, you're a drug I'm finding hard to resist," she whispered softly to his sleeping form.

"Then stop trying to resist," he whispered back as his eyes popped open to meet hers. They held the same burning passion as her own. He had quietly allowed his senses to take over for his eyes. In his mind he could see her beautiful face masked in concentration as she massaged his flesh. In her touch, he knew her yearning. And the ache in her voice spoke of the raging need inside of her. Damien reached out drawing Lacey to him. He aligned her long body against his as his mouth covered hers. The contact of their lips was soft and gentle. For several minutes they did nothing more than press their lips together, then Lacey sighed in that feminine way that women do to signal their pleasure and Damien lost all control. He covered not only Lacey's lips, but her body as well. He fit his hardness to her softness as he deepened the kiss. He forced her lips apart with the thrust of his tongue and performed an erotic give and take that his body longed to emulate. His hands caressed the length of her body before charting a course to her straining breasts. The satin halter did nothing to hide the fullness of her breasts or the hardness of her nipples. He teased the swollen pebbles while making love to her mouth, and trailed kisses down her neck. He raised his head to look down on her.

Lacey's eyes swept open as Damien began caressing her breasts. She realized that he watched her and fed off her response to his touch. Her hands covered his as she raised her head to kiss him.

Damien took the change in position as an opportunity to release the halter. He reverently lowered it to bare Lacey before him. After admiring her for several minutes, he assaulted her with his mouth. He pulled a plumped nipple between his lips and swept his tongue across it. The feel and taste was the sweetest he had ever known.

Shockwaves swept through Lacey's body from the contact of his lips. Her body arched with each delicious tug.

The insistent ringing of the doorbell interrupted the charged moment. Lacey cried out in frustration as Damien rested his head between her heaving breasts. He cursed before rolling off of her.

"Were you expecting someone?" he asked, breathing heavily.

"No." Lacey managed to sit up. Her halter hung around her waist. Quickly she repositioned it as the doorbell continued to ring.

Damien fastened the clasp around her neck back into place and kissed her neck.

"There. Go let whoever it is in so that I can kill them."

Lacey laughed as she rose from the floor. She raced through the house, wondering about her unexpected guest.

CHAPTER 9

"Paige? What's the emergency?" Lacey asked her publicist as the woman practically ran through the door.

Paige Rivers was a small golden-brown dynamo with a pixie cut and a splash of freckles across the nose. She was one of the best new publicists in the business. Her outgoing vibrant personality was a plus in the business, but also quite deceiving. Paige was as tenacious as they came and cunning, and since Lacey hired her, both their careers had taken off.

"This was just too big to deliver over the telephone," she rushed to say. "I had to come over so that I could see your face when I told you the news. I just can't believe she called. Well of course I can. You're so talented." Her hands moved to the rhythm of her speech. "So, what do you think?"

Lacey stood watching Paige in amazement. All that said on one breath of air. "Paige, I have no idea what you're talking about." Lacey smiled down on her publicist and friend.

"Oh," Paige stated, and lost her train of thought as Damien appeared behind Lacey. She glanced at her friend and noticed her disheveled hair and kiss-swollen lips. The big guy was put back together, but she doubted cherry wine was his choice in lipstick.

"I'm interrupting." Paige's eyes darted between the two.

Lacey glanced over her shoulder as Damien came to stand beside her. The look he gave was intimate.

"Paige Rivers, my publicist, I'd like you to meet Damien Christoval. Damien, my friend Paige."

"It's a pleasure to meet you, Paige," Damien responded, extending his hand.

"The pleasure's all mine," Paige said in between admiring Lacey's man. She had always wondered where her talented friend derived her inspiration and now she knew. "What do you do for a living, Damien?" Paige asked while checking out his physique.

"I'm a fireman."

"A fireman," Paige chimed. *And no doubt Lacey's inspiration for* Rescue of the Heart.

"You were saying..." Lacey tactfully reminded Paige that she came to her home for a reason.

Paige smiled sheepishly at Damien, then Lacey. "Sorry. But like I was saying, I received a telephone call earlier from Olivia's Book Club. She has chosen your new book for her book club this month and wants you in Chicago Monday for filming."

"Oh, my God," Lacey squealed with excitement.

"Baby, that's wonderful," Damien roared with pride. He swept Lacey up into his arms and hugged her.

Paige watched the two. She could tell that the big guy was genuinely happy for Lacey, which would make her job easier. So many men were threatened by a woman's success, and used guilt to keep their partners from achieving their goals.

"Lacey, you do realize that you'll have to fly out tomorrow?"

That got Lacey's attention. She glanced over at Paige, then Damien. He had three days off coming up and she had planned on spending them with him as she always did.

"I can't make it Monday."

"What do you mean you can't make it Monday?" Paige came unglued. "This is Olivia here. When she endorses a book, it soars to the top of the bestseller list. This is an opportunity that you can't pass up."

Damien knew why Lacey didn't want to make the Monday appointment and he couldn't allow her to throw away this opportunity. "Lacey baby, we'll spend the next off days together. This opportunity is too important to your career to miss."

Lacey clutched her fist to her side in concentration. She really wanted this interview, but their relationship was important to her as well. "Let me think about this." Lacey walked away in thought. "Are you sure you're okay with changing our plans?"

"I'm sure and there is nothing to think about. Do you know what would happen to me if my mother were to find out that I prevented you from being on Olivia's show?" He drew his finger across his throat. "It will be off with my head."

Lacey laughed and walked over to hug him. "So I guess I should start packing."

"I'll keep you company," Damien told her.

Paige quickly filled Lacey in on all the details of her six-day trip. She whipped out an itinerary which contained not only Monday's interview, but also brunch on Sunday, lunch on Tuesday, a photo shoot Wednesday, and breakfast with Olivia's Book Club members. She would return home on Friday.

After Paige left, Damien joined Lacey, as promised, while she packed her luggage. It was his first time in her bedroom and neither thought anything of it due to their excitement about her upcoming interview. Damien sat on the floral peach settee by the window which matched the bedspread on Lacey's queen-size bed. He looked on while she ran around the room pulling out clothes and asking his opinion about which outfit to wear on the show. By the time she finished packing, she was the one in need of a massage. But in lieu of that, Damien talked her into stretching back out on the floor in the living room while the soft jazz played in the background. They snuggled for several minutes in silence. Damien leaned over and kissed Lacey sweetly. He then reached into his front pocket and pulled out a key.

"I had this made for you."

Lacey balanced on her elbow, staring at the key Damien held out to her. Slowly she reached out and accepted it. With it in her hand she turned it over for a heartbeat before looking back at him. "Is this the key to your home?"

Damien's eyes searched her face for some hint of her thoughts. He could see concern in her eyes. "Yes, it is, and I want you to feel free to use it anytime."

Lacey was deeply touched by the gesture. Her eyes blurred with unshed tears. "Thank you so much, but I won't use it if you're home. I believe in giving people their privacy, so I'll always knock."

"Lacey, that makes no sense. Use the key anytime."

"No, but thanks for the trust."

"I do trust you baby, and I want you in my life and my home." For a long moment their eyes locked in silent communication. Both were well aware of what else was being stated.

Lacey leaned over, kissing Damien, and excused herself from the room. In minutes she returned with a key in hand and a garage door opener. "I had these made for you last week," she admitted, smiling. "I trust you too, and want you to be a frequent visitor to my home."

Damien accepted the key and opener. He was indeed humbled by Lacey's gift and also to know that their thoughts had been the same. He leaned forward, kissing her once more before saying, "I'll miss you."

"I'll miss you too, Damien."

And the ache of missing Damien had accompanied her all the way to Chicago that day and every trip she took after that. Lacey couldn't wait to get home so that she could call Damien. This trip had consisted of yet another interview, this time a national morning show. Since having her novel selected by the Olivia Book Club, the requests for interviews had been pouring in and sales were on the rise. The interest was fueled by the discovery of her personal relationship with a fireman and the rumor that the novel was about their relationship. Lacey didn't have to wonder who had placed that rumor into circulation. It had Paige's fingerprints all over it. But tonight, all she desired was Damien. As she pulled into her driveway and raised the garage door, she was pleasantly surprised to see Damien's truck parked on the other side of the two-car garage.

A month ago they had exchanged house keys, and in her case a garage door opener, as well. It had proven to be a wise move considering the hours they spent at each other's homes. Both, however, were very mindful of the other's privacy and only used the key when the person wasn't home. Actually, that had been Lacey's stipulation. She wasn't comfortable simply walking into Damien's home just because she had a key to the door. Damien had conceded the point and returned the respect.

Lacey entered her home through the door which led from the garage to the kitchen. She called Damien's name but received no response. There was a large pot sitting on the stove. As she moved further into the house a light was coming from the spare bedroom down the hall. She carried her carryall bag with her as she went in search of Damien. For the life of her, she couldn't imagine what he would be doing in this room. It wasn't finished like the rest of the house. It had become a catchall for all the other things in her home that she didn't quite have a place for. So what could Damien be doing in there?

"Damien?" she called from just outside the door to the bedroom.

"Hi baby, come on in."

Lacey slowly pushed the cracked door open and stepped through. Her mouth immediately fell open as she glanced around the new home-office Damien had prepared for her. A built-in desktop in frosted glass ran the length of the wall to the right of the door. Shelving in the same glass covered the wall above the desk. Her many reference books filled the space. On the opposite wall, oak file and storage cabinets with glass doors, held her financial records and notes for future projects. Another countertop with storage underneath, housed her

85

printing supplies. And that new computer that she had dragged him along to check out with her, was now waiting for her next work of fiction.

"Oh, Damien," she cried as she examined every inch of her private space. It was obvious to her that the man paid attention to everything. The walls were painted in the warm pale salmon that she had debated about using in the dining room. Poster-size blowups of her many book covers decorated the walls and the green plants that she loved so much filled vacant space. At the windows he had wooden shutters so that the natural light wouldn't be hampered.

"Happy Birthday. I hope you like it," Damien said from behind her. He had silently watched as she took in every detail of the room.

Lacey turned watery eyes on Damien as she walked into his arms. "I love it," she wailed as the dam on her emotions broke.

"Whew! I was worried."

"There was no need to be," she said glancing up at him. "This room is perfect just like you are. But how did you know it was my birthday?"

"Daniel gave me a heads up several weeks ago." Damien couldn't help the smile on his face or the swell of his chest. Lacey's words always had that affect on him. She made him proud to be a man.

"I have chili simmering on the stove," he said.

"Can we eat it back here?" Lacey asked excited. "I don't want to leave my special room."

"Sure we can, I'll be right back."

Lacey remained in the office checking out every minor detail. It was apparent that Damien had worked hard to accomplish this transformation before she returned home. And she knew that he had done every inch of the work, because that was the type of man Damien was. He always gave of himself.

Damien returned carrying a tray with bowls of chili and all the fixings. He sat it on the countertop; then joined Lacey who was still exploring the room.

"I can't believe you did this for me."

"Kenneth helped me assemble and install the pieces. I think it turned out pretty good."

"I knew you hadn't paid to have this done. It has your loving touch to it," she said as she turned to face him. She slid her arms around Damien's neck and drew his mouth to hers. Through the kiss she tried to express the joy that was in her heart.

After their meal, they eventually returned to the living room where they snuggled on the sofa. Damien was lost in thought while Lacey's head rested against him. He still hadn't told her about her resemblance to Sara or the depth of his feelings. It was time for her to get reacquainted with his family as the woman in his life and not his friend, the writer. But there was a chance that someone would let the secret slip. He felt awful for deceiving her, but was so afraid that she wouldn't believe him when he said that it was she he saw when he looked at her. When he confessed, he wanted her to care so greatly for him that it wouldn't matter. Phillip kept telling him that he was playing with fire and should end it with Lacey, and fast. But that wasn't an option.

Lacey had one last scheduled trip before the holiday season set in. After that trip, he promised himself that he would come clean with the truth. He wanted Lacey to spend the holiday season with him and his family, and there was no way he could ask them to lie for him. So with his decision made, he relaxed beside her as they shared a quiet moment.

CHAPTER 10

"Thanks, big brother, for helping me redecorate the nursery for a third time," Phillip Christoval said to his brother. "I don't know why Robin insists upon changing things with each baby. It's not like the kid is going to know its siblings had the same wallpaper."

Damien chuckled because he had heard this all before and knew that despite Phillip's complaining, his brother would do anything for that wife of his. He and his wife had been married longer than Damien and Sara. They'd married right out of high school, but both had gone on to earn degrees. Their years of struggling and sacrificing had only made them closer. Damien, not for the first time, admired their commitment to each other.

Robin had been a partner in an accounting firm. Her busy schedule and long hours sometimes kept her away from their growing family, but the love and support of her husband made conditions possible for her to build the business of her dreams. And by working together, the business was finally doing so well that she was now able to work half a day.

Damien hadn't realized that Phillip was watching him or the odd expression on his face, until his brother inquired about it.

"You look as though you are a million miles away. What's going on with you? Is Lacey not turning out to be the woman you thought she was?"

Damien stared hard at his brother. For some reason he got the distinct impression that his brother didn't want his relationship with Lacey to work. "Lacey is the woman I thought she was, and far more. Why don't you want me with this woman? Every chance you get, you're trying to talk me into leaving her."

Phillip hadn't realized that his actions had been so obvious. He tossed the wallpaper brush to the floor as he sat in Robin's rocking chair. "It's not that I don't want you with this woman, Damien. I want you happy."

"Lacey makes me happy."

"And Sara made you happy in the beginning, too." Phillip watched his brother squirm.

"What do you know about me and Sara?" Damien's eyes narrowed on his brother.

Phillip leaned forward in the chair. His fingers were clasped together as he chose his words carefully. "I know that her career was more important than yours or you. I know that after ten years of marriage, you were still waiting to have children. I know that she wanted and lived a life that we weren't brought up in or even desired. I also know that despite your love for her, you weren't happy."

Damien expelled a long breath not knowing what to say. What could he say when his brother was right on all accounts. He merely shook his head. "You're right."

"I'm afraid that this Lacey is not only similar in appearance, but also in nature. She's an author on the rise. Look at all the flying around that she has been doing. When is she going to decide that being with a fireman isn't enough? When will she no longer desire the children that you so desperately want because they will interfere with her busy schedule? I don't want to see the hurt in your eyes again that you so valiantly tried to hide with Sara, because of this Lacey."

Damien had always loved Phillip. It had been the two of them for a couple of years before Holly was born and their closeness remained until today. He knew that his brother was concerned, but he also knew deep in his heart that this relationship with Lacey was completely different from the one he had with Sara.

"Lacey isn't like Sara. Her beauty is quiet and subtle. She gives as much to me as I give to her. We share our lives and our interests. Sara and I practically led separate lives." He glanced across the room to where Phillip watched him closely. "It's my fault that you haven't met Lacey and gotten to know her. But that's about to change. I'm going to tell her about Sara and then we are going to spend the holidays with the family. All I ask is that you give her an honest chance. She's not Sara and I don't want you taking your feelings for her out on Lacey."

Phillip pursed his lips as he contemplated his brother's words. He could tell that Damien was far too involved with this woman to turn back now. "You have my word and I'm glad you're coming clean with her."

"Me too, because it has really been eating me up inside."

"I just hope she takes it well."

"You and me both."

It was a week before Thanksgiving and Lacey was in Orlando speaking to a women's group that was sponsoring a writer's workshop, dinner, and book signing. Several women writers from all genres were speaking as well as conducting the workshops at the event. She had made quite a few new friends but she wished that she were on the sofa with Damien locked inside his arms.

Lacey entered her suite exhausted and lonesome. The fast paced schedule, numerous events, and social gatherings filled with friendly faces and wonderful accolades still couldn't replace her time with Damien. They took turns calling each other when they were separated and tonight was Damien's time to call. Lacey tried to be patient until he phoned, but she missed him. She stepped out of her heels and slipped on her house shoes while she waited. Tomorrow's schedule was in her satchel on the desk. She thought about retrieving it, but wasn't in the mood.

She missed Damien. She missed his beautiful hazel eyes and the way they shimmered in the light. His large presence was a constant in her life and her anchor when things became difficult. She missed hearing his deep masculine voice and the soothing comfort it offered. She whispered to the room that she missed him, but her brain screamed that she loved him.

Lacey fell into the nearest chair trying to steady her runaway nerves. She was shaking with a sudden fear as the enormity of the revelation set in. Her mind flashed back to Calvin and the first time that they had told each other of their love. An engagement soon followed. She had been young and foolishly in love, believing that love conquered all. But six months later, she had learned a valuable, yet hard lesson. Love comes and it goes. Now here she was years later, right where she had started. However, she was wiser now and would put the breaks on this relationship. Just then her cell phone rang from the side pocket of her satchel, and she knew that it was Damien on the other end. She watched as its piercing sound appeared to become louder. Three times it rang before finally falling silent. She released her breath only now aware that she had been holding it.

Lacey finally rose from the chair and headed to the bathroom. At the door, she remembered that her phone was still on and returned to the desk. She ran her hand into the side pocket of the satchel and removed it. With a tap of her thumb it was off. In a numb and confused state, she returned to the bathroom.

Damien was worried. Lacey hadn't answered her cell phone. She should have been in her room by now. He was in his office at the firehouse pacing the floor.

"What has you so upset?" Kenneth asked joining him.

Damien turned facing his friend. He shoved his hands into his pockets to keep from reaching for the telephone once more. "I can't reach Lacey on her cell phone. She's in Orlando for a book conference, but she's usually in her room by now. I hate it when she's in those big cities. I worry."

Kenneth roared with laughter as Damien looked at him like he had lost his mind.

"What the hell is so funny? I tell you that I haven't heard from Lace, and you're laughing?"

"Damien, has anyone informed you that you're head over heels in love with that woman?"

"What?" Damien asked as the impact of Kenneth's words struck him right between the eyes. He collapsed on the battered sofa in his office. His hazel eyes searched Kenneth's which were filled with humor. "Where was I when this happened?" He gave Kenneth a bewildered expression.

"I'd say, staring into Lacey's big sherry brown eyes." Kenneth laughed as Damien nodded his head.

"I knew from the moment I looked into those eyes that we would end up in love, but the realization that it has happened, just caught me off guard. We've been so busy with the upcoming holiday season and trying to fit time into our schedules to see each other, that I didn't realize that it had happened."

"You always did know what you wanted," Kenneth said taking a seat. "I remember the first time you saw Sara. Do you remember what you said to me?"

Damien laughed at the memory. He had been a sophomore in high school. "I told you that I was going to marry that girl."

"And you did."

"Yeah, I did," Damien said a little sadly.

"You had a good marriage, Damien."

"Yes, we *had*."

"You and Lacey can have the same thing."

Damien looked over at Kenneth shaking his head. "No, we can't. What Lacey and I have is vastly different from what Sara and I shared."

"How so?"

"For one thing, they are different women, with different temperaments. Sara was fiery and the take charge type. I admired her ability to set her sights on what she wanted and charge right ahead and get it. I guess we had that in common. But, you know, sometimes you have to slow down and evaluate a situation and determine if it's really what you need or simply something you want."

"And I take it Lacey's an evaluator?"

Damien smiled thoughtfully. "Yes, she is. She doesn't say anything, but the contemplation is there in her eyes. You can almost see the wheels turning inside her head. But you know that when she does make a decision, it's a wise one."

"Is she in love with you?"

Now that's the question, Damien thought to himself. "I'm willing to say that she is, but there are times when I feel as though she's weighing the pros and cons of our relationship."

"That's a hell of a thing to say," Kenneth reprimanded Damien.

"It's the truth. She was engaged a while back and the guy broke up with her. Lacey doesn't go into great detail, but I know in my gut that he left scars. In her book *Brush Strokes*, the heroine appears to be your average widow, but underneath you realize that she's a fragile creature that had been hurt badly. She's afraid of involvement and tries to remain friends with the hero. But before she knows it she finds herself in love with him."

Kenneth looked at Damien expectantly. "And the point?"

Damien rolled his eyes. "The point, Kenneth, is that Lacey is the widow. She's fragile and afraid of involvement. And although she and I practically share every moment together, I don't think Lacey is aware that she loves me. But all I have to do is look into her eyes, see the way she smiles, or feel the tenderness in her touch to know that she does."

"You haven't slept with her?"

"No." Damien shook his head. "What Lacey and I have is worth taking our time and getting it right."

"Damn, you are in love."

Lacey returned to the bedroom stronger. Remembering Daniel's words of advice, she had had a private conversation with herself and decided to let nature have her way. She couldn't protect her heart because it already belonged to Damien. The only thing she had accomplished by not taking his call was to make herself absolutely miserable. Damien wasn't Calvin, and until he gave her reason to doubt him, she would have faith in the love she had found with him.

She sat on the bed as she thought of him. His little thoughtful touches were done to make her life easier. She thought of the home-office that he had created for her. Then there were the many errands that he ran so that she wouldn't have to leave a work in progress when the ideas began to flow. Or the many late night runs for chocolate ice cream that he made unselfishly. Heck, she couldn't even recall the last time she'd put gas in her vehicle. Damien had taken it upon himself to see to the upkeep of her vehicle as well. *God, I've been blind. Damien loved her too,* she suddenly realized. Lacey rushed into the sitting area of her suite and grabbed her cell phone. She quickly turned it on and selected Damien's number.

"Hello."

"I love you," she whispered at the sound of his voice. And for the first time she wasn't afraid of the future.

"I love you too, Lace," Damien whispered reverently. "I was worried when I couldn't reach you."

"I turned off my cell phone."

Damien waited for an explanation. When none came, he asked.

"Why did you turn it off?"

"While waiting for you to call, I realized that I was in love with you and became frightened."

He had been right. "Are you still frightened?"

"No."

Lacey let herself into Damien's home. She had caught a late night flight from Orlando so that she could be here when he arrived from work. She wanted to be able to tell him that she loved him the moment he walked in. She carried her luggage back into the master suite. Damien's home was larger than hers with a spacious floor plan. She remembered the first time that she had been here. It had taken Damien a month into their relationship before he invited her, but on that day he had prepared dinner for her. They had eaten on the screened patio. Candles and soft music had created a romantic atmosphere that she was unfortunately unable to enjoy.

"Is your steak all right?" Damien had asked from across the linen draped table. He watched Lacey closely and could tell that something was bothering her. He wanted her to feel comfortable in his home.

"It's perfect," Lacey replied as she reached for her wine glass. She looked at the backyard with its beautiful landscape.

Damien laid his fork down beside his plate. He reached across the table and grabbed her wine glass. Taking it from her hands, he placed it on the table. "What's wrong, baby? You've been so quiet this evening." Damien's eyes scanned her face.

Lacey started to lie, but then decided to tell the truth. "I'm a little uncomfortable being in your wife's home. I keep seeing the two of you together like we are now." She gave Damien a sad little smile as she withdrew her hand and rose from the table.

"Is that all?" Damien said with relief. He followed her across the room and pulled her into his arms. "Sweetheart, Sara and I didn't share this home. After her death, there was no way that I could continue to live in our old home, so I sold it and purchased this one."

"But it's so huge. You have four bedrooms and that large family room, not to mention this spacious backyard."

"Families need room to grow," Damien explained. His eyes were locked with hers. "It's an investment and has great resale value."

Lacey listened to his explanation, but felt that there was more meaning to his reply. She felt the stirring of butterflies in her stomach and discreetly rubbed it. She repeated Daniel's words inside her head and didn't go looking for trouble.

However, after getting to know Damien and falling in love with him, Lacey walked through his home knowing the full meaning of his words. He wanted a family that she couldn't give him. But she had come this far on faith and she would travel further with it in her heart. Damien was worth fighting for and she had no intention of letting him get away from her. She shook off the depressing mood and retraced her steps back into the master suite. In her luggage she located her latest purchase from Victoria's Secret and laid the sheer garment on the bed. She was taking the next step with this relationship, and she wasn't holding anything back. Damien had to know that her love for him ran deep.

CHAPTER 11

Around six in the morning, Damien pulled up in front of his home and spotted Lacey's SUV in his driveway. His pulse rate increased as he realized the woman of his desire was in his home and waiting for him. She hadn't been due back into town until later on this afternoon, but obviously had gotten an earlier flight. He quickly opened the front door and shed his jacket. He draped it on the closet door handle as he went in search of Lacey. The house was quiet so he knew she wasn't in the kitchen and since he was in the living room, he knew she wasn't there. He headed toward the family room in the rear and found it empty as well. That left only the bedrooms and considering one held gym equipment and the other two were empty, that only left his bedroom. The realization that Lacey could possibly be in his bed shook him to the core.

Damien walked slowly down the hallway to his master bedroom. His footsteps were muffled in the thick tan carpet. As he rounded the corner to his bedroom, he took a fortifying breath for what greeted him. He stepped into the doorway and his heart swelled with love. Lacey lay curled in his bed watching him. She was a vision he wouldn't soon forget.

"I thought I heard you come in," Lacey said looking at him. She wore a beautiful smile on her face.

"Didn't mean to wake you." Damien didn't budge from the doorway because he didn't trust himself to not walk over to the bed and strip Lacey bare.

Lacey watched Damien standing like a sentinel in the doorway. His eyes were piercing and his features strained. He showed indecision in the desire to join her. Lacey realized that the next move was hers. She threw the covers back and stepped out.

"I was waiting for you," Lacey whispered as she extended her hand in his direction.

Damien was long and hard as he watched Lacey rise before him in a sheer white gown that hid absolutely nothing. Not even the small triangle thong covering her treasure.

"Are you sure about this, Lace?" he asked admiring her lovely brown body.

Lacey was sure that she had never loved a man the way that she loved Damien. "I love you, Damien," she responded while staring into his passion-filled eyes.

"And I love you, Lace," Damien answered as he pushed away from the door and walked in her direction. He pulled his shirt over his head and tossed it to the floor. A few steps more, his belt buckle opened. By the time he stood before Lacey, all she had to do was lower the zipper and help him step out. He stood proud and erect in black bikini briefs as he reached out taking her hand.

Lacey tightened her grip, and backpedaled toward the bed. As the back of her legs came into contact with the mattress, she sat down and scooted to the center of the bed making room for Damien. Their eyes connected and communicated the depth of their emotions as he crawled in beside her.

"You are so beautiful," Damien stated reverently as he raised his hand to caress Lacey's face. He leaned in, kissing her sweet lips.

"You make me feel beautiful," she whispered back, closing her eyes as he caressed the length of her neck and down lower to her breasts.

"You have on too many clothes."

Lacey smiled. "It's hardly anything."

"If it keeps me from touching you, it's too much," Damien lowered his head to the dark nipple peaking through the sheer fabric. He tugged on it with his lips leaving wetness.

"Then take it off," Lacey boldly stated as she met his dark smoldering eyes when he raised his head. She watched with anticipation as Damien's large hands slowly began to release the tiny pearl buttons that ran from breast to waist. His hands shook slightly as he released the button holding the folds across her breasts. As it fell apart, he swept a hand across the exposed flesh, weighing the right breast in his hand.

Damien had never felt anything softer than Lacey's brown skin or more pleasing to his touch than the feel of her breast in his hand. He had to fight to go slow and not rip the damn gown open as his head was telling him to do. He knew the prize awaiting him was well worth the delay, but what a tortuous test of control it was. So, with gritted teeth, he released another one of the blasted buttons. And when they were all free, he folded the garment back over Lacey's dainty shoulders and down her arms until her hands were out. Then, like a man on drugs, he sought his fix from the breasts before him.

His fingertips became instruments of pleasure as they caressed and taunted the sensitive flesh of Lacey's upper body. While his hand created magic, he allowed his mouth to remind Lacey of what was coming. The erotic play had her squirming with desire. But there was more.

Damien covered Lacey with his body and wrapped his arms around her. In a move that stole her breath, he rolled placing her on top. He smiled up at her when their eyes met. With his hands, he slowly slid under the gown still draped around her waist. He found the tiny swatch of fabric she called underwear and tugged it down over her hips and further down her legs. When he could reach no further, Lacey did a little shake and they dropped to the floor.

Damien noticed the sudden glow in her sherry eyes as she watched him. That little shake of hers had stirred more than she bargained for and it now lay throbbing against her belly.

"Did I do that?" Lacey's mouth twitched with suppressed laughter.

"You most certainly did." Damien's voice was deeper. "And you're going to get it." He swatted her bottom playfully.

Lacey wiggled in his hands. "Promises, promises." But before the words could leave her lips, Damien had her pinned beneath him. Rising up on his haunches, he tugged the gown down and off, letting it fall to the floor. He stood up, locking eyes with Lacey as he removed his briefs and stood before her nude. Desire registered in her eyes as she examined his body and reached for him. But before joining her on the bed, Damien retrieved protection from the nightstand drawer and sheathed himself. Lacey forced him over onto his back as he returned to the bed. She then proceeded to rain kisses across his chiseled chest, defined abdomen, and even lower. The pleasure she was giving was new for him and he closed his eyes until he could take the pleasure no more. He reversed their positions and returned the favor. At the hairline covering her feminine treasure, Damien noticed a thin scar hidden in the sandy curls which ran from pelvis to pelvis. But Lacey's pleasurable moans were music to his ears and the scar was quickly forgotten. He needed to be inside. With a skilled move, he eased into Lacey's tight passage and set a rhythm that the headboard tapped out against the wall.

Lacey wrapped her legs around Damien's hips as he thrust inside of her. The pleasure he was giving, she had never experienced before. Calvin had been young and clumsy, but Damien was loving her with a man's attention to detail and a skill to do the job right. She was experiencing pleasure and pain all at the same time. Her body no longer responded to her brain. Damien was doing the talking, not with his mouth, but with his body, and she knew that he was laying claim to her body and soul.

The tempo escalated. The glorious payoff was just in sight. Damien, braced on his arms, looked down on Lacey as she received him. The expression on her face was one of sheer rapture. He wanted to see her eyes when they fell over into paradise. He needed to know that her love for him was real.

"Open your eyes," he whispered as he thrust into her with a demanding rhythm and was rewarded when her eyes slowly fluttered open. There in the depth of her sherry eyes he found his answer. In response his hips thrust at an increasing pace until their bodies were bathed in perspiration and they both shook from the power of their lovemaking. They clung to each other, rocked to the core by the ecstasy they had found.

"I love you," Lacey gasped as desire rippled through her body.

Damien kissed her damp neck. He mustered the strength to raise his head to look at her. "I love you, too." Damien cupped Lacey's face in his hands as he kissed her passionately.

Lacey stared in wonder as Damien pulled away. Tears glistened in her eyes as she stroked his face and then his chest. Her lips trembled as she tried to express her thoughts.

"I never knew that it could be that way. That another person could have such control over my body, make me feel so good."

"Ah, Lace, you sure do know what to say," Damien whispered, covering her lips once more. He rolled onto his back taking her with him. Lacey laid her head on his chest listening to his heartbeat.

"Lace, it's been a long time since anyone has loved me so unselfishly and completely with their heart as well as their body."

Lacey caressed his damp chest. "I know, three years."

Damien glanced down at Lacey. It was now or never to clear the air, he thought. They were one after making love so intensely. Surely she would know that his love for her was real.

"Let's shower, and then talk. There's something you need to know." Damien rose from the bed and leaning over, picked Lacey up and carried her into the bathroom. Several passionate kisses and caresses were exchanged before the two finally showered. Afterwards they returned to the bedroom where they began picking up their discarded clothes. They laughed and giggled playfully as they passed each other. With the glow of their lovemaking still twinkling in their eyes, Lacey retrieved fresh clothing from her luggage while Damien gathered clothing from the dresser and closet.

"Hey, what were you going to tell me?" Lacey asked while she zipped up her jeans.

Damien buttoned his pants and pulled on his shirt, leaving it open. He placed his hands on his hips as he turned to face Lacey who stood in jeans and a bra. "Let's sit down." He motioned to the foot of the bed.

"You look so serious," Lacey said. She sat down beside him and took his hand. "It can't be that bad." She smiled. "We've just made incredible love. There is nothing you could possibly say to me to ruin this moment."

Damien hoped she was right. "I tried to tell you this right up front..." The telephone interrupted their conversation. Damien swore, but didn't make a move to answer it. "Like I was saying..." The telephone rang again. "I've got to answer that," he said reaching for the phone.

"Hello."

"Uncle Damien, my Dad's here. He and Mama are screaming. I'm scared."

Damien could here the fear in his nephew's voice and the shouting in the background. "Where are your brother and sister?"

"DeMarcus is with me, but Mama has Raye."

Damien fastened the buttons on his shirt as he walked around the room locating his shoes and searching for his car keys. "You two stay in your room. I'm on the way." Damien slammed down the phone and sat on the bed pulling on his shoes.

"Steven's back?" Lacey asked. She grabbed her purse and removed her keys.

"Yeah, and he and Holly are going at it. Damn, I can't find my keys," he roared.

"We can take mine."

Damien's head swung around in Lacey's direction, but she was already walking out of the bedroom.

"Lacey, where are you going?" He followed behind her.

At the door she paused just long enough to grab her jacket and toss his to him. "With you."

"Baby, just let me have your keys. I don't know what I'm going to find over there. My folks are out of town and Holly's there alone. I really need to go."

"Then let's go," Lacey ordered and opened the front door. She heard Damien close the door behind him as he followed. She unlocked the car door and climbed in behind the wheel. "You're angry and not in any shape to drive."

"You're probably right." Damien closed the passenger door and buckled in as Lacey backed out of the driveway.

Damien jumped out the vehicle before it came to a complete stop. The front door of his parents' home was wide open as angry voices flowed out. He stormed in and headed in the direction of the voices coming from the kitchen. Lacey was right behind him.

"I want you out of my life, Steven. We're done," Holly yelled. She clutched a crying Raye.

"I made a freaking mistake," Steven yelled over Raye's crying. He had Holly cornered by the sink. "Oh, I forget, the great Christovals don't make mistakes."

"No, we don't, you jerk."

"I've had enough of your smart mouth," he shouted balling his fist in a threatening manner.

"Steven, if you hit my sister it will be the last thing that you do," Damien growled as he stormed into the kitchen. He placed himself between Holly and Steven. "You need help man. Your marriage is over. Get over it and move on."

"Please just go," Holly cried. She ran from the kitchen with Raye clutched to her chest. She met Lacey standing just inside the living room with the two boys who had come out of their room when they heard Damien's voice.

"I'll take Raye," Lacey told Holly as she reached for the crying child. She rubbed the baby's back while cooing to her. She could tell that the child was sensing her mother's fear and reacting to it.

Damien followed Holly. "Baby, take the kids back to the bedroom," he said to Lacey.

"Wait a damn minute, those are my kids too!" Steven railed as he swept into the room. He charged in Lacey's direction, but was cut off by Damien stepping in his path.

"You need help, man. Your family is terrified of you," Damien tried to make Steven see the truth. "Let Lacey get the kids out of this environment. They don't need to see the two of you going at it like this."

"Please, Steven," Holly begged. "Damien's right."

Steven had always resented the position Damien held in the family. His brothers and sisters all looked to him for advice. And his parents thought he walked on water. The man made life difficult for other mortals to follow and no man should have to compete with his wife's brother for a place in her heart. But he had, until he had grown tired of not measuring up.

He glared at Damien protecting his children against him, their father. The man had no right interfering. And he was about to tell Damien exactly that until he moved slightly to the left, giving Steven a clear view of the woman called Lacey.

"I'll be damned. I thought I was looking at Sara," Steven said, capturing the adults' attention.

Lacey looked at the man like he had lost his mind. "Come on kids, let's head back to your room."

"Not yet, sweetheart," Steven called out.

"Let's go into the kitchen and talk this out, Steven," Damien tried to usher the man out of the room, but Steven shook Damien's hands off.

"Oh, no you don't. You're always giving advice, but it seems to me, brother-in-law, that you're the one in need of counseling. You can't get over Sara, so what do you do?"

"Steven!" Holly tried to shut him up."

Steven waved a dismissive hand. "Don't Steven me. I'm not the one who has gone out and replaced my dead wife with a carbon copy. Hell, I had to look at this woman a long time before I remembered Sara was shorter."

"What? What is he talking about, Damien?" Lacey asked as the fear in her rose. She watched Damien glance at Holly, then back to Steven. "No!" Lacey cried out as she placed Raye on her feet. She told herself it wasn't true. Steven was just angry and trying to upset everybody.

Damien tried to remain calm as he felt his whole world spinning out of control. "Lacey, please take the kids..."

"You take the kids, Damien," Lacey shouted. Her stomach was tied in knots. "I want to know the truth." She glanced at Holly for help and received only her bowed head. "Damien. Please, is he telling the truth?" Her voice cracked as she pleaded for an answer. Her eyes were filled with hurt and suppressed tears.

"It's true, Lacey. Why don't you look in that photo album on the table behind you. Melinda calls that her wedding book. There are four photographs. Holly and my wedding photograph, Phillip and Robin, Trent and Rhonda, and you guessed it, Mr. Perfect and Sara," Steven told Lacey with a satisfied smile. He was enjoying every

105

moment of Damien getting his comeuppance.

Lacey looked behind her and spotted the white wedding album. On stiff legs, she took a few steps to reach it. Her hands shook as she reached for the album.

"Lacey, please trust me," Damien said as he came up behind her. He covered her hand on the album with his.

"Is it true? Do I look like Sara?" she whispered. Her heart was breaking because she already knew the answer.

"Yes." Damien watched as Lacey flipped open the wedding album.

She stared into a face so similar to her own that it took several minutes for her to notice the slight differences. She covered her mouth with her hand, afraid that she would be sick. Images of this morning swam before her and she felt dirty. With a shattered look that would stay with Damien always, Lacey ran for the front door. She unlocked her car door and was climbing inside by the time he reached her.

"Baby, you're too upset to be driving," Damien tried to talk Lacey out of the vehicle.

"Get away from me," Lacey screamed as she shoved at Damien's chest. The tears were flowing freely. She could barely see. But there was no way in the world that she could stay there.

"You're going to kill yourself," Damien screamed back frightened. His heart was in his throat.

Lacey turned toward Damien with fire in her eyes. "Damn it, I am not Sara. She's the one who died in the car accident. I survived, Damien. Me, Lacey Rebecca Avery, wouldn't give you the satisfaction of completing that circle, now get out my way."

Damien stood numb as Lacey's words pummeled him like physical blows. He realized that nothing was going to be solved today. Lacey was hurt and beyond listening to an explanation. He cleared the door, but maintained a hand on the door handle. "Drive carefully, *please.*" Damien didn't try to hide his fear.

Lacey swiped at the tears running down her face aware that Damien was indeed concerned. She inhaled deeply and got her emotions under control. Barely looking his way, she nodded and pulled the door closed. She started the vehicle and backed out of the driveway. With her dreams shattered and her soul battered, Lacey drove away leaving her fantasy of happily ever after behind.

Damien remained in the driveway watching as Lacey disappeared down the street and around the corner. An emptiness settled in the pit of his stomach. He wanted to scream, but the only person he had to blame for this situation was himself. Sure, Steven had taken pleasure in ruining his relationship, but in the final analysis, all of it was his own fault. He prayed Lacey would be safe and open to talking tomorrow. As angry voices reached him out in the driveway, Damien exhaled a breath and returned to the house.

"You don't think, Steven. You just do what makes Steven happy at the moment, then, when things fall apart, you want to say I'm sorry and everyone is supposed to welcome you back."

"Ordinary people make mistakes, Holly. But I guess you wouldn't understand. Your whole damn family is perfect," Steven spat. He struck a defensive stance when Damien returned to the living room.

But Damien was too concerned for Lacey's safety to be angry with Steven. He ordered the children to their rooms and when they were finally out of the way, he focused in on Steven and Holly.

"Steven, you and my sister are divorced. You left her and your children for another woman, so be a man and lie in the bed you made. If you want to see the children, call Holly to set up visitation like the divorce decree stipulates. Now get out." Damien walked to the door and opened it.

Steven wasn't proud of himself or his actions, but he would be damned if he told Holly or Damien that he was sorry. Instead, he made arrangements to visit the children next weekend and left without another foul word.

CHAPTER 12

"You should go after Lacey." Holly tried to persuade Damien as they sat in the kitchen holding hands. She hated what Steven had done and felt that it was all her fault.

Damien smiled weakly at his sister as he patted her hand. He could see the guilt in her eyes as well as her concern, but this was his fault. "Steven couldn't have upset Lacey if I had told her earlier in our relationship about her resemblance to Sara." He laughed dryly. "But you know what's so funny about this whole thing, is that I was in the process of confiding the truth when Gabriel called."

"Oh, Damien, I'm so sorry."

"Would you stop apologizing? Things happen for a reason and I just have to figure out the reason for this mess. But be assured, I'm not letting Lacey get away that easily. I know she's hurt and confused, so I'll let her have today, but first thing in the morning, I'll be on her doorstep pleading my case."

Holly observed her brother closely. She could see real fear in his eyes. Although he talked of fighting for his relationship with Lacey, he wasn't convinced of winning her back. Holly twirled one of her micro braids around her finger with nervous energy. This was all her fault and she had to fix it.

"You're in love with Lacey, aren't you?"

Damien glanced over at his sister and smiled. "Very much. I didn't think I could feel this way again."

"It's my guess that she loves you as well, and from the look of hurt on her face, it ran deep. A love like that isn't easily swept away."

Damien watched Holly fidget. He presumed that she spoke of her love for Steven. "You know Holly, no one is telling you how to handle your relationship with Steven. If you believe the two of you can work things out, then you have to try."

Holly shook her head vigorously. "I can't accept him back into my life or my bed, knowing that he could walk away again. I deserve so much better than that."

Damien was happy to hear his sister's words. For a moment there, he was afraid she was beginning to weaken to the man.

"You're right, you do. And Lacey deserved better than what I did."

"She does, so what are you going to do about it?"

"First thing I'm going to do is call her friend, Daniel, and make sure that she arrived safely. I'm sure she was headed to him when she left here. Then I'm going home and wait patiently for tomorrow and a chance to apologize." He rose from the table and grabbed the wall phone. He retrieved the business card that Lacey had given him with Daniel's number on the back. He had used it to call and thank Daniel for the beautiful birthday creation. Damien dialed the number and waited. He placed the card on the table.

Lacey drove to Daniel's gallery with the intention of going inside. But after glancing through the window and noticing the number of people browsing the floor, she knew that now was not the time. And besides, she was too embarrassed to tell Daniel how foolish she had been. She returned to her vehicle and drove away. She would have to handle the situation on her own. Going left, she headed for the interstate and in the direction of home. As she drove along, an idea came to her. She hit the programmed number on her cell phone and waited for her call to be answered.

"Paige Rivers Agency."

"Paige, it's Lace. Is it too late to book me as a panelist for the convention in DC?" She drove home, now with a purpose.

"Not at all. Actually, the chairwoman phoned this morning and asked if you would reconsider. There were several requests for your participation."

"All right, phone her back and if she agrees, make the arrangements and give me a call back on my cell phone. I'm headed home now to pack."

Paige knew that something was wrong and wouldn't be a friend if she didn't ask. "Lacey, what happened with you and Damien?" There was a long moment of silence before Lacey answered.

"He's not the man I thought he was."

"Lacey, that man loves you. Brothers like him don't come around often. You better be sure of what you're doing before you throw a man that fine back out there."

Lacey wasn't sure she liked or appreciated the sound of Paige's voice as she spoke of Damien. But then, recalling how he had used and hurt her, she decided that she didn't care who wanted Damien Christoval. "Look, Paige, if you want a shot at the man, go for it."

Paige was caught off guard by the abrasive reply. She did find Damien extremely handsome and under ordinary circumstances would be putting the moves on the man, but Lacey loved Damien, whether she was willing to admit it right now or not. "I do have pride, Lacey," Paige replied with a hint of hurt and anger in her voice.

Hearing both, Lacey regretted her thoughtless words. "I'm sorry, Paige. I didn't mean that the way it sounded."

"Forget it. Hey, look, if you two are having problems, now is not the time to leave town."

"Now is the perfect time, because it'll give me a chance to think without others trying to influence my decision. I won't deny that I love Damien, but..." There was another long pause. "He hurt me in a way that I never expected." Lacey's voice was low and laced with pain.

"I assume you don't mean physically."

111

"No, of course not. Damien would never physically harm me."

"I don't believe he would intentionally hurt you either."

"See, it's comments like that that I don't need. I know you're trying to help, but I have to figure this out on my own."

"All right, I'll make the arrangements and give you a call back shortly."

"Thanks, Paige." Lacey disconnected as she left the interstate. A few turns later she pulled into the garage of her home, but didn't get out of the vehicle right away. She thought about how her day had started and ached with desire from the memory, but then thoughts of Damien's deceit snuffed out the desire. Finally, she headed inside and went directly to her room to pack. She pulled up short as she realized that her favorite pieces of luggage were at Damien's house. Not to be outdone, she dug around in the back of the closest for her older set of luggage. It wasn't as convenient with wheels and easy store pockets, but it would do.

By the time Paige's call came through confirming her booking and reservations, Lacey was ready for her four o'clock flight that evening. She stored her luggage in her vehicle and headed over to her parents' home. She gave her mother a copy of her agenda and all the necessary information to reach her in case of an emergency. Lacey left her parents' home and headed to the airport after skillfully avoiding her mother's questions about Damien and her sudden change in plans. When she was finally seated on the airplane, she allowed herself to think about all the events of the day and what she wanted out of life. She hoped to reach a decision by the time the flight arrived in the nation's capital.

"Overstreet Gallery."

Damien braced for the verbal assault that he knew Daniel would give him on hearing his voice. "Daniel, this is Damien. I know I was wrong, but please tell me Lacey reached your place safely."

"Damien, I don't have a clue as to what you're talking about, but I suggest you start explaining quickly, because I haven't been able to reach her all day." The words rushed from Daniel's mouth. The gallery was finally quiet and so he was free to sit down and talk.

Damien tried to end the call. He was alarmed by Daniel's response. "Not now, Daniel. I need to find Lacey. I'm worried about her. When she left me she was extremely upset and really had no business driving, but she wouldn't listen to me."

"What in the hell did you do to her?" Daniel demanded angrily. "And don't you dare hang up on me."

Damien knew there was no getting away from Daniel without an explanation, so as fast as he could, he told him the complete story. As expected, Daniel tore into him.

"How could you do that to her? She trusted you like she hasn't trusted anyone in a long time," Daniel shouted furiously. "Is it Lacey you're in love with, or are you just looking for a substitute for your wife?"

"Don't be ridiculous. I love Lacey, Daniel, and I have to find her so that I can apologize and explain. But more importantly, I want her safe."

Daniel listened as Damien pled his case. Although he was extremely angry with the man, he was convinced of his love for his friend. "If Lace didn't come to me, then she must be beyond hurting. I'm guessing that she's probably embarrassed as well. You don't know what she has been through. Try her parents' home. Lacey may have gone to her mother." Daniel quickly recited the Avery's address.

"Thanks, Daniel; I swear you won't regret giving me their address." Damien hung up the telephone. He took a moment to tell Holly where he was going and to ask for the use of her van. With keys in hand, he rushed from the house.

"Call me if you find her," Holly shouted from the front porch as Damien slid behind the wheel of her mini van and was soon gone. She returned to the kitchen to collect her weary thoughts. The business card with Daniel Overstreet's phone number and address written on the back caught her attention. Picking it up, she slipped it into her pocket, and went to check on the children.

Laura Avery wasn't surprised to find Damien Christoval on her doorstep. She had actually expected him earlier and considering how fast her daughter had been moving, Lacey was expecting him to be right behind her as well. As she unlocked the door for Damien, Laura could see the doubt in his eyes and the strain on his face. He looked as miserable as Lacey had when she arrived. She stepped aside and welcomed him into her home.

"I was wondering how long it would be before you showed up," Laura commented over her shoulder as she led the way into the den.

She introduced Damien to her husband, Mark, who sat in the recliner reading the newspaper.

"Honey, this is Captain Damien Christoval, Lacey's friend."

Mark Avery gave the young man a piercing stare before rising from his chair.

"It's a pleasure to finally meet you, Mr. Avery." Damien extended his hand.

Mark Avery unfolded from his chair to stand equal to his daughter's young man. He grasped the extended hand in a firm handshake. "Nice to meet you as well, young man. Won't you have a seat?"

"Thank you, sir." Damien perched on the edge of the sofa as Mrs. Avery sat down beside him. He could feel her curious eyes on him. Unable to stand it any more, he asked. "Mrs. Avery, I take it from your comment that you've heard from Lacey?"

"Sure have and seen her too. She raced in and out of here on her way to the airport." She looked accusingly at Damien. "Now I'm not going to ask what happened between you and Lace. You're both adults and don't need me in your business. But I tell you, Damien, that I will not tolerate my Lacey being hurt."

"Mr. and Mrs. Avery, I don't want to hurt Lacey. I love her with every fiber of my being."

"Well something sent my daughter running." Mark Avery spoke up drawing Damien's attention. The look on the man's face was fierce.

Damien leaned forward, resting his arms on his thighs. He threaded his fingers together and returned Mr. Avery's piercing gaze. "You're right, and I want to apologize and try to explain."

"I hope you can because Lacey was hurting," Mr. Avery commented.

Damien lowered his eyes to the floor. "I never intentionally meant to hurt her," he whispered more to himself than to the Averys. "Please tell me where she is so that I can speak with her. I know if I could just talk to her, that we could straighten things out. What she and I feel for each other can't be swept away so easily."

Mrs. Avery knew that Damien's pain was real. His love for her daughter was evident in his dejected expression and the slump of his shoulders, not to mention the fear in his voice. However, before she divulged Lacey's whereabouts, she had to be convinced one hundred percent that his love was unconditional. She glanced over at her husband to seek his opinion before telling Damien where Lacey was.

Mark Avery knew a suffering man when he saw one and Damien Christoval was definitely suffering. His Lacey had finally found a man worthy of her. He nodded his permission.

Laura Avery prayed she wasn't making matters worse for Lacey. She placed a comforting hand on Damien's arm. "I'm going to tell you where she is. I just hope I don't regret it later."

"You won't."

Laura nodded her head. "I hope not, because my daughter has been hurt in a way no woman should, and as her mother, I want it known that the next man who hurts her will answer to me."

Damien locked eyes with Laura Avery and knew that she was the one to fear and not Mr. Avery. This was a mother protecting her young.

"I know Calvin hurt Lacey," Damien said.

Laura and Mark exchanged glances. "I'm sure that's all Lacey told you," Laura commented.

"No, she didn't go into details," Damien admitted and wondered about what he didn't know. "Tell me what he did." He looked pleadingly at them both.

"It's not our place," Laura answered. "But, what I will tell you is that my daughter's emotions are fragile, and she needs the love of a good man." She patted Damien's arm. "I believe you're that man."

Damien was humbled by her words. He covered Mrs. Avery's hand. "You don't know how much that means to me. You won't be sorry."

"You'll find Lacey in Washington D.C."

Holly Christoval-Porter entered Daniel Overstreet's gallery a little before closing. She had deliberately selected that time of day because she hoped to find Daniel Overstreet available to speak with her. As she walked into the gallery, she was immediately enthralled by all the marvelous creations. Paintings, carvings, weavings, pottery, sculptures, and artwork she didn't know the proper name for filled the gallery. Holly found herself browsing like an interested buyer.

Daniel observed the dark beauty from the alcove of his office. She was tall like Lacey, but with generous hips that commanded a man's attention. Curves in all the right places accentuated the jeans and knit sweater she wore. Her head of braids was tilted to the side in concentration as she circled around a piece of abstract art and he couldn't help laughing or walking in her direction.

"It's called Disposable America," Daniel explained as he joined the woman.

Holly's head came up at the sound of the deep masculine voice behind her. She spun around to greet the man joining her and froze. Her mind went completely blank as she stared into the most beautiful brown eyes she had ever encountered on a man. Thick dark lashes framed their beauty in a golden face made for gracing magazine covers. The silky texture of his close cut beard and dark head of curls tempted her fingers to caress them. Forcing air into her lungs and quelling the temptation, Holly took a much-needed deep breath.

"Oh, I thought it was a bag of trash." She smiled over at him.

Daniel laughed. Her hazel eyes were hypnotic and doing a number on his senses. "It is. Daniel Overstreet," he said, extending a hand.

Holly placed her much smaller hand into the golden one. "Just the man I wanted to see. Holly Christoval-Porter."

"Christoval?" Daniel whispered. "As in Damien?"

"Yes. I'm his sister and it was my ex-husband who was responsible for hurting Lacey."

"No, Damien hurt Lacey." Daniel arched a brow in her direction. "Your ex-husband simply told the truth."

Holly gave a sad little laugh. "Steven has never told the truth in his life. He's selfish and mean-spirited. He wanted to hurt Damien because he's jealous of our relationship."

"Well, from the sound of your brother's voice when he called me in a panic, I would say that Steven succeeded." Daniel slid his hands into his pockets.

Holly tucked a wayward braid behind her ear. "Lacey was devastated. And poor Damien was beside himself with fear, then I overhead the conversation that you two had, and I felt I had to explain what happened." Holly looked beseechingly at him. "Damien loves Lacey. He hasn't officially said anything to the family, but we all know that he's in love with her. It's just a matter of time before he introduces her to the rest of the family and asks her to marry him."

Daniel looked pleased. "I hope you're right because Lacey has been hurt deeply and I know she loves him as well."

"I know," she glanced at him. "I only pray that Damien can make Lacey forgive him."

"Stop beating yourself up over this." Daniel reached out taking her hand without thinking. "This isn't your doing."

Holly looked at their joined hands trying not to place value in the current of energy racing up her arm. This man was too gorgeous not to have a woman or two in his life, she told herself as she fought down the desire pulsing inside. And besides, she was a divorced mother of three with no business thinking of a man.

"Thank you." Holly removed her hand. "Well, I should be going." She looked at Daniel and smiled.

"It was a pleasure meeting you, Holly. I'm sure we'll be seeing each other again," Daniel expressed with male confidence.

"Perhaps," Holly found herself saying flirtatiously. Her dark eyes gave Daniel a smoldering once over. Quickly exiting the gallery, she couldn't believe what she had done, nor could she explain the girly giddiness she felt flowing inside.

CHAPTER 13

Saturday afternoon, Lacey gathered her leather tote and note cards. The panel discussion on the evolution of African-American literature had been informative and a success. The attendees' questions and comments had been thought provoking, spurring several lively debates between panelists. The liveliest had included Lacey and a new provocative author, Brian Snead. His hard edge writing and language was in complete contrast with Lacey's. Brian had labeled Lacey's writings unrepresentative of the African-American community, to which she had fired back that she wrote of the world that she knew and that he was stereotyping his own people. The debate had become so lively with the audience taking sides, that the moderator finally put an end to the discussion. The audience had given the panelists a standing ovation with thunderous applause.

Lacey did her best to leave without another word being said to the narrow-minded Brian Snead. She shook hands with the moderator and once again thanked the chairwoman for welcoming her on the panel at short notice. When reminded about dinner with the other panelists, she lied and claimed to have other plans for the evening. The chairwoman had actually looked relieved to know that she wouldn't have to play referee over dinner.

Lacey slipped out the door of the convention room and practically ran to the bank of elevators on the opposite wall. She pressed the up button and encouraged its rapid descent. When the doors swept open and no one boarded with her, she said a silent thank you. What she desired most at the moment was peace and quiet. She still hadn't decided what to do or how to feel about Damien's deception. The doors of the elevator finally began to close and she settled against the back of the car. Just when the doors were nearly closed, a hand shot through the meager opening, triggering the sensor. The doors promptly slid open. She saw Brian Snead standing there smiling when they opened. He stepped onboard and gave Lacey a chastising shake of his head.

"You wouldn't be avoiding me now, would you?" Brian asked while watching her closely. Lacey Avery was a beautiful woman who intrigued him.

Lacey couldn't stop the sneer which flashed across her face when the doors opened and revealed Brian. She watched as he pressed the already lit fifth floor button.

"Mr. Snead, you give yourself too much importance. Like I told the chairwoman, I have plans for the evening."

He released a knowing laugh as his piercing gaze examined every detail of her face. "Lacey, you are a terrible liar."

"Look, Brian, it's no secret that we rub each other the wrong way, so let's just ride to our floor in silence and part without more verbal sparring."

"I rather enjoy matching wits with you."

"Whatever," Lacey mumbled under her breath. Brian was beginning to really annoy her. As they reached the fifth floor, the bell chimed their arrival, followed by the doors opening, and Lacey breathed a sigh of relief. She quickly stepped off and headed to the right in the direction of her suite.

"Have dinner with me," Brian said, following behind her. His room was in the opposite direction and around the corner.

Lacey kept walking. She neither accepted nor declined. She was hoping the man would get the message and realize that she wasn't interested.

"I'm not leaving until you say yes," Brian persisted from behind her. He admired the sway of her hips.

Lacey struggled to maintain control over her temper, but the man

was really getting on her already fragile nerves. The last thing she needed or wanted was another man in her life. She still hadn't decided what
to do with the one she already had. With her back to the suite door,
she pasted on her best public smile.

"Mr. Snead, it has been interesting meeting you and I wish you
much success with your writing, but dinner is out of the question."

Brian forced Lacey against the door as he stepped in close. His dark
eyes held an arrogant cockiness. He raised his hand and clasped a
strand of Lacey's auburn hair. He stroked it seductively while holding
her gaze.

"Why, pretty Lacey? Do you have a man inside waiting on you?"
He spoke in a low caressing whisper.

"As a matter of fact she does," Damien's masculine voice came from
behind them as he threw open the door to the suite. Lacey fell into his
waiting arms.

"Damien!" Lacey couldn't believe he was there with her.

Brian stared at the big man standing with his arm wrapped posses-
sively around Lacey's waist. From the murderous look in the guy's eyes,
Brian knew that it was time for him to leave. "Ah, well...I see you have
company. Have a good evening." Brian made a hasty retreat down the
hallway.

Lacey spun around and stepped into the suite. She deposited her
tote on the desk, just inside the door. She continued over to the large
window. She didn't pretend to be interested in what was taking place
outside. Her interest lay right there in the room with her. On hearing
Damien lock the door, she turned facing him.

"What are you doing here and who let you into my room?"

Damien took his time responding. He wanted to enjoy the view.
Lacey was safe and in one piece. The red wool pantsuit flattered her
willowy build by accentuating the bust line and defining the waist with
a tie belt. Her long legs were encased in pleated-cuffed slacks with side
pockets. Damien greedily drank his fill of her.

"I came to apologize and salvage our relationship. A romantic maid allowed me in." He tried for a smile, but failed. "Who was that guy?" he asked, catching Lacey by surprise.

Sherry brown eyes darted in his direction. Lacey struck a defensive pose. She folded her arms before her as she half turned in his direction. *He looked good,* she silently noted. The gray slacks and bulky yellow sweater complimented his complexion. The familiar scent of his cologne managed to do strange things to her nerve endings despite her attempt at being unaffected by his presence. She longed to be back in his arms the way they had been yesterday morning.

"No one important." She walked to within inches of him. "You should be leaving." Lacey didn't quite meet his eyes. She wasn't strong enough.

"We have to discuss what happened."

"What's to discuss? You lied and used me." Her brows arched accusingly.

Damien moved closer with the intention of caressing her face, but Lacey stepped backward avoiding his touch.

"Don't put your hands on me."

Damien stared, bewildered. He slowly lowered his hand back to his side. He tried to hide the hurt he was experiencing. "I never lied to you. My feelings for you are real. I love you."

The timbre in his voice was different than normal. It was softer with a desperate edge. Lacey tried to ignore its effect. "How can you say you love me, when the only reason you're with me, is because I look like Sara. It wasn't me or my looks that attracted you. It was my resemblance to your precious wife." Lacey's voice cracked with hurt.

Damien wanted to wrap her in his arms. He hated that Lacey was in pain. "Baby, I won't lie to you. Yes, when I first saw you, I immediately thought you were Sara and that I was being given another chance to save her. Then I really looked at you and you begged me not to leave. I saw the most beautiful sherry eyes and heard the sweetest voice.

When I took your hand, Lacey, something inside of me came to life."

"Please spare me." Lacey waved a dismissive hand. She didn't dare believe him.

"I was afraid to tell you the truth and get this reaction. I didn't want to lose you."

Damien could sense her weakening but knew that she wouldn't go down easily. He had to come clean about his marriage if he was going to win Lacey back. She had to know it was her that he loved.

"If you remember there were several times that I tried to tell you. The night of my party being one, and that time in the truck bed outside the station, being another. Yesterday morning I was in the process of telling you about your resemblance to Sara when the phone interrupted."

"How convenient." Lacey sassed.

"There are things about my marriage that you don't know that I would like to share with you."

Lacey didn't want to hear about their special love. She had heard about it from others and was tired of listening. It was time to give Damien something to listen to.

"And there's something about me that you don't know," she hurled back. Her resolve was glacier, as were her eyes. She automatically shut down her emotions in preparation for the condemnation she would probably receive. "I may look like the replacement model for your perfect, wonderful Sara, but you see, you selected a damaged model. If this hadn't come up, it was only a matter of time before you threw me back." She swallowed hard on those words. Her secret would be out in a moment and Damien would be gone for good.

Damien didn't have any idea as to what Lacey was referring. Looking at the rigid way she held her body and the detached look in her eyes, he knew that whatever it was had to be extremely painful for her to say. He moved in on her. There was nowhere for her to go and Damien could suddenly sense her fear. It scared him to death because he didn't understand where it was coming from. Lacey knew that he would never physically hurt her. He reached out cupping her face with his hands. Lacey tried to pull free.

"Don't run from me, Lace. You have to know there is nothing to fear from me."

Lacey stopped struggling as she stared into his hazel eyes. They were clouded with concern and she was moved; however, telling herself that it wouldn't last once he knew the truth, she braced herself for the fallout.

"I thought there was nothing to fear from Calvin as well, but words can sometimes be more powerful than blows."

"I'm not Calvin," Damien grunted angrily.

"And I'm not Sara," Lacey replied just as heatedly. "The sooner you know the truth, the sooner we can both go our separate ways."

"I'm not going any damn where," Damien stated defiantly.

Lacey gave a sad laugh as she shook her head slowly. Damien still cupped her face. "You will when I tell you my secret."

Damien shook his head no. "There is nothing you can say to me to make me give up on us. I love you, Lacey. It's you I want by my side, in my bed, building a life together—a family."

"Oh God," Lacey wailed at those last words. She pulled free of Damien's grip and ran into the bedroom of the suite. She perched on the edge of the bed crying silently.

Damien followed not sure of what he had done or said to elicit such a response. His heart was racing with fear because for the first time, he could sense the end of their relationship. He got down on his knees before her. He took her small hands, which were clenched tightly with nervousness, into his, and coaxed them into relaxing. He threaded their fingers together. He needed the connection.

"We can't work this out if I don't know what's wrong." Damien's voiced wobbled, conveying his fear. "It's more than my not telling you about the resemblance to Sara, isn't it?"

Lacey nodded, yes. She wouldn't look at him. Her head and eyes were downcast as her shoulders slumped with the weight of her secret. Damien knew she was near the breaking point and kept pushing. The sooner this secret was in the open, the sooner they could hopefully deal with it.

"Tell me," Damien whispered. He squeezed their fingers together lightly.

It was now or never, Lacey thought. In the end it wouldn't matter because Damien would leave her just like Calvin had. The only difference this time was that she really knew what love was and had found it with Damien. At the moment, however, she wasn't necessarily convinced that his love for her was true, but she knew that she would always love him.

"I may resemble your Sara," Lacey began softly. "But unlike Sara, I can't give you the children that I know that you want. You're a man who loves family and with me you won't have that." She raised her eyes to his. "I can't have children, Damien. The accident destroyed my chance for a family and if you stay with me, I'll destroy your chance as well." Lacey exhaled. The truth was out. "So now you understand what I mean when I say I'm the damaged model."

Damien's eyes narrowed as the gravity of Lacey's words sank in. Then he lowered his head as he pulled his hands free from hers to stand up. He took several steps back and didn't utter a sound.

Lacey's eyes followed him. Her heart broke when Damien pulled away from her. Some part of her had prayed that he would respond differently than Calvin. In a way he had, she conceded. He hadn't verbally attacked her inadequacy as a woman.

She fought back the tears because they were useless. Her last bit of hope that Damien had really loved her was now gone. He hadn't spat venom like Calvin had, but she felt more alone than ever. This was definitely the last time she gave her heart to anyone. Love and marriage hadn't been written in the stars for her. The path that had been chosen for her was that of romance writer and it would have to do.

"I'm sorry. I should have told you the truth up front. I could have saved us both some time. You could have searched out another Sara look-alike. A real woman," she whispered, recalling Calvin's words.

Damien's head came up so quickly that Lacey thought he would have whiplash. However, the moment his eyes zeroed in on her, the thought was banished. He was angry. The hazel eyes that she loved so much were now glowing with a rage that frightened her. Lacey rose from the bed uncertain of Damien's intention.

He couldn't believe what he was hearing. Damien was so angry that he wanted to hit something. Lacey was like a skittish animal poised for flight and he had never hated a person as much as he hated this Calvin.

"Lacey Rebecca Avery, you are more woman than any man has the right to pray for in his life. Don't you ever let me hear you say otherwise." Damien glared at her. His hands were perched on his male hips. "And if you call yourself damaged one more time, I'll take you across my knees and paddle that pretty little backside of yours."

Was she hearing him correctly? Lacey stared at Damien as though he had lost his mind. "I can't have children, Damien," she repeated.

"I heard you the first time. What do you expect me to do? Run—walk—leave without a word?" He gave her a painful glare. "You sure don't think much of me as a man, if you believe I would walk away because of something beyond your control."

New life was breathed into Lacey on hearing Damien's words. She grasped him around the waist as she faced him. "You're wrong. I think you are a wonderful man who deserves a family of his own."

Damien glanced into Lacey's waiting face. Her sweet lips trembled with emotion and he knew that they would make it. He ran a thumb tenderly across her lips. "Baby, families come in all sizes, colors, and bloodlines. Families are created out of love, caring, and respect. I believe we have enough of all of those things to share with a couple of children out there. Social services are overrun with children needing good homes."

"But what about the family name?" she asked, a little unsure.

Damien looked at her quizzically. His dark left brow hiked curiously. "What do I look like? Royalty? I just want a wife who loves me and a couple of kids to call me Dad. Can you help me build that family, Lacey?"

"Yes, if you're sure that it's me you want."

Lacey, you do resemble Sara a great deal, but that is where the similarities end. I have gotten to know the sweet woman inside of you who nurtures our relationships, respects the job I love, and allows me to be and feel like a man. I love you, Lacey, and want only you." Damien tipped her chin up. "Now the question is, do you still want me?"

"Oh yes, Damien," Lacey cried as she threw herself into his arms. He wanted her just as she was. The floodgate on her emotions opened as the reality of the situation hit her.

Damien held her against his chest lovingly while she cried. He knew the relief she was experiencing because he had been fearful of losing her as well. He swept her up into his arms and returned to the bed. Sitting with his back against the headboard, he held Lacey while she cried. His fingers gently combed through her hair while deciding where to start with his own confession.

CHAPTER 14

"Lacey, I apologize for not telling you about the resemblance. But after I got to know you and knew that I wanted a relationship with you, I was afraid you would leave me like you did."

Lacey smiled sheepishly. "I was hurt and confused. I suddenly realized that your family had kept your secret and I felt foolish. I could imagine them laughing at my stupidity."

"Sweetheart, no one was laughing. Actually my mother instructed me to come clean from the start. So did my brother, Phillip." Damien paused before telling her the rest. He kissed her silky head. "Phillip suspected the truth about my marriage."

Lacey stared at him. She wasn't sure where he was headed.

"Sara didn't want my children," Damien informed Lacey about his relationship with his wife. It was time to eliminate all secrets and misconceptions.

Lacey's eyes widened as she searched his face for answers. She swept away the remnants of her tears. "I'm sure she did." She caressed his handsome face tenderly. The love she felt for him was expressed in her gentle touch.

"Sara's career became everything to her. It was more important than our marriage, our dreams of the future, hell, it was more important than me." Damien glanced off into the room. It was difficult to verbalize what he had known for several years before his wife's death.

"The woman would have to be insane not to want you." Lacey kissed him passionately; then sat back watching him. She could see the pain in his eyes and knew what it must be costing him to divulge such hurt.

He watched her watching him. Sweeping the hair away from Lacey's pretty face, he wondered how he had gotten so lucky to find her, and how he had ever thought she resembled Sara. The spirit around her was so vastly different. It was quiet and gentle, yet radiated her inner beauty to those around her. Her writing career was a vital part of the woman that she was, but it never overshadowed what they had or shared. He never felt second to it or like an embarrassment to Lacey.

"Sara was headed to see me at the station the day of the accident. When I arrived on the scene, I recognized the car immediately." He paused as the pain of that day returned.

"You don't have to say any more," Lacey whispered.

Damien nodded yes. "I do. You have to know the truth." He drew in a deep breath and said, "I found divorce papers on the front seat beside her. She was on the way to the station to serve me with divorce papers personally."

Lacey was speechless. The silence between them seemed to grow louder before she turned on his lap so that she faced him head on. She could see the pain Damien tried to hide. If Sara were alive, she would tell her a thing or two about commitment. "I'm sorry she hurt you, but she didn't deserve you." Lacey fell silent. Eventually she laughed dryly. "Here I was jealous of the woman. I wanted a love like the two of you shared."

Damien said nothing for several minutes while watching her. He caressed her lips with his thumb once more. "What we have is so much more. When I'm with you I feel important in your life, not like decoration. We enjoy simply being together as opposed to surrounding ourselves with other people. When we're apart, we're miserable and can't wait to be together. You make me feel good about my profession, the decisions and dreams I've made for myself. But more importantly, I feel needed by you. Not that you can't take care of yourself," he explained, "But that I complete you and you me."

129

"We do," Lacey said with a smile.

"Sara stopped needing me. Her ambition and career replaced my love. I wanted the love we used to share when we were first married. I wanted her to *need* me more than anything. I wanted her to need my strength to lean on, my ears to listen, my mind for advice, and my arms for shelter." He glanced away briefly; then looked back at Lacey head on. "All she needed from me was to smile at the appropriate jokes and not to embarrass her in front of her co-workers. My job was no longer good enough for her. It wasn't prestigious or lucrative enough for a lawyer's spouse. She didn't understand that I love what I do. She wanted me to take my masters degree and use it in a career that would bore the hell out me, yet wouldn't be an embarrassment to her."

"You are no embarrassment," Lacey declared emotionally. She kissed Damien deeply, wanting to soothe his hurt.

Damien broke the kiss and leaned back observing her. Lacey loved him completely. There was room for him, her career, and the family they both wanted. He smiled to himself realizing that he hadn't actually asked her to marry him, but it was understood that she would. He reached out tilting Lacey's chin up so that she was looking right at him.

"Tell me about the day Calvin visited you in the hospital."

Lacey responded with a shiver that ran the length of her body just thinking about that day. Damien drew her into the wall of his chest. He wrapped his arms around her as she began speaking.

"I had been learning a new routine with a difficult tumbling pass for the championships. I was practicing when I fell. My timing was off and I didn't quite know where I was on the beam. So when I tumbled and flipped in the air, I was in the wrong place and came down crashing into the beam. I was rushed into surgery with internal injuries."

"That's where you got the scar," Damien said remembering it just at the hairline.

"Yes. The damage was severe. Later that night I was rushed back into surgery because of hemorrhaging. By the time it was over, I was left unable to have children. The doctors didn't tell me right away, but when they did, I was devastated."

Tears ran down her face as she recalled the pain of that news. "I told Calvin what the doctors had said when he came that evening. He didn't say a word. He just sat there staring at me. Then he said this couldn't be happening to him. I tried to console him by reaching for his hand." Lacey took a deep breath as her voice trembled. "He pulled away and walked out of the room. The particular day you asked about, was actually two days later. Everyone had been at my side through the operations and my bad news. Daniel practically moved in."

"But not Calvin," Damien stated. He kissed the top of her head still on his chest.

"No. When he did show up that day, he was like a stranger. He never touched me. He never asked how I was doing. He stood at the foot of my bed and proceeded to tell me why he couldn't marry me." The tears came freely now. "He reminded me that he was the only male in his family and it was his responsibility to make sure the Maxwell line continued. He told me that he needed a real woman for that and that I no longer qualified. I was good to look at, but when a man crawled into bed, it was a woman he craved, not half of one." Her shoulders shook as she sobbed uncontrollably. "Then he was gone."

Damien used several colorful words to describe Calvin and his actions. He held Lacey close while she cried. "I love you Lacey and you are a beautiful, desirable woman that any man would be damn lucky to have. Let go of that pain once and for all. Calvin isn't worth the heartache."

"I know, but it hurts," she whispered. After a while she said, "He has three little girls."

Damien roared with laughter. He thought it served the jerk right. Although to have three daughters still made him a lucky man, but considering what Lacey had told him, he suspected that old Calvin was greatly disappointed. He and Lacey remained snuggled together until they drifted off to sleep.

Lacey was the first to awaken. The clock read eleven. She eased off Damien's lap and headed into the bathroom. She turned on the shower while she removed her clothes. When she was bare and about to step in, Damien appeared in the doorway just as naked. Their eyes connected and conveyed their love.

"Mind if I join you?" He flashed that killer smile Lacey loved so much.

"I would be delighted."

"Yes, ma'am you will be," Damien promised as he came up behind her. He swatted her bottom playfully. Under the warm pulsing spray of the shower, Damien and Lacey reaffirmed their love.

With soapy hands, Damien lathered Lacey's heated body from head to toe. He allowed his slippery hands to tease and tantalize every erogenous zone on her body. Behind her ears, the hollow of her neck, that spot on her arm, and her sensitive dark berry nipples had all been treated to his attention. Her responsive spinal column, delectable belly button, that area just at the base of her abdomen, and the all-important bend of her knees were administered to as well. On and on it went until the rinsing. Then Lacey received his full manly attention. He lifted her into his arms and pinned her against the shower wall. With her legs wrapped around his waist, he was free to love her at his own pace. Shifting her position so that their angle was just right, Damien growled fiercely when Lacey welcomed him inside. Her body enveloped every inch of him deliciously. He thought he would lose it before it started, but forced himself to hold steady and concentrated on making love to her mouth. It was sweet and responsive.

Lacey thought she would die with wanting. The feel of Damien inside of her, but not moving, was driving her crazy. The length and girth of him, filled her to overflowing. She could feel the pulsing power just waiting to be released. A blinding desire raced through her and she tightened helplessly around him.

Damien's fingers dug into her bottom as he began a thrusting motion which pushed Lacey firmly against the wall of the shower. With nowhere to go, she took the force of his loving, unable to stop the spiraling of sensations overtaking her body. Thrust after thrust, Damien came into her until Lacey cried out with pleasure and he bathed her with his love. It was the first time that they had made love with nothing between them and he found himself a little sad that the possibility of new life wasn't there. Lacey wanted and accepted all of him. She wanted babies and there wasn't a thing he could do to give them to her. Life sometimes wasn't fair, but then as he looked into her sated face all aglow with love for him, he knew that he still had much to be thankful for.

"I thought we were over yesterday," she whispered.

Damien leaned forward and kissed her. "I was afraid I had lost you forever," he responded back when they parted.

"We share everything from this point," Lacey declared.

"Everything," Damien answered with a thrust of his hips. The rhythm began again, with just as much intensity and need. Once again they reached paradise together.

All through the night the couple made love. There were no secrets hanging between them and the loving was better than the first time because of it. Their hearts freely expressed that which was hidden inside. Damien learned that Lacey's appetite matched his own. When she wanted him, she didn't wait for him to initiate things, but took matters into her own talented hands. They had collapsed into a lover's heap and drifted off to sleep.

The next day, Lacey and Damien strolled along the Tidal Basin arm-in-arm, oblivious to the crowds of tourists milling around. They strolled at a comfortable pace, with no concern about the time or destination. They were in love and simply sharing the moment together. The weather was unseasonably warm and made for a beautiful day of sightseeing. Damien had never been to the nation's capital and was eager to see all the monuments and museums. Lacey played tour guide, since she had practically grown up in the city. Her mother's sister lived in neighboring Arlington, and she had made plenty of visits through the years.

Lacey led Damien to a local Mom and Pop restaurant for lunch where they maintained a steady stream of conversation. There was so much about themselves that they both finally felt free to share. Damien was telling Lacey about his last conversation with Phillip.

"He was concerned that I was getting myself into the same type of relationship," Damien explained to Lacey. "I never realized how intuitive my brother was. There I was, believing that I was putting up the perfect front and he knew all along that my marriage was in trouble."

"Did you tell him about the divorce papers?"

"No," Damien replied shaking his head. "You are the only person I have trusted with that information." Damien met Lacey's understanding eyes.

"Why, because you believe you have to be strong for everyone else?" Lacey covered his hand and caressed it.

"Partly, but then...," Damien paused while he gathered his thoughts. "My family has always looked to me for support and guidance. Being the oldest, my siblings always came to me when they were having problems, and my parents felt I was mature enough for them to run things by me. So, as I grew older, I continued the role.

"But you never learned how to depend on others," Lacey enlightened him. "You carried the weight of your failing marriage alone, needlessly. You said to me last night that Sara didn't need you. Did it occur to you that your family might feel the same way about you?"

Damien looked at Lacey stunned. The thought had never occurred to him. "I guess I've done them a disservice as well."

"You have." Lacey smiled over at him. She wove her fingers into his. "But it's never too late to change."

"Have I told you how much I love you?" Damien leaned over and kissed her.

Her eyes conveyed her love and happiness as they sparkled brilliantly. "I'll never get tired of hearing it."

The couple shared a dessert while discussing the upcoming holiday season.

"I was thinking about our hosting Thanksgiving dinner for our families. It will give them a chance to meet and also to get to know us as a couple," Damien suggested.

Lacey immediately liked the idea. She clasped Damien's hands as she smiled over at him. "I love the idea. I'm looking forward to seeing your mother and sisters again. I really enjoyed meeting them after the accident."

Damien brought Lacey's hands to his lips and kissed them. "They were ecstatic about meeting you as well. They knew I was interested in you, but they were concerned as to the reason.

"Hopefully, seeing us together on Thanksgiving will put their fears to rest and provide them with an opportunity to get to know me and *us* better." She searched his eyes. "Do you want to have dinner at my place?"

"I think my home would afford us more room. You forget, there are a lot of us Christovals."

She nodded conceding the point. "Your home it is then."

CHAPTER 15

It was a week before the big Thanksgiving gathering. Holly stood nervously on Lacey's doorstep waiting for the door to be answered. She had come to apologize for the ugly scene at her parents' home with Steven. She had liked Lacey immediately upon meeting her, and was relieved to hear from Damien that they had managed to work through their problems. Now she could only hope that Lacey was as forgiving for her role in that painful moment.

The release of the front door lock drew her attention. As it opened, she stood there surprised to see Daniel Overstreet returning her appraising stare. He looked more handsome today, if that were possible, than the first time she saw him. He was dressed casually in blue jeans and a sweatshirt. He wore no shoes on his sock clad feet. His glossy curly locks were a little longer and gave him a carefree appearance befitting an artist.

Daniel stood in the open doorway unable to believe his good fortune. He had thought of Holly Christoval-Porter constantly since meeting her at his gallery. Vibes of attraction had passed between them despite an aura of cautiousness surrounding Holly. Now, as she stood before him just as pretty as he remembered, Daniel was determined to break through that reserve. The spirits were telling him that the life partner he sought was hiding behind that very wall.

"It's a pleasure to see you again, Ms. Christoval," Daniel spoke, breaking the silence. He had deliberately not used her ex-husband's name. They were divorced and it was time Holly stopped hiding behind her non-existent marriage.

She was the picture of feminine temptation dressed in a curve hugging red sweater dress and high-heeled suede boots. Her neatly maintained braids were twisted into an attractive knot atop her head which added to her alluring appearance.

"Daniel...," she said flustered, as she clutched her purse to her chest. Her eyes fluttered nervously. "I mean..."

"Daniel is fine," he answered with a teasing smile. Taking her hand, he led her across the threshold, through the foyer and into the living room. "Lacey is doing some shopping for the big day," he said as a way of explaining his answering her door.

"And she left you in her home?" Holly glanced down to his shoeless feet. She wondered, not for the first time, about his relationship with Lacey. She knew from Damien that Lacey looked upon Daniel as a brother, but failed to say how he felt about Lacey. After all, Lacey was a beautiful woman with a girlish figure unaltered by childbirth, not to mention an exciting career.

Daniel flashed a knowing smile. It wasn't the first time his and Lacey's relationship had been questioned. "For the record, Holly, Lacey is like a sister to me. There is not, nor has there ever been, anything romantic between us."

"I wasn't implying that there was," Holly worked to explain. She was a little rattled that he was able to read her so easily.

"Maybe not, but you were wondering." Daniel indicated for her to have a seat on the sofa. He opted for one of the chairs across from it.

Holly didn't answer right away. Instead she examined the room. It was stylish and classy, like Lacey. The cream pillow-backed sofa was plush and comfortable. The chairs across from it were bold in a warm brown and cream stripe. An oversized, dark wood ornate table divided the two. Writing magazines were neatly arranged on the tabletop, as well as the current issue of Ebony. Numerous candles in various shades of peach, brown, and cream were positioned throughout the room as well. A few green plants here and there added to the beauty of the room. On the mantle were several silver framed pictures; an older couple, probably her parents, was in one, Lacey and Damien in another, and lastly a picture of her and Daniel.

"Yes, I was," Holly answered, barely looking at him. She continued examining the room.

Daniel respected her honesty. "Well, just so there's no misunderstanding between us, I find myself extremely attracted to you, Holly."

That got her undivided attention. Her hazel eyes widened as they swung back to stare at Daniel. "What?"

This time Daniel was the one slow to answer. He opted to observe her expressive face for a moment. "I'm attracted to you, Holly," he repeated with sincerity. "I'd be honored if you would join me for dinner—say Saturday night?"

Holly couldn't control the excitement which coursed through her body. Daniel Overstreet, in all his handsomeness, was inviting her to dinner and had just stated that he was attracted to her. The womanly spirit inside of her became buoyant at the prospect of a man's interest. Then her thoughts switched to Steven. The betrayal and pain he had inflicted caused her spirit to crash back to Earth and the reality of her life.

"I can't," she blurted out and searched for an excuse. "My father is recovering from surgery and I've been assisting my mother with taking care of him." The words, though plausible, spilled out unconvincingly.

Daniel knew a brush off when he heard one. However, this was something other than disinterest. In Holly's hazel eyes, he had seen the spark of desire to say yes. This refusal had more to do with her failed marriage than him. "How long has it been?"

Holly didn't have to ask what he was referring to because she knew. Looking him square in the eyes, she answered. "Six months."

Daniel nodded in response to her answer. He rose from the chair and walked over to the fireplace. Six months wasn't a long time to be completely over a failed marriage, especially when you were the injured party. Intellectually he could understand, but emotionally, he couldn't allow her to walk away.

"No strings," he heard himself say as he turned back around to face her. He crossed the room in few steps and sat beside her. Leaning forward so that his arms rested atop his thighs, he glanced over at her. "Take this time to get to know me as a friend." He forced a casual smile despite feeling anxious about the turn of their conversation.

Holly picked up on the undercurrent in his voice. She almost relented, but then forced herself to stick to her decision. "You're looking for more than friendship, Daniel. I have children to consider, a demanding job, a questionable future to map out, not to mention an ailing father."

"There will always be excuses to hide behind, Holly." Daniel watched as she wrestled with the truth of his words. During her silence he admired her beautiful brown skin and wished for the right to caress it. But it was her eyes which held the greatest interest. They were so very expressive and open with honesty. He knew instinctively that his future was with this woman.

Holly rose suddenly from the sofa. Daniel's intense examination had her nervous and uncertain of her decision. It conveyed of a deep, honest interest that, if allowed, could pull her in.

"I wanted to apologize to Lacey."

"What do you have to apologize for?"

Holly fidgeted. "I allowed my bad marriage to interfere with Lacey and Damien's relationship." She shifted her purse from one arm to another.

"You're no longer married," Daniel softly reminded her. "You're also not responsible for your ex-husband's behavior."

"Of course you're right, but old habits are difficult to break." She forced a weak smile as her eyes fluttered nervously.

"Break this one." Daniel moved in a little closer. His hands were safely shoved into his pockets. "Give us a chance, Holly."

"Oh, Daniel, you don't know how badly I want to take that chance with you." She stood before him visibly confused.

"As the commercial says, *Just Do It*." Daniel stroked her cheek.

Beseechingly, Holly met his beautiful brown eyes. "Give me time," she requested softly.

"Not the answer I wanted," Daniel replied as he dropped his hand. "But you're worth the wait." His voice was laced with heavy emotion.

Holly's eyes blurred with unshed tears. It had been a long time since a man had made her feel desirable and wanted. "I should be going. Would you tell Lacey that I stopped by and that I'll call later?"

"No problem," Daniel answered as he held the door open. He stepped aside as she walked out onto the porch. He followed and stood watching as she made it down the sidewalk to her minivan parked in the driveway. As she prepared to enter the vehicle, he called out. "I'll see you at Thanksgiving dinner."

Those words stopped Holly dead in her tracks. She swung around to face him. Her face registered surprise. "Of course, Lacey invited her *family*," she managed to say over the lump in her throat. How the devil was she supposed to ignore the attraction between them for an entire day in close confines?

"Yes, she did," he called back with pure male satisfaction. Despite her desire not to see him socially, Thanksgiving with the family was an event she couldn't miss. It also provided him with time to work on dismantling that wall of reserve she hid behind.

Daniel remained on the porch well after Holly drove away. Peacefulness settled over him as he found himself wondering what *Turkey Day* would bring.

Thanksgiving Day dawned sunny and bright. There was a cool crispness to the air which enhanced the feel of the holiday season. The Christovals arrived around noon in a convoy of mini vans. Mr. and

Mrs. Christoval arrived with Holly and the kids. Patrice rode with their brother Trent and his wife Rhonda, who had driven down from Jackson the night before with their two children. Phillip and his family were pulling up the rear.

Lacey stood beside Damien on the porch greeting everyone as they entered Damien's home. She had spent the previous night with him and together they had worked side by side in the kitchen preparing for today's meal. A traditional menu had been planned with all the trimmings. Just before calling it a night, Damien had given the house a final vacuuming while Lacey set the dining room table with china and crystal for the adults. For the children she had chosen to use a table purchased while on a trip in Japan. A slab of an indigenous tree had been sanded and polished to a high gleam, then encased in acrylic. Eight low stools in the same type of wood with animal carvings circled it. Placemats depicting the first Thanksgiving sat under inexpensive harvest patterned plates. Bamboo styled utensils accompanied the place settings. For a centerpiece she had made a decorative arrangement using Indian corn and a turkey shaped wicker basket filled with foil wrapped candies. Stepping back, Lacey had surveyed her handiwork and liked what she saw.

"The little ones are going to love that table," Damien had commented coming up behind her. He placed his arms around Lacey's waist as she leaned back against him.

"It turned out nicely, didn't it?"

"More than we ever had," he said tightening his hold. "We got the card table and dishes we were afraid to use."

Lacey laughed, recalling holidays spent at the kids' table. "There's additional seating if you want to join them."

Damien had laughed and tightened his hold around her waist. "That's tempting, sweetheart, but I prefer to be close to you."

Now, as they sat side by side at the dining room table, Lacey was grateful to have Damien so close. The reception from the Christovals had been friendly and genuine. She had been embraced more that day than she could ever remember before, but as she had observed the Christovals, she realized that they were an affectionate bunch. Her own family, as she glanced at her mother, father, Daniel and his parents, were not nearly as affectionate. They loved each other and hugged occasionally, but nothing on the scale of the Christovals. These people hugged when greeting, they hugged in passing, they hugged when talking. As Lacey looked on, she realized they hugged for no reason at all other than as an expression of their love for one another. And today, she and her family had been included.

Well, almost. Phillip Christoval hadn't warmed to Lacey. Upon introduction he had been cool and cordial, but behind his penetrating brown eyes, Lacey had been keenly aware of being assessed. His wife, Robin, on the other hand, had been just as friendly as the rest of the family. The two had clicked and fallen into easy conversation once Robin realized that Lacey wasn't uncomfortable being around a pregnant woman. But Phillip remained aloof and assessing. He was there when she visited their mothers in the living room. He was there when she checked on the children out in the sunroom. She had spotted him while she and Daniel huddled in companionable whispers in the hallway. And when she and Damien sneaked off to the bedroom for a private moment, he had been the first face she saw as they returned to the kitchen. Now, sitting around the table over dinner, Lacey had had enough. His suspicious eyes followed her every move while he gauged her actions. It was time for the two of them to have a serious conversation.

Damien and the others noticed the silent surveillance by Phillip and picked up on the undertone of tension between him and Lacey. In an effort to ward off trouble and protect his lady, Damien had pulled his brother aside and instructed him to back off. For a moment or two he had, and the tension in the air abated. Damien had even asked him what he thought of Lacey.

"On the surface she appears okay. But then, so had Sara," Phillip responded dryly.

Angered and aggravated, Damien dragged Phillip down the hall for a private conversation.

"Phillip, let's get a couple of things clear between us. One, Lacey is not Sara. Two, I don't appreciate the silent treatment you've been giving her, and three, I love that woman and I will not tolerate your behavior much longer." Damien allowed the dark intensity of his eyes to convey his seriousness.

Phillip had always been able to read Damien and now was no different. Okay, so his brother was in love with this Lacey, but that wouldn't stop him from discovering what type of woman she really was. He had discovered with Sara that sitting back and observing her actions had conveyed far more about the woman than words. Sara was a lawyer—a manipulator of words and could make one believe almost anything with her legal tongue. Now this Lacey was a writer and no doubt skilled with whipping up the right words for any occasion. No, he didn't want to talk. He instead would sit back and observe her deeds.

"Look, Damien, I know you believe you know this woman and that you're in love with her. If she turns out to be as great as you say, I'll welcome her into the family. But if her actions prove me right, I'll give her hell." Phillip turned to walk away but was halted by Damien's firm grip on his upper arm. He glanced back, meeting his brother's brooding eyes.

"You hurt Lacey and it will be you on the receiving end of hell, my brother." Damien released Phillip; then stepped around him as he returned to the living room.

Now, as they sat across the table from one another, he had had enough of the spy routine and was about to put Phillip in check when Lacey tossed her napkin on the table and scooted her chair back.

"Phillip, may I speak with you in the den, please?" Lacey asked politely. Her tone of voice never indicated how very angry she truly was.

Damien gazed at Lacey as he rose from his chair. "Baby, I'll handle this."

Lacey smiled over at him. She could see the love in his eyes as well as the concern. She patted his arm lovingly and assured him that she could handle the situation. "Phillip and I will only be a moment," she assured him. "You all go ahead with the meal."

Robin swatted at Phillip's hand. She had warned him before leaving home not to cause trouble. But Phillip was unaware of his wife's anger or the many eyes watching him curiously. Lacey Avery had his undivided attention at the moment. He sensed that she was about to show her true colors and he couldn't wait to tell Damien *I told you so.*

"Shall we?" Phillip pushed his chair in and quickly fell in step behind Lacey. He was barely aware of the hum around the table.

Daniel was the first to speak. "I feel sorry for the brother." He laughed. "I know that look of Lacey's and he's in for one good butt chewing."

"I don't know, Daniel," Holly responded from her seat next to him. The two of them had been inseparable all evening thanks to Daniel's persistence. "Phillip has been known to chew a little fanny himself."

"That may be." Daniel smiled over at her. "But Lacey is the wronged party here. Your brother has been rude, suspicious, and stand-offish towards her all day. It's obvious that he dislikes her," Daniel defended Lacey vehemently.

Holly didn't appreciate Daniel talking about her brother. "Who do you think you are talking about?" Holly's voice rose as she turned on Daniel.

"I'm the closest thing Lacey has to a brother and I don't appreciate the way Phillip has been playing the great protector. Hell, Damien's a man. He doesn't need his brother interfering." Daniel gestured in Damien's direction.

Indignant, Holly pushed her chair back as she stood over Daniel fuming. "Well, it's obvious that you don't have siblings, because if you did, you would know that we look out for each other."

"For your information, Holly Christoval, I have two brothers. You would know that if you would accept my dinner invitation and stop hiding behind your family and a million excuses," Daniel shouted out of frustration.

Hands on hips, Holly squared her shoulders while her eyes blazed. "I am not hiding behind my family or excuses."

"Sure you are. A sad tune as I recall. Shall I recite it? My mother needs help with my father, the kids...," he recited as he ticked off each one on his fingers.

"I'm not singing a sad tune," Holly shouted back. "Just because I'm not melting at your feet, you're upset."

"You're right, I'm upset. I've finally found a beautiful, desirable, intelligent woman that I know is perfect for me, and she's too afraid to give love a chance again," he shouted.

At the sound of the collective heartfelt sighs around them, Holly and Daniel realized where they were and that they were now the center of attention.

"Um, Holly, I think this conversation can wait." Daniel smiled over at her.

Holly nodded vigorously in agreement. "This wonderful meal is getting cold. You heard Lacey, eat up." She returned to her chair and dove into her plate of food. Daniel followed suit.

The dining room erupted into laughter as Lacey and Phillip were momentarily forgotten.

Lacey faced off with Phillip in the den. His stance was unyielding and an attempt to intimidate, but Lacey wasn't threatened. She raised her chin, meeting his gaze head on.

"Damien informed me that you have some misgivings about our relationship. Considering the secret that he hid from me and your being privy to that information, I can understand your initial concern. But the secret is out and Damien and I are in love."

"But how long will that last?" Phillip interrupted her. "Until you're a household name, selling millions of copies of your books and no longer consider Damien in your league?"

How dare he? The question pushed Lacey over the edge. She had been trying to hang on to her temper, but the ugly, insinuating question had snapped the reins on her restraint.

"How long will your marriage last, Phillip?" She pointed a finger at him. "Can you place a time limit on it? No, you can't. The only thing you can do is cherish the love that you have and pray that it survives all the obstacles and hardships life throws your way. But in your heart you know that there has never been a greater love or one so worth fighting for than the one you have." Her hand covered her heart. "I'm not Sara and I don't appreciate being judged. I love Damien and there is no better man. My writing is what I do for a living. It doesn't greet me at the door from a long lonely trip. It doesn't slide into bed with me at night to cuddle. It doesn't listen to my dreams or my fears, and it definitely doesn't return my love. Damien does all that, and so much more."

Lacey walked to the window, pulling the sheers back and looked out into the back yard. It was a yard for children, but there would never be any, at least not of her body, romping in the yard.

"I can't have children," she said, glancing back at Phillip.

"Damien told us. I'm sorry."

"I'm not looking for pity." Her sherry brown eyes locked with his. "What I wanted was love and acceptance. I found that with Damien." Her eyes misted with tears as she continued to speak. "I don't care if Damien washes dishes for a living. For the love he has shown me, I would fight you and the devil himself if either one of you tried to come between us. Now, I don't plan on leaving so I believe it's best you and

I figure out a way to get along. Don't you?"

Phillip couldn't help the smile which spread across his face. This feather of a woman was standing her ground and he had no doubt that she meant every word. "Damn. I think my brother finally got it right." He swept Lacey into a warm embrace that surprised her. He stepped back looking at her. "You and I are going to be great friends, Lacey. All I have ever wanted for my brother was the love and respect he deserves. He has that now with you, so I can sit back and relax."

"That you can do because Damien's in good hands," she declared, smiling up at him.

"Are you okay?" Damien asked as he joined Lacey later in the kitchen. She was preparing a tray for desert. It was the first moment since her meeting with Phillip that he had been able to catch her alone. His hand caressed her neck as he now stood beside her.

Lacey dropped the knife she had been using to slice cake and turned, focusing on Damien. "You can wipe that concerned look off your face. Phillip and I only want what is best for you." She smiled and leaned over kissing him quickly. "We both decided I was it." She winked and laughed.

Damien joined her in laughter. "He means well." He drew Lacey into his arms and caressed the length of her back.

"I know, but truthfully we gained a mutual understanding and I believe we are well on the way to becoming good friends."

"I sure hope so, because families are an important part of any relationship, and I would like for ours to get along."

Lacey moved out of Damien's arms. "Oh, they are," she informed him and began ticking off each observation on her fingers. "Our mothers and Mama Overstreet have had their heads together all evening. I'll give you one guess as to what they're whispering about. Now our fathers have made it no secret that they're both into football. If those two don't stop quoting statistics trying to prove who knows more, I swear I'll scream. Then there's Daniel and Holly who believes no one sees the glances they are shooting at each other."

Damien laughed heartily. He asked, "So what do you think about those two?"

Lacey leaned against the counter, folding her arms. "I personally believe Daniel will be good for Holly and the kids. He's not a flighty artist, but a good man with strong family values."

"That's good to know because that's exactly what my sister and her children need." A sudden smile crept across his face as he moved closer to Lacey. His body pressed her against the cabinet. "Speaking of kids, the children all think you're pretty terrific." He leaned down to nibble on a studded lobe. "Gabriel thinks you're kind of pretty."

Lacey laughed as she squirmed against him. "And what do you think?"

"I think you're kind of pretty too." Damien kissed her.

"They're good kids. I'm enjoying getting to know them, and that little Gabby." Lacey looked up at him with longing in her eyes.

Damien caressed the side of her face wishing that he could give her the one thing in life that she wanted. "She's beautiful, isn't she?" he spoke of Phillip's two-year-old daughter. She had a cinnamon brown complexion, with thick long braids, and large hazel eyes. "She's definitely going to be a heartbreaker when she grows up," Damien commented.

"Yes, she is."

"Hey, Lace, what's holding up that desert?" Daniel waltzed into the room with a trail of little people following behind him.

Lacey and Damien both jumped and separated as their private moment was shattered. "It's right here," she said spinning around and grabbing the tray. "If you little people will follow me please," she spoke to the children in a formal voice which set off their giggle boxes and led the way to their table.

"Sorry, man," Daniel apologized for interrupting.

"Don't be." Damien smiled over at him. "Lacey and I have a life-time of private moments like that ahead of us."

Daniel liked the sound of that. "Does that mean you'll be popping the big question?"

"It does indeed," Damien replied, then retrieved the other tray and headed out into the living room where the adults were gathered.

CHAPTER 16

"Did you have to select the biggest tree on the lot?" Damien huffed as he struggled to get the large spruce into Lacey's home. "Where do you want this thing?"

"Over in front of the window," Lacey directed. She followed behind him with an armload of presents.

"Why the need for such a large tree?" Damien asked as he collapsed on the floor in front of the window. He waited for a response while Lacey ran back out to the vehicle for another load.

"I have a lot of Christmas presents," she said upon returning. She deposited her packages and stood above him. "I need a tree large enough to handle all these gifts."

Damien laughed and shook his head. He tilted his head back looking up at Lacey. She was radiant. Her eyes twinkled with a child's enthusiasm for the holiday. "Did it ever occur to you that you didn't have to buy all these gifts?"

"Don't pretend like you didn't enjoy yourself," she challenged as she dropped down beside him. She reached for one of the shopping bags. "I saw you playing with the remote control cars." She waved the box in front of him.

"Okay, they were a lot of fun and Gabriel is going to enjoy them."

"I'm sure he's not the only one," Lacey said from behind her hand.

Damien laughed as he rifled through another plastic bag. Finding what he was searching for, he turned the tables on Lacey. "And just who did you purchase this doll for?" He waved the eating, crying, and wetting doll before her."

"Give me that." Lacey reached out, taking the doll. She laid it reverently across her lap. "This is for Raye. Every little girl should have a doll like this." She tried to look innocent.

"Right. I'm sure Holly will thank you for more diapers to change." He roared with laughter when Lacey elbowed him in the gut. He grabbed her around the waist and lowered her to the floor. Covering her body, he kissed her passionately. The day had been one he would cherish always. "I love you so much," he whispered as he pulled back. His large hand stroked her hair while his eyes took in Lacey's loveliness.

"I love you too." Lacey lay on her back looking up at him. She was overwhelmed by the depth of love visible in his eyes. "Thank you for giving me such happiness."

Damien leaned down and kissed each cheek. "I plan on giving you years of happiness, baby." Once again he thanked the man upstairs for bringing this woman into his life.

"You really want to make me happy?" Lacey asked with a hint of wickedness in her voice. She smiled and rubbed her body up against him.

Damien warmed to the idea Lacey's body was conveying. "Definitely."

"I'm glad to hear it because these presents have to be wrapped and the tree decorated." She smiled impishly at him and laughed.

Damien rolled his eyes and flopped back onto the floor. He enjoyed hearing Lacey's laughter. "Where do we start?"

"The tree first, then the presents." She rose from the floor to retrieve the decorations. Her heart was overflowing with love and excitement. She could hardly wait to see the children's faces when they opened their gifts on Christmas morning. And she had Damien to thank for the joy she was experiencing.

Christmas at the Christoval home was just as hectic and noisy as

Thanksgiving at Damien's. Lacey and Daniel's families had joined the Christovals. The kids were running around playing with their new toys from Santa while the adults exchanged gifts from under the tree. Damien and Lacey had chosen to open their gifts for each other privately at her place before they had headed over to his parents' home. It was their first Christmas together and they wanted to share the special moment together.

Now, as Damien and Mrs. Christoval handed out gifts, Raye was close by removing the diaper off her doll while Lacey looked on. She sat on the floor with Gabby in her lap. The three had bonded Thanksgiving Day and had almost been inseparable today. A stack of gifts sat to the right of Lacey. One gift remained under the tree and Damien was the one to hand it out. It was a small box wrapped prettily in gold holiday paper. He approached Lacey drawing her curious attention. He removed Gabby from her lap.

Lacey glanced at Damien oddly. She darted a quick glance around the room and noticed that they had become the center of attention. She could feel her heart rate increase.

"What are you doing?" she whispered low so that only Damien could hear.

He smiled boyishly as he knelt before her. "Giving you a token of my love." He placed the small box into Lacey's hand.

Lacey stared down at the small gold box. She imagined what was inside. Her hand shook just thinking about it. "I thought we had already exchanged gifts," she said to Damien. Her eyes were overly bright.

"This one was special and I felt our families should be gathered around when I gave it to you." His voice was just above a whisper, yet radiated with emotion.

Lacey swallowed hard. She glanced down at the small box in her hand and proceeded to tear the paper away. A black velvet box was exposed. Slowly, she opened the lid to reveal the diamond it contained.

Tears blinded her vision as she launched herself into Damien's arms. "I love you," she whispered against his chest.

"I know, but will you marry me?" Damien asked. His own vision was a little blurry.

"Yes! Oh, yes," Lacey cried even harder. It was a moment that she had once believed would never be hers. But here today, amongst their families, Damien had made her dream come true.

The room immediately erupted into words of congratulations. Everyone gathered around as Damien removed the two-carat diamond from the box and took Lacey's trembling hand into his. Proudly he slipped the ring onto her finger. Leaning forward, he kissed her hand reverently. With his eyes on Lacey, Damien beamed joyously as he said to the room, "We're getting married, folks."

"Do you want a long engagement?" Lacey asked Damien. She was lying with her head resting on his chest and their feet intertwined. They had returned to her house after dinner, and were now stretched out on the sofa cuddling before the fire.

"Absolutely not," Damien replied as he pulled Lacey on top of him. "I want to marry you tomorrow." His eyes caressed her face.

"Tomorrow, huh?" Lacey planted her chin in his chest and looked up at him. "How about the first of February? It will give me a month to plan a small wedding."

Damien rolled his eyes dramatically. "A month? Lacey baby, I want to wake up to you beside me."

"A month, sweetheart." She kissed his chest exposed through the open collar of his shirt. "Just imagine the wedding, followed by the honeymoon night that I could plan for us."

A dark brow rose as Damien glanced down at Lacey. "I thought the honeymoon was my responsibility."

"It is, but you can't plan anything special by tomorrow. Now in four weeks...," she paused and gave him a suggestive wink.

"Point made," he relented, rolling over and pinning Lacey beneath him. "Prepare, my sweet, for a honeymoon to remember."

The telephone was ringing. Lacey rolled over reaching blindly for the offensive noise.

"Hello."

"Hi baby, sorry I woke you, but I wanted to hear your voice before I started my shift," Damien apologized. It was a week into the New Year and he was back on duty.

Lacey smiled at the sound of Damien's voice. The rich deep timbre rumbled through her body, stirring the flames of desire. "Just think, in a couple of weeks all you'll have to do is roll over and give me a proper wake up."

"Lacey," Damien groaned into the phone. "Don't start or I'll have to make a detour on the way to work."

Lacey gave him a sultry laugh. "I wish you could, but I'm dress shopping with our mothers and your sisters today." She glanced at the clock for the time. "As a matter of fact, I should be getting dressed right now. We're meeting for breakfast before tackling the boutiques."

"Well, don't let me stop you from dress shopping. The sooner this wedding takes place, the sooner I can give you that proper wake up." His voice was low and seductive.

This time it was Lacey who groaned. "Maybe I can skip breakfast."

"Don't you dare or you'll have our mothers hot on our trail."

Lacey gave an exaggerated huff. "I'll stop by the station after shopping. I love you."

"I love you too, baby."

"Be safe," Lacey whispered before disconnecting. Scrambling

quickly, she was dressed and ready for a day of shopping in record time. She pulled on her jacket and located her purse on the table in the living room. A search revealed her keys in the side pocket. With keys in hand she was off.

Lacey and Holly were the first to arrive at McElroy's Restaurant for breakfast. It was a local favorite perched in the middle of the harbor overlooking the soothing gulf water. Securing a table, they placed orders for coffee and juice with the waitress while they waited on the others to arrive. The conversation turned toward Daniel. Lacey had wondered how long it would take Holly to ask about him. From the little Daniel mentioned, she knew that Holly was putting up roadblocks, despite her obvious attraction.

"How's Daniel doing?" Holly asked innocently. "I haven't seen him around in awhile." What she really wanted to know was had he given up on her. Since the holidays, she hadn't seen or heard from Daniel Overstreet, and his absence was starting to concern her. She had taken his phone calls every other day for granted and the occasional flower deliveries. Now, without a word from him in several days, she nervously wondered if she had allowed a good man to slip away.

Lacey sipped her orange juice while watching Holly over the rim of her glass. It was obvious to anyone with two good eyes that the woman was definitely interested in Daniel.

"He's been out of town scouting new artists. He was due back last night," Lacey explained. She waited to see what Holly would ask next.

"So you haven't spoken to him?"

"No. Daniel keeps a fast pace when he's on one of his searches."

That explains it. "He's a very nice man, your friend." Holly stared down into her cup of coffee. She wanted to say that she had missed him and looked forward to hearing from him. Instead, she said nothing more.

"Holly, if I'm out of line, please say so. But it's obvious to anyone who looks at you that you're attracted to Daniel. I know you've been hurt and that you're trying to put your life back together, but there is no need for you to do it alone."

Holly looked at Lacey across the table. The two were fast becoming good friends. "I do like Daniel and a part of me wants to go with what I'm feeling. However, I have children who have had their world torn apart and I just feel as though I have to focus my attention on them."

"I completely understand." Lacey assured her. "But they have you to lean on and I know you have your family, but there isn't anything wrong with you having that special someone who's there just for you."

"No, there isn't. Steven was supposed to be that person," she whispered.

Lacey reached over and covered her hand. "It's okay to still love him."

"That's just it. I don't love him," Holly confessed. She tucked a braid behind her ear in a nervous habit. "I was hurt by his actions, but other than that I don't feel anything for the man at all and that frightens me. We have children. Shouldn't I feel something?" She looked to Lacey. "What does that say about me, if I can feel nothing for the man I was married to for years, yet at the same time feel girlish giddiness at the mere thought of Daniel?"

Lacey smiled with joy. It was so wonderful to hear Holly confess her true feelings for Daniel. "It means that maybe your marriage was over a long time ago and it took his betrayal to force the issue."

Stunned because Lacey had hit the nail right on the head, Holly stared wide-eyed at her. "How did you know?"

"I'm an observer. Maybe that's what makes me a good writer." Lacey shrugged her shoulders. "I remember some of the things Steven said to you about Damien and your family. It was apparent that he was jealous of them and placed that burden on you."

Holly nodded in agreement. "He did. From the moment we were married, it was as though he expected my family to disappear and not

157

be a part of my life."

"I would guess that he and his family aren't close?"

"No, they're not. But it was the closeness of my family that Steven said he admired.

"Maybe he did. However, without experiencing the give and take of the family unit, or the unsolicited advice simply because you are loved, he didn't know how to handle it. He didn't understand that he didn't have to compete for your love because he already had it."

"Was that my fault, Lacey? Did I not tell him enough or show him? Even when I knew my marriage was changing, I still loved him."

"I'm sure you did both those things, but a person has to be willing to learn how to accept love. People assume it's a given. I know from personal experience that it isn't."

"How so?" Holly asked intrigued by the confession. When she looked at Lacey, all she saw was this confident woman with a fabulous career and couldn't imagine her doubting that she was loved.

"After my broken engagement because of the accident, I didn't believe there was a man who could really love me. I couldn't have children and so I saw myself as less valuable. Fortunately, I've had the pleasure of meeting some really nice men and the one or two that I dated, were extremely nice. One in particular I would even say loved me."

"So what happened?"

Lacey smiled a sad little smile as she glanced out the window overlooking the gulf. "I ended the relationship because I couldn't accept that he loved me. I hadn't shared the fact that I couldn't have children and so, in my mind, his love was suspect. I didn't want to stick around to see what would happen if and when I told him."

"You were afraid he would reject you, because you couldn't have children and so you pushed him away first." Holly mulled this over. "In a sense, Steven did the same thing. He knew family was important to me as well as fidelity. So out of fear of my not loving him as much as my family and being rejected, he did the one thing that would make me leave. He had an affair."

"That would be my guess," Lacey replied.

"So why did you become involved with Damien?" Holly asked with great interest. She planted her elbow on the table and cupped her chin with her hand. She had to hear this.

Lacey's eyes swung heavenward as she thought how to respond. Formulating an answer, she responded. "Because my best friend told me that I couldn't control life. He said that you had to live it and allow it to happen." She smiled remembering the actual words. "Thanks to Daniel's sage advice, I have the love that I've always wanted."

Holly liked that. "Maybe it's time I put that same advice to use," she said as her eyes sparkled with new inspiration. They quickly changed conversation as the other members of their party began arriving.

"I don't like any of these dresses," Lacey wailed several hours later. She stood draped in a sea of white and pearls. The gown, though pretty, wasn't her style or flattering to her willowy figure. After hours of searching shop after shop with no luck, she was upset and completely frustrated. This was the third bridal boutique. She had an image of what she wanted in mind and knew that she would recognize the right dress when she came across it, but so far the selection of dresses had been lacking. She turned to the women accompanying her. "Let's try Deedy's Bridal Boutique. I hear she has a wonderful selection."

"A friend of mine purchased her bridal gown from there," Patrice said. "It was absolutely gorgeous."

"Okay then, let's head over there and see if she has something gorgeous waiting for me." Lacey returned to the dressing room to remove the dress. As she did so, she said, "Otherwise, I'm going to take Damien up on his suggestion of a quick marriage at the courthouse and get it over with."

"You will do no such thing, Lacey Rebecca Avery," Laura Avery scolded her daughter. "I have waited a long time to see my daughter walk down the aisle and you are not going to take that away from me. Do you hear?"

Lacey laughed because she could imagine the look of horror plastered on her mother's face. A courthouse wedding was definitely not to Laura Avery's liking. "It was just a suggestion, Mom."

"Well you can forget that idea young lady."

"Amen," Melinda chimed in.

The women piled back into Lacey's SUV and drove across town to Deedy's. The moment they pulled up in front of the two-story shop, Lacey had the feeling that her dress was inside waiting for her. Entering the boutique they were greeted by a friendly attendant who led the way to the bridal gowns. They also sold special occasion dresses. Upstairs was everything a bride would need for her special day. Gowns, headpieces, gloves, jewelry, undergarments, and shoes were all available. Melinda and Laura took a seat on the overstuffed settee and allowed the young women to search through the plastic encased dresses. They smiled to each other at the girls' excitement. Finally, Lacey squealed with delight as she removed a dress from the rack. Through the clear plastic case, she admired the heavenly creation of white satin, lace, and sea of pearls. The shoulders and arms of the dress were of the most delicate lace with a sprinkling of pearls along the way. The scalloped neckline, trimmed in that same lace and white pearls, covered the most beautiful white silk which started at the breast and flowed gracefully to the floor. The cinched bodice and waistline would complement her svelte figure. The straight cut gown would also enhance her appearance. A modest train would follow behind her as she made her walk down the aisle. *This was the dress.*

"I've got to try it on," Lacey spoke with excitement. The attendant quickly selected a headpiece, inquired about shoe size, and then ushered Lacey into the nearest dressing room where she assisted her into the dress. When the last pearl button had been fastened down the back and headpiece and shoes were on, Lacey glanced at her image in the mirror. For a moment she couldn't say anything. The reflection staring back at her was like a dream come true. The dress and headpiece were beautiful and just what she wanted. Tears formed in her eyes as the realization that her dream was finally coming true. Her watery eyes concerned the attendant.

"If something isn't just the way you like, I'm sure we can alter it," the young woman rattled on.

Lacey smiled at the attendant through the mirror on hearing her concern. "The dress is perfect. The tears are just of happiness. I've been searching for the perfect dress all day and it was here waiting for me."

The woman sighed, visibly relieved. "Deedy's aims to please. Why don't you give the ladies out there waiting on you a preview?"

Lacey nodded, then opened the door and stepped out.

Laura Avery was the first to spot her daughter. Her eyes instantly filled with tears. Her beautiful daughter made a stunning bride. "Oh, baby, you are beautiful," Laura whispered in awe.

"Damien isn't going to be able to take his eyes off you," Melinda added.

"Girl, that dress is *da bomb*," Patrice added in her youthful exuberance.

Only Holly hadn't commented and now Lacey faced her. The two had shared a great deal today. She reached out her hands to her. "So what do you think?"

Holly pushed the memories of her wedding day to the back of her mind with all the dreams she had carried down the aisle with her. This was Lacey's day and she would do nothing to ruin it. She clasped Lacey's hands as she smiled. "I think you are the prettiest bride I have ever seen and that my brother is the luckiest man alive."

"Thank you," Lacey whispered. "So, everyone agrees, this is it?"

161

A chorus of approval rang out. Lacey and the attendant quickly set about selecting bridesmaids' dresses, then something special for the mothers. By the time everyone was outfitted, it was late into the afternoon. As the women approached the service counter, they were laughing and joking. The day had been wonderful and filled with the excitement of love. Behind the counter a small television was on. The volume was low. As Lacey waited for the attendant to ring up her purchases, an image of a raging fire lit the screen. A reporter stood to the right of the shot.

"Could you please turn up the volume on the television?" Lacey asked.

"Sure, no problem."

"Repeating," the reporter was saying. "The number 10 Warehouse at the Port of Gulfport is engulfed in flames. Around three thirty, a worker reported flames coming from one of the interior rooms. He tried to extinguish the blaze himself but was unable to. Now as you can see behind me, it is out of control. We are told that this warehouse contains automotive components for one of the new automotive plants. There are four fire engine battalions battling this blaze. I see engines from Biloxi just arriving to assist."

The camera panned the fire trucks on scene. The number 24 Engine practically leaped off the screen as the women realized that Damien and his men were fighting that ferocious fire.

Damien descended the ladder from the roof with axe in hand. The ominous glow of the fire was only now starting to light the darkening sky. The hellish heat from the raging fire below could be felt through the insulation of their gear. He and his men ran back over to the engine and quickly removed their breathing mask and air tanks. Breathing deeply he unhooked his radio and quickly linked up with the Chief.

"This is Christoval, the roof venting is complete. Engine 24 will move in from the east entrance," he relayed.

"Copy 24," the Chief replied. His voice could be heard dispatching orders to the other engines. Damien continued to listen so that he would know the position of each engine crew. Then, on the Chief's command, they all moved into the block-long wooden warehouse.

Manning the 600 foot attack lines which were connected to the engine, Kenneth and Howard, one of the younger guys from the station, were the nozzle men for 24. It was their responsibility to knock down the flames as quickly as possible. Perched to the side of the metal doors, Damien gave the order to slowly open them. Pike poles were used to accomplish this. The melting heat rolled over the firemen as the doors were opened. The men prepared to enter the burning inferno. Thick choking black smoke hindered their ability to see the dangers lying ahead of them. The roar of the firestorm inside was nearly deafening, but to the men of Engine 24, it was a familiar companion. By keeping one's ear tuned to the sound of the fire crackling and swallowing up oxygen, one could ward off possible danger. The slightest change in the rhythm could signal a fire was intensifying.

Kenneth and Howard hit the water beating back the flames licking around the doorway. When they were extinguished, they inched further into the pit of hell. One behind the other, the men of Engine 24 entered the burning structure, all knowing the routine; vigilance and safety first. The nozzle beat back the flames while Damien and his men pulled down fire from stacked crates and interior walls. They were fortunate not to have to search for missing employees since all had been accounted for. Howard sprayed to the left, while Kenneth swept to the right. The molten reddish-orange flames swayed to their own rhythm in defiance of the firemen's efforts. Smoke, black and thick, and no doubt toxic, billowed as more of the aged warehouse was consumed by fire. After nearly twenty minutes inside, Damien signaled for three of his seven men to take a break. When they returned after five minutes, another three rotated out. He and Kenneth were the last to leave.

"It's dangerous in there, man," Kenneth huffed to Damien as they removed their breathing apparatuses. Their faces were covered with sweat.

"I hate these types of calls," Damien commented as he sucked in air. "Those damn stacked crates make me nervous."

"I know what you mean. I'm afraid if I hit them too hard with the water they'll all topple over on top of us. And who knows what's inside of them." Kenneth hoisted the tank back on as he and Damien prepared to re-enter the building.

"Ready?" Damien asked.

"Ready."

The two rejoined their team just as they were entering a narrow passageway. Crates were stacked nearly to the ceiling in this area. The signed packing labels indicated the crates contained automobile seats that were highly flammable and combustible. As the men battled the flames desperately trying to crawl up the crating, a loud explosion came from somewhere in front of them. Damien grabbed his radio to inform the Chief, but before he could complete the transmission, a call for help came across the radio. The assisting Biloxi squad was trapped by falling crates. Damien and his men proceeded in their direction at a fast pace. Time was of the essence in a blaze like this.

Directly ahead, a wall of crates had toppled before Engine 24. The crates were burning out of control creating a wall of fire, and somewhere inside was the Biloxi squad. Using their poles while the nozzle men bathed the flames, Damien and his men began digging through the debris. The crates were heavy but not unmovable. It wasn't long before they had located the six trapped firemen. All were intact and accounted for, but they had lost their nozzle somewhere under the crates. They quickly joined up with Engine 24. Suddenly the sound of the fire changed. The dull, almost soothing roar of the fire grew louder in intensity as flames soared to the height of the ceiling, consuming everything in its path. The ceiling overhead looked like the gates of hell, churning with molten flames. Minor explosions one by one could be heard coming from the rear of the building as combustible items fueled the ferocity of the fire-breathing storm, signaling the massive eruption yet to come.

Damien turned to his men, but was caught on something jutting out. Unable to see how to remove the trapped left sleeve of his jacket, he yanked on the garment and heard it tear away. All was done simultaneously while he yelled from behind his mask, "Flashover!"

Each man knew the potential danger if they didn't immediately clear the area. Running for their lives the men exited the building. At the door, Damien counted twelve instead of thirteen. Glancing behind him, he saw Howard trapped under a fallen crate. He returned inside for his man with no regard to the wall of fire rumbling from the rear of the building in their direction. The ground around the warehouse shook from the powerful explosion that followed.

The sales attendant had completed the transaction minutes ago, but just knowing Damien was fighting that fire, no one had moved from the television. Now they all stood with their eyes glued to the screen searching for a glimpse of Damien. Then, an enormous flash of light filled the screen as the building exploded.

The camera stayed focused on the inferno for several minutes before swinging away from the fire and back to the excited reporter. "I've just been informed that two firemen are down. They were caught inside the warehouse when a firestorm, known as a flashover, occurred." The reporter paused and listened as someone whispered into his ear. "We have confirmation that the two injured firemen were from Engine 24," he went on to say.

Cell phones began ringing. First Mrs. Christoval's, then Lacey's, followed by Patrice's and Holly's. No one moved as their panic-stricken glances collided. Laura Avery wrapped her arms around her daughter for strength. One by one, the women answered the call that would forever be etched into their memory.

CHAPTER 17

The five women raced into the emergency entrance of the Mobile Burn Center. Damien and Howard had been transported to the center by Life Flight. As they entered the building, Lacey didn't remember anything of the forty-five minute drive over. She had been on automatic pilot in her quest to reach Damien. Prayers from the front and back seats of her vehicle had been sent up to Heaven on his behalf. Uniformed firemen lined the corridor of the emergency room. Their uniforms indicated that they were from Mobile and the surrounding areas. But despite their locations, their grief stricken faces indicated that they were all brothers at heart.

Kenneth spotted the women first. He broke away from the other men to meet Mrs. Christoval and Lacey. Just as he approached the women, the Christoval men came barreling through the automatic doors.

"How's my baby?" Mrs. Christoval asked Kenneth. She had a grip on his arm that was nearly cutting off the circulation.

"He's alive, but hurt badly," Kenneth told her honestly.

"Dear God," Lacey wailed as she stood in her mother's arms. Her watery eyes connected with Kenneth's. They were filled with visible fear.

"What the hell happened?" Phillip asked of Kenneth. He and his father had arrived just as Kenneth began talking to the women.

"Flashover. One of the men didn't make it out. Damien went back in for him, but before he could clear the doorway of the building with Howard, it exploded."

"How is Howard?" Lacey asked remembering his excitement about the baby.

"The same as Damien."

"Poor Katie," Lacey whispered.

Kenneth guided the family to the private waiting room that the hospital had set aside for them. They were soon joined by a very pregnant Katie and Howard's family. The mothers embraced and shared prayers. Lacey and Katie sat off to the side holding each other's hand. Katie kept whispering that Howard had to make it because they had a baby on the way. Lacey was envious. Despite her love for Damien she would never carry a part of him inside of her as a testament to their love. She needed air. As she rose to seek peace outside the waiting room, a doctor rushed in. He hurriedly approached the Christovals gathered around.

"I'm Dr. Randall. Damien has been badly injured, but he's alive. His left arm has suffered third degree burns and we have treated it as best we can for the moment. He's sedated and will probably be in and out of consciousness for several days. It's best with this type of injury to allow the body to rest and heal. He's in ICU under the watchful eyes of our talented nurses. Now I know you all want to see him, but we have to be careful about germs and infections, so I'm only going to allow, his wife, Lacey to go back. Damien was talking about a wedding and asked for her. Is she here?"

"I'm here," Lacey answered. All eyes turned to her, only now remembering the wedding they all had been eagerly anticipating. Laura clasped her daughter's cold hands while the doctor watched Lacey sympathetically.

"Damien and I are due to be married in February," she informed the doctor. "So I'm not family. His parents really should be with him."

The doctor nodded. He knew how difficult it had to be for her to say that. Bending the rules he told her to follow them. Lacey smiled brightly as she thanked him and followed behind Mr. and Mrs. Christoval. They were led to an area outside of ICU where they were issued sanitary masks. Dr. Randall explained the need for the masks.

"We have to be careful of infections to the burn site and the patient's strained immune system. This is only a precaution for a day or two." When they entered Damien's room, the beeping sound of the monitors greeted them. The window blinds were partially open. The moon was out and shining brightly. Its beauty caused Lacey to recall a night when she and Damien had sat in the back of his truck cuddled together. As she focused her attention on the still body lying in the perfectly made bed, she wished that they were back in the bed of that truck. But they weren't. Damien was lying in bed sedated. His left arm was bandaged and elevated while the right lay on top of the covers with IV lines dripping life-sustaining fluids into his damaged body. Dr. Randall walked in removing the chart hanging at the foot of Damien's bed. He turned toward the Christovals and Lacey.

"He's not in any pain at the moment. We're giving him a Morphine-based drip which will control the pain. For the time being, infection is our enemy. That's why he's receiving topical antibiotics on the wound surface. Coupled with close monitoring and debridement treatments for the removal of dead skin, they're our best defense against the septic burn wound."

Mrs. Christoval sobbed openly as she ran a hand across her son's brow. Mr. Christoval stood beside her. His lean face lined with worry for a son he couldn't help.

"Damien's in good hands here," Dr. Randall tried to convince the Christovals. "He's a strong healthy man. He'll pull through this." His blue eyes were warm and encouraging. To Lacey he patted her arm saying, "You'll have that wedding." He left the three of them to visit.

At the moment Lacey couldn't even think about a wedding with Damien lying so still in bed. This wasn't the energetic, take charge man that she had come to know and love. This man was battered and bruised and now in need of another's strength. Lacey was fortified and determined to see Damien through his recovery. She wasn't under the misguided notion that it would be easy, but was positive that with the good Lord's help, Damien *would* recover.

Mr. Christoval escorted his teary wife out of the room. Lacey was left alone with Damien. Moving from her position just inside the doorway, she walked over to the bed and looked down on her love. His beautiful face was nicked and bruised. Lacey looked around the room for somewhere to sit. A chair was over by the window. She left his side, grabbed the chair and placed it beside his bed. She covered Damien's uninjured hand while sitting down. The warmth of his skin was reassuring. He had survived.

A nurse tipped into the room a short time later. She informed Lacey of the visiting hours and asked her to leave. Reluctantly, she did. Back outside in the waiting room she discovered that Mr. and Mrs. Christoval had been taken to a nearby hotel to rest, and that her father and Daniel had arrived while she had been with Damien. Daniel separated himself from Holly, whom he had been consoling. He greeted her with open arms and a reassuring hug. They stood in the middle of the floor locked in an embrace. Lacey cried for the man she loved while taking comfort in Daniel's strength. When she was finally in control of her emotions, she stepped out of his arms.

"How is he?" Daniel asked. He led Lacey to a nearby chair.

"Sedated." Lacey pulled her hair back from her face in frustration. She felt so completely helpless. "I was just sitting beside his bed hoping that he sensed that he wasn't alone." Her voice held a weary tone.

"I'm sure he knew that you were with him."

"I hope so." She looked over at Daniel. "I remember how lonely the hospital can be."

"Look around," Daniel ordered. Christovals, immediate and extended now filled the waiting room. "Damien isn't alone. All these people are here praying for him. They're aunts, uncles, and cousins."

Lacey smiled for the first time since leaving Damien's side. It did her heart good to see that Damien was so loved. "He's a good man."

"Yes, he is."

"He has to be all right, Daniel," Lacey sobbed, breaking down once more. Tears tracked down her face as she collapsed into her friend's arms. "The doctor said infection is the enemy."

"He'll pull through this, Lace," Daniel whispered softly. His large hand stroked the length of her back soothingly. "Damien risked his life for another man. Surely unselfishness like that has to be rewarded."

"I'd like to think so," she replied on a sniff. "But bad things happen to good people."

Daniel grabbed Lacey by both arms and sat her back so that he could face her. "Stop all this negative thinking. Damien needs you positive and in fighting spirit. That man is going to need you like never before. Do you understand me?"

Lacey was instantly ashamed for giving in to a moment of weakness. Daniel was right. Damien would need her strength and faith to help him recover. "I understand and thanks for being my best friend."

"Always, honey." Daniel smiled, using his thumbs to wipe away her tears.

"I love you."

"I love you too, Lace." He suddenly rose from his chair and walked back over to where Lacey's father sat. He came back with an overnight bag. "I hope you don't mind, but I had my mother pack you a bag. I figured you would be spending the night here at the hospital," he explained as he passed Lacey the nylon bag.

A smile lit her face. "Thank you so much for thinking ahead." She relieved Daniel of the bag. "You're right; I will be spending the night here. I want to be here when he wakes up."

It had been three long days since the fire. Damien had been placed in a semi-conscious state which allowed the staff the ability to perform the painful removal of burned skin. They went in and out of his room each day, performing one task after another. And every day they informed the family that Damien was getting stronger and that it wouldn't be long before he was fully awake.

That time came on the fifth day of Damien's hospital stay. Lacey had awakened stiffly around six in the morning from a catnap in the ICU waiting room. The caring nursing staff had provided her with blankets and pillows. After visiting with Damien each morning, she would return to the near-by hotel room that Daniel had secured for her. There she would shower and change clothes. But until then, she grabbed her over-sized handbag and made her way to the ladies room down the hall. Inside she splashed water on her face, removed the travel toothbrush kit, and proceeded to brush her teeth. With the comb she kept in the side pocket of her bag, she stood in front of the mirror and swept her hair up into a neat ponytail. Dark circles lay underneath both eyes. She hadn't slept well last night and knew the reason why. Dr. Randall had given her the straightforward facts about Damien's condition and recovery. It would be a painful and difficult struggle, but not one that the couple couldn't overcome, together. Those last words gave her the strength to press on. Lacey retrieved the small make-up case from the bottom of her bag and applied a light application of concealer under her eyes in an attempt to camouflage her exhaustion.

Lacey entered Damien's room at the first visiting hour of the day. She expected to find Damien still under the effects of the sedative, but to her surprise he was awake, eyes on the door. Lacey quickly walked across the room surprised and elated to see his beautiful hazel eyes on her. She sat down in the chair next to his bed and took his right hand into hers.

"Hi sweetheart," she whispered softly. Her voice resonated with emotion.

"How bad is it?" Damien asked with heavy lids. His voice was rough and raspy from lack of use.

"You're going to be fine."

Damien's eyes searched her face for a moment; then turned to look at his left arm hidden under white bandaging. "How bad is it?" Damien asked again in a more demanding tone. His face showed agitation.

"Calm down. I'll get the doctor for you." Lacey rose to leave.

"Wait!"

Lacey turned around. She walked back to the bed. In his eyes she saw his fear and wanted so badly to remove it. "You're going to be fine, baby." She leaned over, placing a kiss on his brow. When she withdrew, he was watching her closely.

"Where am I?"

"You're in the Mobile Burn Center. You arrived five days ago."

"Five days? Howard. Did he make..."

"Howard is in the room across the hall. You saved his life."

Damien was becoming exhausted. He nodded in response. He was thankful to know that he hadn't lost a man.

"I'll get the doctor for you." This time Lacey left the room. She walked the quiet corridor relieved that Damien was awake. She would locate the doctor for him, and then call his parents at the hotel. But as she arrived at the nurse's station, Dr. Randall was just getting off the elevator.

"Dr. Randall," Lacey called drawing his attention.

"Good morning, Lacey. How are you doing?" He smiled warmly.

"Better. Damien is awake and asking questions. He's concerned about his arm."

Dr. Randall could see the worry in Lacey's eyes. It was obvious to him that she loved Damien Christoval very much. The young man would definitely need her love and strength to see him through this difficult time. "Well, let's go address his questions."

They walked side by side in silence. Just before reaching Damien's room, Dr. Randall turned to Lacey. "When his parents arrive today, I want you to go to that hotel room your friend reserved for you, and get some sleep. Not a nap, young lady, but sleep. Damien is going to need you healthy." His blue eyes conveyed his seriousness.

Lacey smiled guiltily. "I promise." Together they entered Damien's room. He was lying quietly with his eyes fixed on the door. "Damien, this is Dr. Randall."

Damien's eyes locked onto the gray-headed man with intensity. "How bad is my arm?"

Dr. Randall didn't answer right away. Instead, he removed the chart from the foot of the bed and read over the nurse's annotations. When he was finished reading the chart, he replaced it, then moved around to the side of the bed facing his patient. "Mr. Christoval, I won't lie to you and say that your recovery is going to be easy." The door opened, interrupting his thought.

Mrs. Christoval rushed into the room with her husband trailing behind her. Her hazel eyes searched the bed, and then filled with tears when she noticed Damien was awake. "Hi, baby," she said as she pushed past Lacey to get to Damien. She kissed his lips with motherly affection. "You had us all scared."

Mr. Christoval reached out touching his son's hand. "It's good to see you awake, son."

"It's good to see you too, Pop," Damien replied. He recalled a moment just as the world around him exploded, thinking that he wouldn't ever see his parents or Lacey again. Then everything had gone black. He blinked his eyes rapidly. His emotions were running rampant at the moment and he fought the tears threatening to fall. "Dr. Randall was about to tell me how bad my arm is," Damien informed his parents.

Lacey yawned unexpectedly. The sound of her exhaustion drew everyone's attention. "Excuse me, Dr. Randall," Lacey interrupted before he could get started. "I'm going to take your advice."

He smiled at her, understanding. He could tell that she was

exhausted. "I don't want to see you back here until later this evening," he ordered.

Lacey nodded with a smile behind her hand as another yawn attacked her. She walked over to Damien and leaned down close to his face. "Dr. Randall has explained your condition to me already, so I'll leave you and your parents alone to talk with him. I'm going to the hotel and get some rest, but I'll see you later."

"Okay." Damien raised his right hand to her face. His eyes searched hers lovingly. "Bye."

"Bye, sweetheart."

Lacey hugged Mrs. Christoval, glanced one last time at Damien and left the room. Phillip was there in the corridor. Quickly informing him that Damien was awake, she ran to catch the elevator going down before the door closed.

Phillip entered the room as Dr. Randall was informing Damien of his condition. "As I was saying, recovery won't be easy. There is some muscle damage, but the first thing we have to do is keep that arm from becoming infected. For that we are giving you topical antibiotics and debridement treatments daily. We have covered the wound which will aid in the fight against infection. Your bandages will be changed daily. If all that goes as expected and the healing process takes place, we will assess the need for skin grafting, tackle any scarring which develops, and start you on exercises to regain mobility, immediately." He provided them with a quick overview.

"What happens if the arm becomes infected?" Damien asked with concern.

"We'll deal with that when the time comes," Dr. Randall tried to skirt the subject. There was no point in causing his patient needless worry. "With today's medicines we can tackle anything."

"You're dodging the question, doctor," Damien growled. "I want to know what I'm up against."

Dr. Randall's admiration rose for the man lying in bed. He had heard the courageous story of Damien single-handedly returning into the burning warehouse to rescue his man, but the frank desire to know the details of his condition was indicative of his courageous nature. "Mr. Christoval, if the antibiotics and the debridement treatments fail to keep the wound septic free and the infection spreads, then the only alternative would be to amputate."

"Amputate?" Mrs. Christoval wailed. She leaned back into her husband's embrace. "You can't just cut off his arm," she cried.

"Mrs. Christoval, amputation is the last resort. So far, the antibiotics are working. Let's not go borrowing trouble." To Damien he said, "Your burns are third degree; however, you're a healthy man. I believe together we can fight off infection. In time, after the healing starts to take place, I will get a better idea about scarring and will decide upon a course of treatment. The next step will be to get you moving. The physiotherapist will lead you in exercises to maintain the mobility in that arm. I won't lie to you and say that it won't be painful, but it's a necessary process to help you regain the use of that arm." Dr. Randall paused for a moment to allow all that he had said to settle in.

"If I have an arm," Damien mumbled.

"Damien, please remove that thought from your mind. You're healthy and strong and I intend to keep you that way. Do you have any more questions?"

Damien had plenty, but didn't know where to begin. The word *amputate* kept floating around inside his head. He was a fireman. What would he do if he were to lose his arm? And what good would an arm be if it didn't work properly? "I'd like to be alone," he announced abruptly.

"Of course," Dr. Randall replied. This was a normal response. "Before I leave, are you in any pain?"

"No. Whatever you're giving me is working."

"You're on a morphine-based drip for the time being, but we're going to have to take you off shortly."

"Because it's addictive," Damien commented knowledgeably.

"Yes, but we have other pain management medications. I'll be around until noon. If you have any other questions, have the nurse page me. By the way, you're being moved into a private room." Dr. Randall nodded for the Christovals to follow him.

"Damien, don't you want me to stay with you?" Mrs. Christoval asked.

"Pop, will you take Mom outside?" Damien ordered without looking at anyone.

Mr. Christoval knew his son had a great deal to think about and to accept. His eldest son was so like him—used to being in charge and in control. His own illness had taught him to take each day as it came and how to accept help. It wasn't an easy lesson to learn, but he had learned it. Now Damien would have to learn the same lesson.

"Come on, Melinda. Damien needs some time alone."

Phillip had remained silent while the doctor spoke. He now stood beside the bed. His eyes were focused intensely on his brother. He could see the fear in Damien's eyes that he was fighting so gallantly to hide. "How about if I just sit quietly with you?" Phillip asked.

"I'm not a child, Phillip. Please leave," Damien barked. The look in his eyes dared argument.

"Damien, don't do this."

"Get out!"

"You can't shut everybody out."

"Damn it, will you leave?" Damien was now bellowing. His raised voice caused his father to rush back into the room. Without a word, he grabbed Phillip by the arm and led him out into the hallway.

Damien watched as his father and brother left the room. Once the door was closed, he was able to deal with the fear that was suffocating him. His eyes filled with tears at the prospect of possibly losing an arm. He asked himself, *What have I done so wrong to deserve a fate so awful?* Then his thoughts switched to Lacey. It was obvious from the circles under her eyes that she was exhausted. No doubt she had been with him since arriving at the hospital. What condition would she be in by the time he recovered?

He loved her. More than he ever thought possible. And one look into her sherry eyes and he knew that he was loved as well. She would be at his side every step of the way through his recovery. Confident that he could face whatever the doctor and his staff threw at him, Damien was less confident about his ability to tolerate pity from Lacey. He was her man, her protector, and now here he was relying on others for help. Exhaustion tugged at his body. His eyelids fluttered close. For the moment, his injury was forgotten.

CHAPTER 18

"Damien shouldn't be left alone, Pop," Phillip said to his father as they sat out in the waiting room. He paced the tiled floor with worried energy. His brother was obviously afraid.

Mr. Christoval approached his son. He laid a comforting hand on his strong shoulder. "I've been where Damien is. It isn't easy going from being the caregiver to the one receiving the care. As men we place value in our ability to do and be there for the people we love. We're strong and capable of doing anything, and then something like this happens to you and your entire world is turned upside down. You begin to question the quality of your future. How will people treat you? Will they think less of you?"

"But Pop, we're family," Phillip cried in anguish. "Doesn't he know that we love him?"

Out of this tragedy, Mr. Christoval was once again getting the chance to practice his parental nurturing. It had been some time since any of his children had needed that fatherly reassurance. He touched his son's handsome face. "He knows that he's loved. Damien's fear is not only the possibility of losing an arm, but losing our respect as a man. How others see us sometimes determines how we see ourselves."

"Is that how you felt?" Phillip asked with a new interest.

John Christoval's face reddened with shame. It was something how it took Damien's injury to make him see his illness and recovery clearly. "Yes, that's exactly how I felt. I was the father—the head of the Christoval household and there I was being handled like a newborn babe. My wife—the woman I love and vowed to protect, was now assisting me with my bath. How do you think that made me feel? Then my own sons were ordering me around. Don't do this, don't do that. I had to sit on my sorry behind and watch my children shoulder my responsibilities."

"But we were only trying to help," Phillip explained.

"I know that. But at the time your spirit is so low that you don't see things as they truly are. I'll be honest with you. I felt sorry for myself. I felt as though I had lost everything that I had worked so hard to accomplish—respect, admiration, and pride."

Phillip saw his father in a different light. He had always thought of his father as the super human who could do almost anything. Now he realized that John Christoval was just a man with fears like everyone else.

"So what about now, Pop? Do you still feel that way?"

John chuckled. "Hell, no! I'm beginning to enjoy watching you boys take care of my lawn and other chores around the house; leaves me with more energy for your mother." He winked.

Phillip blushed with embarrassment.

Melinda laughed at her son's reaction, but it was John's moving words describing how he had felt during his illness that touched her heart.

Lacey arrived back at the hospital in time for the five o'clock visiting hour. She had slept more soundly than she had in days. Dressed in a pair of blue slacks and a rose sweater that Damien particularly liked, she stepped off the elevator feeling better. A nurse recognized Lacey and informed her that Damien had been moved to a private room on the sixth floor. She returned to the elevator. On the sixth floor, she located the waiting room and peeked inside to find Damien's parents. She greeted them both upon entering and inquired about Damien.

"He had a rough morning after speaking with Dr. Randall, but just a moment ago when we visited, he seemed in good spirits," Mrs. Christoval told her.

"My boy is geared up for the long fight," Mr. Christoval added.

Lacey smiled with relief. "That's a good sign. Together we'll have him back on his feet and home where he belongs."

"You're right about that. Now run on and see him before the visiting hour is over," Mrs. Christoval encouraged her.

Lacey nodded in agreement. She left the waiting room headed toward Damien's room. She felt a sense of relief knowing that he had been upgraded to a room on the ward. That had to be a positive sign.

The private room was decorated in green and blue speckled wallpaper. It was cheery and a definite improvement from the sterile white of the ICU. An armoire was just to the right as she entered, and the bathroom directly across from it. Next to Damien's bed, which was to the right of the room, was a plush recliner in a darker shade of green. It would help to make the hours of sitting more comfortable. On the window side of the room was a wooden nightstand containing the telephone. A desk/table combo with chair in the same wood veneer was positioned in the corner opposite the bed. She could utilize it for writing.

Damien was awake and staring out of the window. He didn't have to turn around to know that it was Lacey entering his room. He would know her Givenchy fragrance and the sound of her soft walk anywhere. Everything about the woman he loved was etched in his memory—from the warm sherry color of her eyes, to the shape of her beautiful breasts, and her soft cries of passion. He could also envision the dark circles under her eyes.

"I'm back," Lacey called out as she eased into the chair beside the bed. She reached out covering Damien's hand.

"You shouldn't have come."

"What do you mean I shouldn't have come?" Lacey stood. She reached across his body to grasp his chin. With a gentle touch, she turned him to face her. "I love you and you're lying in a hospital bed recovering from a terrible injury, and you say I shouldn't have come. Just tell me where I should be?" Her eyes danced across his face. She

181

couldn't get enough of looking at him. She had come too close to losing him.

Damien had to admit that Lacey looked much better after a little sleep, but how long would that last if his recovery was long and drawn out? "You should be in bed sleeping. You need more than just a nap."

"And I feel much better after a couple of hours in a real bed." She smiled at him. "How are you feeling?" she asked stroking his face.

"I'm not in pain, if that's what you're asking?" He pulled his chin out of her grasp. "Don't you have a deadline to meet?"

Lacey sensed his agitation. "Each day you get better, sweetheart."

"Why is it all of sudden everyone is a shrink? Get out of my head, Lace," Damien commanded. He focused once again on the view outside of his window.

"Talk to me."

"I'm tired, Lacey. This is my first day awake and I'm worn out." He didn't look at her.

Damien was asking her to leave. Lacey's spirits took a nosedive. "Okay, I get the message. I'll be outside if you should need me." She searched his face for answers. Had she said something to upset him? She didn't think so, but it was quite obvious that he wanted her gone. A gnawing feeling began in the pit of her stomach that would last over the next couple of days. Each subsequent visit was much like the first. His demeanor didn't improve. If anything it was slowing getting worse; however, Lacey attributed his bad temperament to the painful treatments he was receiving daily. She had read all that she could on the treatment of burn patients, and knew that the majority of the treatments aimed at helping the patient could be quite painful.

On this day, Damien watched the nurse change his bandage with detachment. He tried to see the wounded arm as someone else would. It was disfigured, discolored, and disgusting. He had wanted to regurgitate the first time he caught sight of his arm. As he continued to watch the dedicated nurse bandage his arm as though it was normal, he wondered what Lacey's reaction would be. Would she react like the nurse as though nothing had happened or would the sight turn her stomach as it had his own?

Who was he kidding? Damien asked himself later when he was alone. Of course she would be disgusted by the sight of his charred flesh. Oh, she would pretend not to notice because that was the type of woman his Lacey was, but she would notice. Her pity would be buried deep in her sherry eyes. But it would be there. He couldn't stand the thought, nor could he bear the thought of her wasting her life with him. The daily exercises still hurt. Hell, he didn't even know whether he had a career to return to. But what he did have was love for Lacey. Deep, unwavering love and he knew what had to be done.

Lacey entered the room an hour later carrying a large bouquet of flowers. She was talking a mile a minute. A brilliant smile was plastered on her face as she searched for a clear surface. Well-wishers had sent Damien flowers, plants, stuffed animals, and many other expressions of love. She finally placed the flowers on the windowsill, then turned back to face him.

"How was your morning?" she asked with effervescence. Her novel had climbed into the number six spot on the bestsellers list and she was overjoyed. *Rescue of the Heart,* despite being written prior to their meeting, eerily resembled their relationship, and for that it would always hold a special place in her heart.

"How do you think?" Damien growled out. "The nurse scraped some more dead flesh. Is that what you wanted to know?"

Lacey's eyes narrowed. She counted to ten before speaking the biting words which she so desperately wanted to set free. From her reading, she knew that people responded differently to crises in their lives; however, she never thought Damien's attitude would be so negative. But that was where she came into the picture. As the woman who loved him, she would bolster his spirits and remind him that he had so very much to fight for.

183

She eased down on the bed beside Damien. She loved him—missed him. "You know that's not what I meant. Look around you. Don't you see all the love in this room?" Lacey's outstretched arms spanned the area.

Damien's dark eyes zeroed in on her. He didn't bother looking around. "What's your point?"

Lacey exhaled exasperated. "The point, Damien, is that you have so much to be thankful for." The words came out harsher than she had intended. To lighten the mood, she leaned into him, and with a hand caressed his handsome dark face. Trailing a finger over his lips, Lacey leaned forward kissing him. It started out as a sweet peck. But then all the fear and emotions that she had been dealing with since the fire roared to life inside of her and she needed reassurance. Lacey sought it through the kiss, parting Damien's lips with her tongue as it deepened. She needed this and couldn't get enough. She planted kisses along his jaw, chin, nose, and back to his mouth.

"Stop it. Lacey, stop it," Damien ordered while shoving against her shoulder.

"Kiss me, Damien." Lacey wasn't really hearing Damien's words. She only knew that she missed their closeness and his beautiful smile and caring nature. "I love you," she whispered covering his mouth once again.

"Damn it, stop!" Damien shoved hard against Lacey, nearly toppling her off the bed and pulling over his IV bags.

Lacey snapped out of her love-induced haze. Wide eyes stared at Damien with confusion and a great deal of hurt. She swept her hair away from her face while regrouping. It was a struggle not to break down and cry. "I'm sorry. I didn't mean to hurt you."

You didn't, but I'm about to hurt you. "I know. Maybe you should go," he said without feeling.

"But I just got here."

"Look, Lacey, I'm not in the mood for company." He turned away from her.

Lacey sat quietly on the side of the bed not sure where to go from here. Something was going on inside of him and he wasn't letting her in to help. "Can't we just talk? The way we used to?"

His eyes swung back to her. He could see the fear in her eyes. "There's nothing to talk about." *Only that I love you and can't bear to see pity in your eyes.*

"Okay. What if I just sit quietly in the chair?" *Anything. Just don't push me away,* Lacey thought to herself.

"Suit yourself." Damien turned over giving Lacey his back. After several tension filled moments with not a word exchanged between them, he heard Lacey slip out of his room. He turned over as the door closed behind her. He exhaled a painful breath. Lacey was hurt and he was responsible. It wasn't supposed to be like this. He had vowed never to hurt her, but circumstances were different and what he was about to do was out of love.

Lacey arrived at the hospital feeling stronger the next day. She was determined to force Damien into discussing his feelings. No matter how hard he attempted to push her away, she wasn't budging. They had to deal with this fear before the situation got out of control. More importantly, he had to be reminded of her love.

A nurse came rushing from behind the nurses' station as Lacey placed her hand on the door to Damien's room.

"Ms. Avery, you can't go in there," the shorter woman huffed. "I'm sorry. I really love your books," she said as an afterthought.

"Thanks. What do you mean I can't go in? Is something wrong with Damien?" Lacey's voice rose with her concern.

"No ma'am," the nurse rushed to assure her. She stood there looking slightly uncomfortable.

"So why can't I go in?" Lacey asked while slowly easing the door open.

The nurse reached out grabbing the handle. "Mr. Christoval has

185

barred you from his room," she finally managed to say. Her eyes were sympathetic.

Lacey didn't need her sympathy. What she needed was to see the man she loved. "There's some kind of mistake here," Lacey glared at the woman. "I'm his fiancée. I've been here the entire time that Damien has been hospitalized." Her voice was high, tinged with anger. "I just saw him yesterday and now you're going to tell me that I can't go into his room?"

"Yes ma'am," the nurse responded weakly.

Lacey fixed the woman with a *watch me* stare and proceeded into Damien's room. Phillip was sitting in the chair beside the bed talking with his brother. They both looked up as she stormed into the room with the nurse trailing behind her.

"Damien, tell this woman that it's okay for me to be here."

"I tried to stop her, Mr. Christoval."

"Get out," Damien ordered from the bed.

Lacey faced the nurse. "You heard him."

"No. I want you out, Lacey," Damien clarified. His tone was commanding and without feeling.

Phillip and Lacey both stared at him bewildered. The nurse tugged on Lacey's arm, only to be swatted away like a pesky insect.

"What did you say to me?" Lacey moved closer to the bed. Her eyes locked on to Damien. She searched the depth of his eyes for meaning.

"I don't want you here," Damien enunciated clearly so there was no misunderstanding.

Lacey blinked, but didn't respond. She stood in a daze. Her heart was beating so fast that she was beginning to feel lightheaded.

"Damien, what the hell are you doing?" Phillip asked. Damien's statement caught him completely by surprise.

"You heard me. I don't want her here," he told Phillip, but his eyes never left the woman he loved.

Lacey, coming out of her stupor, finally managed a question.

"Why?"

Damien was becoming agitated. "I don't have to explain myself. I want you gone, now!" he bellowed. To the nurse he ordered, "Get her out of here." His raised voice brought the other nurses running to assist.

Lacey stood rooted in place with tears in her eyes. She was screaming to Damien that she loved him and didn't understand why he was doing this.

Phillip was trying to calm Damien down. Finally with no other recourse, he rose from the chair and grabbed Lacey forcibly by the arms. With little effort he placed her out of the room.

"Lacey, just go," Phillip now screamed at her. "We'll deal with the why later." He rushed back into Damien's room to calm him down.

Mr. and Mrs. Christoval, seeing and hearing the commotion, came running toward Lacey. "What happened? What was all the screaming about?" both asked.

Lacey's head was spinning. What had happened in the span of her absence to make Damien send her away? She needed to sit down before her legs gave way. Walking to the waiting room, she collapsed into the first empty chair. Mrs. Christoval sat down beside her. She took Lacey's balled fists into her hands.

"What happened?" she asked in a soft motherly voice.

That's what Lacey wanted to know. "Damien has barred me from his room. He doesn't want to see me." Her eyes were glued to the tan and brown tiled floor.

"Lacey." Mrs. Christoval shook her hand. "What did you say to upset him?"

Lacey turned tear-filled eyes to Mrs. Christoval. "I didn't say or do anything," she spat out, angered that she would think that she had. "When I was going into Damien's room, a nurse told me I was barred." She continued to recount the details of the encounter. When she was finished speaking, she was all worn out.

Mr. Christoval didn't know what to say. He had an idea as to what was going on with his son, but remained quiet.

"Maybe you should keep your distance for the time being," Mrs. Christoval said. "He's going through a lot at the moment."

Lacey immediately withdrew her hand and rose from the chair. She stood and walked to the other side of the room wondering what had happened to this family she loved and thought she was a part of.

Melinda knew how harsh her words must sound to Lacey, but Damien was her priority. "Lacey, maybe Damien simply requires space and time to deal with his injuries. I'm sure in a couple of days, he'll be missing you so badly that he'll be demanding one of us bring you to him."

Lacey didn't say anything more. She didn't wait around for Phillip to explain himself, or Mr. Christoval to add his two cents. She left the hospital with tears in her eyes, and emptiness in her heart. She drove back to her hotel room not believing how fast things had changed. Removing her clothing, she crawled into bed exhausted and confused. Eventually she fell asleep.

Back in Damien's room, Phillip sat watching his brother try to ignore him. It had been two hours since the scene with Lacey and Damien had yet to explain himself.

"Look man, I know you're scared."

"You don't know a damn thing, Phillip."

"Well, I can imagine."

"No, you can't. You're not the one lying in this bed wondering when and if they will cut your arm off, or if you have a future."

"You're absolutely right," Phillip conceded. "But what you did to Lacey...,"

"You can leave now," Damien interrupted agitated.

"We need to talk about this."

"You need to leave it alone, or you may find yourself barred." Damien didn't say any more. He allowed the threat to speak for itself.

Phillip stared incredulously at his brother. He had never seen this side of Damien before. Even when his precious marriage was crumbling around him, Damien had remained strong and steady. But this vicious side was new and so very different. He wasn't sure how to handle the situation.

"I think I'll leave you alone with your foul attitude." Phillip stood up and left Damien in the room to brood. He returned to the waiting room and was informed by his parents of their conversation with Lacey. He groaned just thinking about how he had treated her, and now his parents. She must really be feeling rejected. He thought to seek her out at the hotel, but changed his mind because he didn't have an explanation for his brother's behavior. He took a seat, praying that in time Damien would come around.

CHAPTER 19

Lacey gave Damien three days to come to his senses. Despite not seeing him, she checked in with the nursing staff daily. She hadn't asked for his family on purpose. After their last encounter, she wasn't sure of their reception. Phillip had called several times and left messages. She hadn't bothered to return them. They had turned on her and though their reasons may have been intended for the best, she was still smarting from the betrayal.

She snuck onto the sixth floor by way of the stairs. Damien's room was two doors down from the stairway entrance. She had selected after lunchtime for her visit because things usually quieted down after the patients were fed. Damien's parents most likely would have returned to the hotel for a little rest, and his siblings were still at work. The early shift of the nursing staff was nearing the end of their day, which made sneaking into Damien's room a great deal easier. She stepped into the hallway and quickly walked to Damien's door. She listened for any sign of visitors. When she didn't detect voices, Lacey eased the door open and stepped inside.

Damien wasn't surprised to see Lacey. He had actually been expecting her sooner. The day and time had come for him to set her free. He took an anxious breath as he watched Lacey come closer.

"Hi," Lacey whispered unsure of the reception.

"Hi," Damien whispered back just as softly. His head and his heart were at war. "What are you doing here?"

Well, he wasn't screaming for her to leave, Lacey thought to herself as she inched even closer. "I think we need to talk. Something more than your injury has happened between us." She paused, looking down at her fidgeting hands. "I love you, but I'm not sure how you feel about me anymore." Her hungry eyes searched his for the love that used to reside in them. For a brief moment she thought there was a flicker of it, but it was replaced too quickly with indifference.

"You're right, we should talk," Damien responded, sure of what he was about to say. "I didn't want to have to say it, but you leave me with no choice."

Lacey prayed for strength because in those brief words, she knew that she would need it. "There's no need to sugar coat it. Just say it; but when you do, look me in the eyes."

You can still change your mind. No, I can't. Not if I love her. Damien raised his hazel eyes to hers and digging deep, he set Lacey free. "Laying here in bed these past weeks has allowed me to do a great deal of thinking."

"About us?"

"Yes, and about what's really important to me. I almost died in that fire. And if I had, what would have been left to say that I lived."

"Oh, God," Lacey cried out, knowing where this conversation was headed.

Damien's eyes never left hers. "I want children, Lacey. I thought I could live without my own, but I realize now that I can't."

Lacey almost doubled over in pain. Damien's words were like blows to the stomach. But finding strength from somewhere, she straightened to her full height. She ran her right hand over her barren abdomen, unaware of the action. Her mind was still processing his words

But Damien noticed the movement and nearly choked on the lie he was telling. He had wounded Lacey the only way he knew that would send her running. "I'm sorry, Lacey, but I tried. Children are important to me and..."

"And we both know that I can't give them to you," her voice wobbled, but she didn't cry. She would be damned if she stood in front of him and cried. "Well, I said don't sugar coat it, didn't I?" She glanced out the window. Anywhere but in the face of the man she loved; the man who no longer wanted her. "There really isn't anything I can say to that, is there?" She finally looked at him and saw her dreams melting away. She inched toward the door. "I guess I should be going."

"Lacey, you'll never know how sorry I am," Damien whispered. He was barely able to speak. His own heart was breaking and yet he knew that he was doing the right thing.

"On the contrary, I do know. At least Calvin was honest and up front with his feelings. He didn't allow me to get sucked into this dream of happily ever after," She tossed out the words, angry and hurt, . Then, regrouping, she reined in her emotions. She wouldn't degrade herself by begging for this man or any man's love. Her engagement ring caught the sunlight streaming through the window. The prism of colors taunted her as they danced before her face. With sheer will and determination, she removed it from her finger, and acting very ladylike, she returned it to Damien. "I won't be needing this."

His gut twisted as he watched Lacey remove his ring. He had been so proud to slip it onto her finger. "It was given out of love."

"A fleeting love; I don't want it." She placed the diamond ring on the bedside table. As she withdrew her hand, Damien reached out grabbing her.

"Lace, I'm sorry." Damien's heart bled inside. *Maybe I should simply tell her the truth that I'm frightened and scared of her not seeing me as a man, but someone to pity.* But in the end he said nothing. He watched in pain as the woman he loved walked out of his life.

Lacey walked to the door and paused. She turned back facing him. "I wish you a speedy recovery." With that said, she left. Her composure crumpled once she was on the other side of the doorway. The tears came in blinding streams—one after the other. The sound of approaching voices forced her to the stairwell. She bumped into a nurse on the way.

"Lacey?" Phillip called out as he caught sight of her disappearing into the stairwell. He chased after her when she didn't stop. Throwing the door open, he found her crying, curled up on the top step.

"Hey, what happened?" He drew Lacey into his arms. He hadn't seen her since the incident in Damien's room.

Resentment caused Lacey to pull free of his embrace. She swiped at her tears as she faced him. "Don't pretend like you don't know. You and Damien talk about everything." She rose from the step.

Phillip followed her lead. He rose too. "I swear I don't know what you're talking about." When she didn't respond, only stood glaring at him, Phillip knew that it was bad. "I thought you and I were friends," Phillip stated quietly.

Lacey tried to gauge whether he was telling the truth or not. And yes, they had become friends, but then, she and Damien had become lovers and now look where they stood. "Your brother broke off our engagement."

"What?" Phillip exclaimed. He couldn't believe what he was hearing.

Lacey realized from his startled surprise that Phillip was telling the truth. He didn't know what Damien was planning. "He doesn't want to marry me," she whispered out. Her voice trembled as she fought against the building tears.

"No. Damien loves you." Phillip moved closer. He rubbed his hands up and down her arms. He knew that his brother was frightened, but to go this far was incomprehensible.

Lacey shook her head no, as a tear slipped free. "He loves the idea of children of his own more." Her voice cracked. She hated feeling weak and out of control.

"What are you saying?"

She took a deep breath then squared her shoulders. Looking into Phillip's concerned eyes she answered, "Your brother has experienced an epiphany."

"How so?"

"The fire made him realize his desire for children of his seed." The tears ran unchecked now.

"Dear God. He broke up with you because..."

"Because I can't have children," she wept. Then without warning, she turned and ran down the stairs without another word.

Phillip started to chase after Lacey. He knew that she shouldn't be alone in the emotional state she was in, but he had to see Damien. He snatched the stairwell door open and stomped out into the hallway. He was furious. He couldn't believe his brother could be so selfish and cruel. Sure, Damien was afraid. His future was one big question, but that didn't excuse what he had done to Lacey. He stormed into Damien's room practically throwing the door off the hinges.

The noise of the knob bouncing off the wall broke into Damien's replay of the scene with Lacey. He was sitting on the side of the bed. He was actually thankful for the distraction because with each memory another piece of him died.

"Do you know what you've done?" Phillip roared. He advanced on Damien with the intent of knocking some sense into him. But as he got closer and saw the withdrawn expression in his brother's face, he knew there was nothing he could do to hurt Damien. "You did this on purpose."

"I had to," Damien responded, resigned. "Lacey never would have left me otherwise."

Phillip glared at Damien. He couldn't believe what he was hearing. "Make me understand this, bro."

"Look at me, Phillip. I don't know what the future holds for me," Damien pleaded. "How could I ask Lacey to face that uncertainty with me?"

"Hell, man, who knows what the future holds? No one, Damien, but it sure is a whole lot better with the one you love by your side."

"I agree, but I couldn't do that to Lacey. I may not be able to use my arm and if I can't, I couldn't bear for her to see me this way."

Things were getting clearer for Phillip. "You ripped Lacey's heart out because of scars?" Phillip shook his head in amazement. "Damien, you should have seen her; she was crushed by your words."

Damien's head fell forward in agony. "Don't you think I know that? I said the words that would drive her away from me. I know she's crushed, but it's for the best. She's free to find someone whole."

"Whole? Man, will you listen to yourself? Do you really want Lacey to find another man? Do you really want to think about another man making love to your woman?"

The very thought of some other guy touching Lacey made him sick. "I'm saving her from an uncertain future."

"All our futures are uncertain, Damien." Phillip released an exhausted breath. He walked around the small room at a loss for words.

"I do love her, Phillip. It was hell saying those words to her."

"You hit Lacey where you knew it would hurt most."

"Yeah, I did," Damien answered feeling lower than low.

"Let me get this straight. You ripped the heart out of the woman you love, because you don't want to saddle her with a man with no future, who just might be scarred. Do I have this right?" His eyes blazed with rage.

"Yes."

"No, Damien," Phillip exploded. "This has to due with you feeling sorry for yourself. This has to do with Damien not being able to rely on anyone else. This has to do with Damien being the only one who can rise above the physical and see beyond other's blemishes and short-comings." Phillip slammed his hand down on the bed beside Damien. His words hung between them. "A real man faces life with the strength of the woman he loves sustaining him. He doesn't rip her heart out."

"Do you want to hear me say that I'm scared, Phillip? Well, I'm saying it," Damien screamed. "I can barely look at my own damn arm without getting sick. How am I supposed to handle the look in Lacey's eyes when she sees it? And what if I can never use my arm properly?

195

Don't be quiet now. You're the one with all the answers."

Phillip pulled the chair over in front of Damien. He collapsed into it. "I don't have the answers and neither do you. What I do know is this. You need to tell that woman of yours that you love her. Then you need to sit her down and explain what you're feeling. I'm betting the two of you can work things out together."

Damien wanted to believe Phillip, but life wasn't that easy for him. His marriage to Sara hadn't been that easy, nor would this situation with Lacey. "I can't. I know that she's hurt right now, but in time she'll forget about me."

"Is that really what you want?"

Hell no! "I'm tired, Phillip. I want to be alone."

"You are alone, Damien. You just threw Lacey away."

Lacey returned to the hotel moving on instinct. She packed her bags in record time; then checked out. The reason for her being there no longer existed, so it was time to go. She tossed her luggage into the backseat of her vehicle and climbed in behind the wheel. Pulling out of the parking lot, she headed for the interstate. She was going home to lick her wounds. When Damien was purged from her system, she would pull herself together and get on with the business of life. The idea was to keep moving until the thought of him no longer hurt.

An hour later, she sat in front of her parents' home. Their cars weren't in the driveway and she was thankful. Although she didn't want to be alone tonight, she didn't feel much like talking at the moment. She let herself into the house. There was nothing more comforting than coming home. Feeling the need to be surrounded by people who loved her just as she was, Lacey climbed the stairs to her old bedroom. She dropped her bags on the burgundy carpet on her way to the bathroom. Stripping quickly, she stepped into the shower and turned on the water.

The pulsing spray helped ease the tension in her shoulders and somehow cleared her mind. When she left the bathroom she was completely exhausted. She quickly located a gown and pulled it on. In minutes, she was buried deep under the covers, seeking peace in sleep.

Laura Avery arrived home around four thirty. She was pleasantly surprised to see Lacey's SUV parked in front of the house. Her daughter hadn't left Damien's side since he was brought into the hospital nearly a month ago. His condition must be improving if Lacey was home.

She entered the foyer calling out to her daughter. When she received no response, she climbed the stairs knowing where she would find Lacey. Laura stopped outside her daughter's room and cracked the door open slightly. Sure enough, there she was with the covers tossed all around her. Laura laughed because it seemed that her daughter's sleeping habits hadn't changed. Lacey never stayed covered. She tiptoed into the room, as she had done many times when Lacey was a child. Grabbing the covers from the floor, she lovingly spread them out over her daughter. She tucked the covers under the foot of the bed then moved to the sides. As she was about to cover Lacey's arms, she noticed her daughter's left hand. It was empty. The diamond was gone.

Laura searched the room for the ring. She didn't find it on the dresser or nightstand. A search of the vanity in the bathroom yielded nothing. With her heart in her throat, she walked back to the bed and looked at her daughter critically. There, around the eyes were the telltale signs of crying. *Lord, what has happened?*

Lacey stirred. She sensed someone was in the room with her. Opening her eyes, she saw her mother easing out. "I'm awake."

Laura halted in her tracks and turned around. She watched her daughter put on a brave face, knowing that Lacey was hurting. Hell, she hurt for the daughter she loved so much. "Feel like talking?"

"Not really." Lacey shook her head. "I just wanted to be with people who loved me."

Laura returned to the bed and reached out caressing her daughter's cheek. Her beautiful daughter had so much love to give and yet, couldn't seem to receive love in return. She had really thought Damien was the one. The day he had arrived at their home begging to know Lacey's whereabouts, she had been so sure that her baby was going to get that happy ending she so wanted.

"Well, you came to the right place." Laura smiled and leaned forward kissing her daughter's cheek. "I'll leave you alone."

Lacey watched as her mother walked away. When she was at the door, she called out, "Mom."

"Yes, Lace," Laura replied, facing her.

"I really tried this time."

"I know, sweetheart."

"This was the last time. It hurts too much to try and fail." Her mother's understanding gaze met Lacey's eyes.

"I hope you're wrong because love is out there waiting for you."

Lacey didn't respond. She just sat there in bed watching as her mother left the room and softly closed the door behind her. Lacey had no intention of getting seriously involved with anyone ever again. Her mother's pipe dream was not hers. Twice, life had taught her valuable lessons about love and she was no dummy. A third disastrous relationship was not necessary to make the point. The message was received loud and clear.

Tonight she would bask in the love of her family. Then tomorrow, she would get back out there in the world and promote her book. Writing had saved her once before and it would pull her through this time as well. She stretched back out and sought the peace of sleep once more.

That night in his hospital room, Damien's thoughts were on Lacey.

He prayed that she was somewhere safe and receiving the love he was no longer able to give. He stared at the blank ceiling trying to figure out why life kept betraying him. He was a good person and tried to be good to others. All he ever wanted was a woman to love him unconditionally.

You had that, the tiny voice inside his head whispered. *I know. But what kind of man would I be if I shackled Lacey to half a man?* You'd be a happy man. A loved man, the voice whispered back.

Damien, alone in the dark of his room, prayed like never before. He asked God for his divine wisdom and guidance. At the moment, his arm was forgotten. Only the void in his life where Lacey belonged was center stage and of importance. But that was his doing. Lacey loved him and would be by his side now, if he was strong enough. However, he wasn't. He couldn't face seeing disgust in Lacey's eyes when she saw him. How would he ever make love to her again with the scars he was sure to carry for the rest of his life? And what about his job? At the moment he didn't have a clue as to what he would do if he could no longer be a fireman. He had made the right decision. He loved Lacey enough to let her go despite the pain it had caused them both. Tomorrow was a new day. It was the day that he would begin focusing on his recovery and trying to map out his life. A life that didn't include the woman he loved.

CHAPTER 20

Lacey left the warm cocoon of her parents' home early the next morning. Collecting her pride and her luggage, she slid behind the wheel of her SUV and headed home. There was no point in hiding out because everyone would find out about their broken engagement soon enough. Turning onto her street, it seemed liked ages since she had been home. So much had happened in a short span of time. She had found the perfect wedding dress and lost the man she loved, all in a matter of weeks. But Damien was alive and despite the current state of their relationship, she was very grateful for that.

Lacey unlocked the front door to her home. Her luggage was deposited in the foyer. She moved into the living room and thumbed through the stack of mail piled on the coffee table. Her mother had been thoughtful enough to bring those items which required her immediate attention to the hospital. Seeing nothing of importance, she left it for later. She returned to the foyer and picked up her luggage. Walking through her empty home on the way to the bedroom, Lacey felt the weight of loneliness crowding in on her. It was a strange feeling considering she had lived alone for years and actually enjoyed having her own space. But now the space and silence were suffocating. There would be no call from Damien to break up the silence, and no visit to fill the emptiness. Lacey realized that she was experiencing the first signs of depression. She pushed the thought away and continued on to her room. She ambled over to the closet and pulled the door open. There, hanging on the inside of the door, was her wedding dress. The delicate pearls caught the morning sunlight filtering through the blinds. Their mocking beauty caused her eyes to fill with tears. The intrusive peel of the doorbell spared her from a bout of serious depression.

Daniel stood on the other side of the door. Holly had given him the news of the breakup this morning, as told to her by Phillip. He had called Lacey immediately and got the answering machine. Worried, he had jumped in his car and come over. Suddenly, the door opened and a teary eyed Lacey fell into his arms.

"Why didn't you call me?"

"I didn't want to see anyone."

"Not even me?" Daniel's feelings were a little hurt.

"I've bothered you enough with my problems. I didn't want to dump this on you too; especially not now that you and Holly appear to be getting closer. Besides, there's no point in crying over spilled milk." Lacey gave a sad little laugh.

"Your love for Damien is more than spilled milk," Daniel said taking Lacey by the hand. He guided her over to the sofa.

"You're right, but it wasn't enough for Damien." Lacey popped up from the sofa and began wandering around the living room. She couldn't sit still.

Daniel rose from the sofa to follow her. Blocking her path, he said, "I don't believe for one moment that Damien doesn't love you. I've seen the look in the man's eyes when you walk into a room."

Lacey smiled sadly as she was assailed by memories. She too knew the look. "I know he loved me because that's the type of man Damien is. He wouldn't have asked me to marry him if he *hadn't* loved me. But the fire happened and he realized that I wasn't enough," she said meeting his sympathetic eyes. "His desire for children was greater than his love for me."

"Children?" Daniel echoed. "He broke up with you because you can't have *children*?" Daniel was outraged. Holly hadn't told him that. "That arm of his won't be his only concern when I'm finished with him." He headed for the front door. His blood boiled with hurt and anger. He had believed in the man and practically shoved Lacey into his arms and this was how he treated her?

"Daniel, no!" Lacey rushed across the room. She blocked his path to the door. "Don't do this. Damien has every right to want children. I want them. Playfully punching his shoulder, she went on. "Besides, I don't think Holly would be very pleased if you confronted her brother." She smiled, trying to lighten the mood though her eyes brimmed with tears.

"This has nothing to do with Holly. You're stopping me because you love the guy."

"You're right, I do. And I love you too. I know the relationship between you and Holly is in the early stages, but I see the potential for something wonderful."

"I do too, but I thought you had found happiness as well." He reached out caressing her face."

"I'm going to be fine. I have my writing to keep me busy."

Daniel didn't believe her, but didn't pursue the subject further. "I read in today's paper that *Rescue of the Heart* hit the number five spot on the bestsellers' list."

"Yes, it did." She smiled proudly, the situation with Damien momentarily forgotten.

"That's a big accomplishment my friend."

"I know. When I got home earlier there were several requests for interviews—television and print."

"Aren't you big time?" Daniel teased Lacey. His beautiful brown eyes sparkled with happiness for his friend.

"That gossip columnist, Blanche McClure, has requested an interview." Lacey returned to the living room and found the letter. She handed it to Daniel.

"What does Paige have to say?"

Lacey ran her fingers through her hair. "You know Paige is for any type of publicity."

"She'll want you to do it, in other words," Daniel commented dryly while returning the letter.

"You've got it." She folded the letter and returned it to the envelope. But I'm not touching this stuff until next week. I need some time to myself."

"You take all the time that you need. Give me a call if you want to talk."

"I will and don't worry about me. I'll get through this."

"Lacey, I can't believe you've been sitting on this for a week. Don't you know this is too great an opportunity to pass up?" Paige followed behind her client trying to persuade her to agree to the columnist's interview. "Girl, this woman has a large readership. She's syndicated across the country."

"Who cares? Her articles are sleazy and her writing is unprofessional. I don't like the way she turns an interview into a smear campaign against the very person she has requested an interview with." Lacey entered the kitchen with Paige hot on her trail. She went to the refrigerator and removed the plate of sandwiches she had made earlier. Dodging Paige, who stood in the middle of the floor trying to change her mind about the interview, Lacey deposited the sandwiches on the table. Plates and utensils were already out.

"Guilty as charged, but the interview is about *Rescue of the Heart.* There's no juicy story there," Paige reminded her.

"Not that you and I know. I'm not doing it," Lacey stated with finality. She poured glasses of iced tea. "Now, concerning the major morning shows, I'll do those. Can you be happy with that?"

"Of course I can." Paige beamed happily. She would have preferred Lacey do the interview with Blanche as well, but the major networks were a definite plus. "You know these interviews are live?"

"Yes, I know—no room for a mistake."

"Are you nervous?

"What do you think?" Lacey turned around to glare.

"Dumb question." Paige laughed.

Lacey finally took her seat at the table and placed a sandwich on her plate. They discussed the interviews while they ate. During the course of the conversation, Paige's eyes repeatedly landed on Lacey's bare hand. Since becoming engaged, the woman hadn't removed that ring for any reason. Unable to sit there without knowing what was going on, she asked,

"Why aren't you wearing your engagement ring?"

Lacey glanced down at her bare hand as the chicken salad in her mouth lost its taste. She had to force it down around the sudden lump in her throat to answer.

"The engagement is off."

"Lacey, I'm so sorry." She reached across the table to cover her hand. "Do you want to talk about it?"

"To tell you the truth, Paige, I'm tired of talking about it. I want to get back on schedule with my writing and forget I ever met Damien Christoval."

"You don't mean that," Paige said watching her. "*Rescue of the Heart* was to be your wedding gift to him."

"Don't remind me." Lacey rolled her eyes heavenward. "It was a dumb idea. Who ever heard of a bride presenting her groom with a book?"

"I thought it was a good idea."

"Yeah well, it wasn't even about us. My hero just so happened to be a fireman."

"Is there any chance of a reconciliation?"

Lacey shook her head thoughtfully. It would be nice if it were that simple. "I'm afraid not."

"All right then, let's focus on something we can control. What are you wearing for the interviews?"

Lacey laughed. She was thankful for the change of subject. At the moment she wanted to forget her troubles and bask in her accomplishment. It wouldn't be difficult to do with Paige's bubbly personality and zest for her job. But when the time came for Paige to leave, Lacey was assaulted by a wave of loneliness. She wanted to ask Paige to stay longer, but knew how pathetic she would sound. So instead, she hugged her friend and thanked her for doing such a wonderful job.

"I couldn't do this without you."

"Well, aren't you lucky that you don't have to?" Paige said with sass. "I'll call and make apologizes to Blanche."

"Thanks."

Damien was miserable without Lacey in his life. The two weeks since their breakup were the most painful he had ever known. His heart longed for her. His soul and spirit cried for their lost half. And though he thought he had done the right thing in sending her away, the desire to have her by his side was no less painful. He replayed the conversation with Phillip over in his head for the hundredth time. Perhaps he had made a mistake. Was it too late to reclaim their love?"

"How are you doing today, Damien?" Dr. Randall asked, entering the room. He was delighted to see his patient sitting in the recliner beside the bed. For the past week, Damien's spirit had been down and it concerned him. He had learned through the hospital grapevine that he and Lacey had broken up. This wasn't the first relationship he had witnessed fall apart under the stress and strain of a burn injury. But this was the first time that he had been wrong about a couple. Usually the signs of a weak foundation were visible right up front; however, Lacey and Damien had appeared strong. It was his guess from Damien's depression that it was he who severed the relationship and was now having second thoughts.

"You tell me," Damien mumbled back. He wasn't in the mood for the good doctor's bedside chatter.

"For a man who arrived here in the shape that you were in, you are making remarkable progress. In no time at all you'll be leaving here. With continued rehabilitation I don't see any reason why you can't return to your life." He hoped Damien was listening to him.

"You're saying that I'll get back the flexibility in my arm?" Damien's heart raced with expectation.

"I don't see why not. The damage to the muscles in your arm was minimal. The stiffness that you're experiencing is mainly from the scarring as you heal, but there are things we can do for that." Dr. Randall watched Damien closely. He could tell that his mind was racing with possibility. "Will you please reconsider speaking to the psychiatrist? Sometimes having someone who isn't family to discuss your fears with can help."

Damien thought about it for a moment. Phillip had said he was too proud to depend on others. Hadn't Lacey told him the same thing in D.C.? Maybe they were both right and it was his pride getting in the way of his happiness. "I believe I will."

Dr. Randall smiled with relief. "You've made the right decision. I'll schedule an appointment for you."

"Thanks, Doc." Damien's spirits suddenly rose.

"My pleasure. Now let's have a look at that arm."

Lacey shook with rage and humiliation. How could Blanche McClure do this? Was this smear job some act of revenge because she didn't accept her offer for an interview? This wasn't good journalism. This was a hatchet job and Lacey was the victim. She held the newspaper in a death grip while she read the headline of the article again.

Author of Love Dumped Again

There in black and write were the intimate details of her life starting with the accident and hysterectomy. The article told of her relationship and subsequent engagement to Calvin and his withdrawal of the marriage proposal after her surgery. Blanche had even contacted Calvin for a comment, but he had had the decency to decline. But his always broke cousin Tyrone, was only too happy to fill Blanche in on all the details. Knowing him as she did, Lacey knew that he had been paid for the information.

The article then focused on Damien and their relationship. A bitter Steven Porter had recounted the incident that had taken place at the Christoval home. He had even provided a picture of Sara. Side-by-side, their photographs graced the pages. Blanche creatively implied that Lacey had been a substitute. A method Damien had used to get over his wife's death.

The next paragraph provided information on Damien's injury. An unnamed source at the hospital informed Blanche about Damien having Lacey barred from his room. The same source recounted word for word their breakup. No doubt the source had been outside the door listening.

And if all that wasn't enough, Blanche implied that since Lace couldn't keep a man, she had turned to writing romances. *Rescue of the Heart,* she wrote, was obviously Lace's desperate attempt to create the perfect ending to her romance with the fireman. However, unlike her fictitious heroine, Lace wasn't woman enough to get her man to the altar.

Lacey cringed at having her entire life laid open before the world for entertainment. Outraged, she threw the newspaper across the room with all her might as the tears began to flow. Now the whole world was privy to her private life. How could another woman do something so vile like this to another woman? And what about Damien? Blanche had named him in her article. Lacey's stomach pitched. She raced for the bathroom where she relieved herself of breakfast. When the heaving stopped, she brushed her teeth and rinsed with mouthwash, then made her way to the safety of her bedroom. She crawled into the middle of the bed curling into a protective ball.

The telephone rang a short time later. Picking up on the third ring she was unprepared for the intrusive questions hurled at her by a reporter from that rag, National Interloper. "What was it like to have a hysterectomy as age 21? Let us tell your side of the breakup with Mr. Christoval. Are you going to continue to date?" The insulting questions and comments kept coming. Finally unable to listen any more, she hung up the phone only to have it ring again. This time she allowed the answering machine to pick up. It was another reporter with another tabloid magazine. She was finally forced to disconnect the phone from the wall. But the silence was short-lived. Insistent ringing of the doorbell drew her attention. She prayed it was her mother and raced to answer the door. Flashbulbs went off in her face the moment the door was opened. For a moment she was paralyzed with shock, but then her mind kicked into gear and she managed to shove the reporters out of her door. Shaken to the core by the turn of events in her life, Lacey collapsed to the floor. She drew her legs up to her chin in a protective manner while she allowed her mind to go blank.

Damien cursed a blue streak when he finished reading the article Phillip had pointed out. He was barely hanging on to his self-control. He wanted to track Blanche McClure down and give her a piece of his mind. This article wasn't journalism. It was exploitation of a woman who had done nothing to deserve it.

"I need your help," Damien said to Phillip.

"What do you need?" Phillip asked. He had known that article would infuriate Damien, but he thought it best that he see it from him rather than hear the hospital staff talking about it.

"First, I need you to track down Dr. Randall," Damien explained as he rose from the recliner in his hospital room. "Then I need you to help me get dressed. I do have clothes here, don't I?"

"Yes, you do, but where do you think you're going?"

"I'm going to the woman I love. This article is going to crush Lacey and I plan on being there for her."

"I'll take you if Dr. Randall gives his okay," Phillip promised Damien. He went to the armoire and removed Damien's clothing. "Don't do anything until I locate Dr. Randall." Phillip headed for the door.

"Sure. And Phillip," Damien said, stopping Phillip's exit.

"Yeah?"

"I want that hospital source found and dealt with," Damien growled. His facial features were hard and menacing.

"Consider it done," Phillip replied. He was more than willing to do anything for Damien. It was just a relief to see his brother's fighting spirit back and his obvious love for Lacey restored. Phillip spotted Dr. Randall at the nurses' station. He quickly informed him of the article and Damien's request.

"I completely understand. My wife is a fan of Lacey's and read the article to me this morning. It was a disgusting piece of journalism."

"So, do you believe it's okay for Damien to leave for a little while?"

"It's just what he needs. With Lacey back in his life and by his side, Damien will heal faster. I'll let the nurses know. But I'll expect him back here by six," Dr. Randall stated with authority.

"He will be. Thanks for everything, Dr. Randall." Phillip returned to Damien's room.

CHAPTER 21

"Look at those vultures," Phillip snarled as he slowly drove passed Lacey's home. Reporters littered the front lawn waiting for the perfect photo. Making two lefts, he parked on the street behind. He and Damien cut through a neighbor's yard and approached Lacey's home from the rear. They opened the privacy fence gate and entered the backyard. Daniel and Lacey's parents were on the patio. It appeared they all had the same idea.

"What the hell are you doing here?" Daniel raged at the sight of Damien. He left the patio to confront him, but Phillip stepped in between them.

"Stop acting like a damn fool, you know why Damien is here," Phillip spoke up. He knew that Daniel was protective of Lacey and understood his resentment, but now was not the time.

"Has anyone spoken to Lacey?" Damien asked, walking around his brother and Daniel. He didn't have time for this. He was concerned for Lacey.

"I tried calling, but the phone just rings," Laura answered.

"That means she disconnected the phone if you didn't get her answering machine." Damien removed his key and unlocked the sliding glass door.

Laura grasped Damien by his good arm halting his advancement. "You hurt my daughter badly."

"I know..."

"I don't want to hear your excuse," Laura cut Damien off. The look in her brown eyes warned of her seriousness. "Don't go into that house unless you're sure of your love for my daughter and plan on marrying her."

"I've never stopped loving Lacey and as soon as I'm able, I plan on making your daughter my wife." He looked Laura squarely in the eyes as he spoke.

"Just as long as we understand each other."

"We do." Damien then proceeded to enter Lacey's home. The living room was empty. He stepped on something and looked down. There on the floor was the morning paper. From its disarray it was obvious that it had been thrown—no doubt in anger. He picked it up. Going through the dining room into the kitchen, he deposited it into the trashcan where it belonged. The others followed him inside. He left the kitchen stepping into the hallway and immediately spotted Lacey.

Huddled on the floor against the front door she sat with her knees drawn up and her head resting on them. She wore an oversized sports jersey which was pulled down over her legs. She sat staring at the blank wall to the right.

"Lacey," Damien called softly as he walked in her direction. The others emerged from the kitchen behind him.

At the sound of her name, Lacey glanced up to find Damien before her. The impulse to rush into his arms flooded her. Then she remembered that he no longer wanted her. She took in his appearance. He had lost weight, but looked better than the last time she saw him. A pressure glove covered his left arm from hand to shoulder. All in all, he was a sight for sore eyes.

"I guess your appearance means that you read Blanche McClure's article." Movement behind Damien caught her attention. At the kitchen entrance, her family and Phillip quietly stood. "I guess you all read the article."

"I was worried about you, baby. When I called you and didn't get an answer I was concerned," Laura Avery came to her daughter. She squatted down in front of Lacey. "Are you okay?"

Tears formed in Lacey's eyes. She hated worrying her mother. "Yes.

I disconnected the phone because it wouldn't stop ringing." She glanced up at Damien. "I'm sorry Blanche named you in her article."

Sensing her daughter and Damien's need to be alone, Laura rose from the floor and returned to the kitchen with the others. "I'll be in here if you need me," she said.

Lacey nodded and turned her eyes onto Damien. He eased down beside her taking Laura's place. He sat to Lacey's left. "Why are you sitting here on the floor?" he asked wrapping his arm around Lacey's shoulders.

"There's no reason to get up," Lacey responded with a shrug of her shoulders. The expression on her face was one of resigned sadness.

"I'm sorry Blanche hurt you."

Lacey raised her head. She turned looking at Damien. "Blanche has angered and humiliated me. *You*, Damien, hurt me." She rose from the floor leaving him where he sat to contemplate her words. In her bedroom, her heart raced with joy just seeing him. His very presence meant that he cared about her, but smart enough not to dream of a happy ending, she accepted his presence for what it was. But she wanted *love*. Love of a good man who would be proud to claim her as his wife.

The force of Lacey's words seemed like physical blows. Damien sat with his head tilted back resting against the door. He realized in those words just how badly he had hurt her. The smiling eyes that he loved so much were now cloudy with sadness. Getting up from the floor, he followed Lacey to the bedroom. It was time to set the record straight and reclaim the love he had thrown away in a cowardly way.

Damien found the bedroom door unlocked. He slowly pushed it open. The soft peach and green tones in the room were warm and welcoming, like Lacey. The ever-present stack of books that she planned on reading in her spare time was still beside the bed. Their eyes met and held. Both were assailed with the memories of their love making behind that very door.

"I'm not up to listening to you explain yourself again." Lacey hoped to halt his advancement into her room. His presence and the rush of memories were wearing her remaining reserve of strength thin.

"I have to explain how and why I hurt the woman I love." He came further into the room and closed the door behind him.

Lacey watched Damien suspiciously from her reclined position at the head of the bed. She could see the strain etched in his handsome face. "You should be in the hospital."

"I'm returning after we talk. I'm actually a lot stronger than the last time we saw each other." Damien immediately regretted the reference to the last time that they saw each other. The pain of that moment would be forever carved into his heart. He eased down beside Lacey's outstretched legs. His starving eyes slowly traveled their shapely length. He remembered when he had the right to run his hands along the brown beauties. But now the look in Lacey's eyes said *don't even think about it.* He hoped after they talked that it would change.

"Talk fast because you look dead on your feet." It hurt to see him so weak. "Here, lie down." Lacey climbed off the bed and indicated for Damien to take her place. She sat on the settee at the foot of the bed.

"Maybe later. Right now I want you to listen to what I have to say. Please," he stressed the word when Lacey gave him the eye.

"Go ahead." Lacey steeled herself for the pain she knew his explanation would cause. She folded her clenched fists into her lap and tried not to fidget with unease.

Damien slid down to the foot of the bed across from Lacey. Taking a deep breath, he looked her squarely in the eyes when he spoke.

"I've been seeing a therapist. Dr. Randall had tried to encourage me to speak to someone about the fire sooner, but I didn't believe I needed mental help." He watched her closely for a reaction. "It all came to a head after the last time I saw you. I hurt like hell, both physically and spiritually. The woman I loved was gone and I had no one to blame for that but myself." He swallowed nervously. "What the therapist got me

213

to admit was that I was afraid."

"Of what?" Lacey asked before she knew it. "I'm sorry." She threw up a hand in apology.

"No, that's okay." He reached out taking a closed fist in his hand. "Initially I was afraid of losing my arm to infection and what that would mean to my career. But what I feared most was how it would affect the way you thought of me."

"Damien, I..."

"Just listen," Damien halted Lacey's comment. "Then when it became clear that I wouldn't lose my arm, it was the scars. On several occasions the sight of my own arm has caused me to become physically ill. It's not a pretty sight." He glanced away as his eyes filled with tears. Quickly gaining strength, he continued. "I pushed you away because I knew you loved me and that you would be at my side no matter how bad things got. And I loved you for that. But in the same breath, I feared it, because I didn't want to see pity in your eyes. I didn't want to see you pretend not to notice my scars, and I didn't want to see you cringe in disgust when you did. So I made sure that you would leave. I hit you with the one thing that I knew you couldn't or wouldn't fight against."

"Children," she whispered.

Lacey's own eyes were cloudy with tears. But they weren't tears of pity or joy. She was downright angry. "How dare you take the coward's way out," she yelled coming out of her seat. "This wasn't about me or how you thought I would react. This was about *you*, Damien, and your inability to accept people's help. The strong, capable, Damien doesn't need anyone. He can take care of everyone as well as himself. Well guess what, Mr. Christoval?" She pointed a finger in his direction. "You're human just like the rest of us. If you had lost your arm, I would have wept with you; then I would have told you that you had an additional two right here." She held out her arms.

"Lacey..."

"Be quiet," she screamed. "You cut my heart out with your words all because you couldn't accept help or love. You must not think very much of me, if you thought I was so shallow as to care about the loss of an arm." She returned to her seat but leaned forward facing him. "Yes, when I look at you, I see this beautiful black man that makes my heart skip a beat. But it's not the external beauty I fell in love with. It's what's inside your heart. The words you express to me, the looks you give, the smiles, and most important, the love." Tears ran freely down her face now.

"You saw my physical scar and you knew of my emotional scar, and yet you loved me; asked me to marry you. Did you think you were the only person who could give unconditional love?" Her hand covered her heart conveying her message.

Damien cried openly for the love he had been blessed with. "I'm sorry, baby."

"I'm sorry too, because you didn't have to face this ordeal alone. I wanted to be there to aid you in any way that you required. If you wanted to scream in pain, I would have screamed right along side you. If you wanted to cry, I would have held you while we cried together. If you had wanted to meet this challenge head on, I would have been beside you cheering you on. But you robbed me of that fulfillment. You took away my chance to express through action just how much I love you." She began to cry in earnest. "You didn't have that right."

Damien cried too. He pulled Lacey from the settee onto the bed beside him. He kissed her wet eyes, her cheeks, her sweet lips. "Can you ever forgive me?" he whispered against her lips.

"On one condition."

"Anything."

"Tell me that you still want me."

"Lacey Rebecca Avery, I have never wanted any woman as much as I want you. I love you, Lace."

Lacey wrapped her arms around Damien's neck for dear life. She was mindful not to hurt his injured arm, but she had to make sure he was back where he belonged, with her.

An hour later, Laura Avery tipped back to Lacey's room and opened the bedroom door. The sight of Lacey and Damien wrapped in each other's arms sound asleep on the bed filled her with joy. She set the bedside clock to alarm at five since Phillip said Damien were due back at the hospital by six. Something told her that neither had had a good night's sleep since the breakup and they would probably sleep the day away. Easing out of the room, she returned to the kitchen and ordered everyone out of the house.

"What are you going to do about that article?" Damien asked Lacey as she helped him back into his hospital bed. They had slept soundly until the clock alarm went off. Both had awakened happier than they had been in weeks.

"I can't sue her because everything she printed was true." She eased down on the side of the bed facing him. "I was asked a month or two ago by one of the women's magazine to write a piece for them about my transition from gymnastics to writing. I had been struggling with the decision, but since that article, I've decided to do it. However, not only will I write about my injury which led me to writing, but I will write about support groups for women unable to have children, adoption agencies, and most importantly, the men who love them." She smiled brightly at Damien.

"In that case, I can expect to see my name in print again." He wrapped his good arm around Lacey's neck and pulled her closer. "I am so very proud of you. I think this article is a wonderful idea."

"Thank you." Lacey lovingly caressed his face with her eyes. "You know, for too long now, I've been held prisoner by that secret. Blanche, in her need to punish me for not agreeing to an interview, actually freed me. There's no need for me to fidget out of worry when women start discussing babies, or that someone is going to ask me how many children I want."

"It seems that we both have learned something today, as well as gained enlightenment." Damien caressed Lacey's outstretched leg because he could. He hadn't stopped touching her or looking at her since they left her house. Their separation had reiterated just how deeply in love with her he was.

Lacey covered Damien's hand. "Has Dr. Randall discussed your prognosis?"

"He says with rehabilitation there is no reason that I shouldn't gain full mobility of my arm. The muscles weren't as severely damaged as they had earlier believed. The restriction of movement is due to the scarring, but physical therapy will help to eliminate that. Barring complications, he believes I'll be able to return to work maybe around the end of the year."

Lacey wasn't too keen on the idea of Damien returning to work, but the idea of trying to convince him to quit, never entered her mind. Damien loved his career choice. It was his bravery, not his carelessness which caused his injury. And because of his unselfish bravery, a man would live to see his first-born child enter the world.

"I am so happy for you."

"For us baby," Damien whispered. "We're a couple. What affects one, affects us both."

"I like the sound of that."

CHAPTER 22

The day finally came for Damien to leave the hospital. He was placed on an outpatient status and given detailed instruction on wound care by the highly trained nursing staff. Now Lacey was by his side. She too had received instruction on how to care for his healing injury. The physical therapist had taught her simple exercises to use with Damien. The dietitian had provided her with a diet plan to aide in healthy recovery. By the time Damien was wheeled out the front door to the vehicle, he was loaded down with literature on burn recovery, supplies, and instructions.

Lacey drove to the Christoval house after leaving the hospital. They were expected for a family gathering to celebrate Damien's release. The hour drive was filled with lively conversation and familiar laughs. Their time alone ended too soon for the lovers. On the Christoval street a river of family vehicles lined one side. A colorful bouquet of balloons tied to the mailbox greeted them. A welcome sign stood in the yard. Pouring out of the front door, the Christoval clan milled around waiting for Lacey to deliver her precious cargo.

"Damien, sit here." Patrice clasped her brother by the elbow as she led him over to the recliner in the den.

"Thanks."

"Uncle Damien," Gabriel interrupted from the side of the chair. "You want something to drink?" His eagerness to please was reflected in his young innocent face.

"That would be great, Gabriel."

"Hey, man, how about a plate?" Phillip asked from the kitchen.

Damien had had enough of this coddling. He was a grown man

who didn't need to be babied. He was on the verge of telling his family this very thing when Lacey's words came to mind. Releasing a breath, he sat back in the recliner and accepted the fact that his family loved him, and wanted to express that love; just like he had done for them numerous times before.

"Sounds good. Place it on the table and I'll be there in a moment."

Lacey sat quietly watching the action around her. She recognized the family's attentiveness as love, but wondered if Damien did. She could tell by his body language that all the attention was starting to bother him, but just as she thought he would blow, he surprised her by accepting the help graciously. Glancing over at him, their eyes connected and silent communication was exchanged.

The slow smile spreading across her face confirmed that he had handled the situation correctly. By accepting his family's help, he was still able to give something to them. He didn't know why he hadn't realized that before, but thanks to Lacey he did now. Rising from the recliner, he called Gabriel over to help him. The child's face lit with pride to be the one chosen to assist. Together they made their way into the kitchen where Phillip had indeed prepared Damien a plate. The others followed as Melinda called everyone to the table.

"Baby, mama cooked your favorites," Melinda informed Damien. She beamed with joy to have her oldest back home. It was a day to give thanks to the Almighty for Damien's recovery.

The adults took their seats around the table. Lacey sat to Damien's right with Phillip to her right. As she eased into her chair, Phillip turned to her.

"Lacey, I've been trying to find a moment to speak with you." His hazel eyes were direct. "I owe you an apology for the way that I treated you that day in Damien's room. I hope you realize it was nothing against you. I just wanted to calm Damien down. I hope you can forgive me," he said placing a hand on her arm.

Lacey glanced down at Phillip's hand. She recalled the pain of that day, and although at the time she had been hurt and angered by his and his parents' actions, she later understood. She placed her hand over his. "There's nothing to forgive. We were all reacting to a frightening situation and doing the best we could. Friends?" she asked.

"No. Family," he replied honestly from the heart. "You've made my brother happier than he has been in years, and during this ordeal you have been at his side every step of the way. We're all extremely lucky to have you in our lives."

Lacey's eyes shimmered with tears. So moved by his words, Lacey threw her arms around Phillip's neck. "Thank you," she whispered.

Damien caught Phillip's gaze over Lacey's shoulder and nodded in appreciation for the love he was bestowing onto Lacey.

"Phillip's words express all our feelings," Melinda added. "You have been all that a mother could ask for her son." Cheers went up around the table in a show of consensus.

Lacey openly wept at the love and acceptance she had found with the Christoval's. She felt Damien give her hand a squeeze. Turning to face him, she was surprised by the depth of love visible in his beautiful hazel eyes. It was a moment that she would always remember and treasure.

Lacey and Holly volunteered to clean up the kitchen after dinner. Holly washed while Lacey cleared the table and placed the leftovers in containers. It was the first time the two had been alone and Lacey was thankful for the opportunity. She was curious about Holly's relationship with Daniel.

"How are things going with you?" Lacey opened the conversation.

"Well, I'm counting the months until school is out." She laughed. "My goodness! I sound like one of the students instead of the teacher."

"Nothing wrong with a little vacation time," Lacey commented. "Have any plans for the summer?"

"No. I think I'll take the kids to Disney World. You know this past year has been really difficult for them."

"You're a brave soul, tackling Disney with three children alone." Pause. "You are going alone?"

Holly glanced over her left shoulder staring at Lacey. She laughed because she was wondering how long it would take her future sister-in-law to get to the real subject. Daniel.

"Actually, Mom and Dad are thinking about joining us."

"Oh."

Holly threw the dishtowel in the sink as she turned facing Lacey. "Daniel and I aren't seeing each other if that's what you wanted to know." She leaned with her back against the counter.

Lacey was wiping off the table and took a seat. "That's your doing because Daniel has made it abundantly clear that he's interested in you."

"Yes he has, and I've admitted my interest in him. But I need time to myself and with my children before getting involved in another relationship. But I promise you, like I did Daniel, that I do plan on living life. I just hope he's there and interested when I get myself together." Holly explained while Lacey nodded in understanding.

"You know, Lacey, I still can't believe you two were never involved. Friend or not, Daniel is one fine man," Holly said saucily.

This wasn't the first time Lacey had heard this. She laughed as she always did. "I grew up with Daniel. I knew the man when he wore braces." Lacey smiled. "I know he's handsome, but I see him through the eyes of a sister. It was his shoulder I cried on through the years, although," she paused to laugh. "When we were children, I was taller. If any kids in the neighborhood tried to pick a fight with Daniel they knew that they had to fight me as well. Sometimes Daniel would be trying to talk his way out of a fight and I would rush in from nowhere throwing punches." She laughed from the memory. "Then he and I would wind up in a huge argument because I defended him. But he was all I had and I wasn't about to allow the other kids to mess with him."

Holly laughed imagining the very lady-like Lacey throwing punches. "Now he defends you."

"Yes, he does. Our roles have reversed, but the love between us hasn't changed. That's the type of man Daniel is. Once he gives his love, it's for life."

Message received, Holly thought, as she glanced at Lacey. "It's not the right time for us."

"I hear you, but I have to tell you that Daniel won't simply disappear. He'll give you time to heal, time to miss him, and then when you least expect it, he'll launch a full scale assault."

"And you've seen him use this tactic on other women?" Holly asked a little let down. She returned to the dishes not wanting Lacey to see her disappointment.

But she had and rose from the chair to join Holly at the sink. Shoulder to shoulder she answered. "Only one woman and I'll allow Daniel to tell you about it. But there's something you should know, Holly. Despite Daniel's good looks, he doesn't chase women. He believes in love and commitment. And he is the most patient man I know. When he wants something or someone, all his energy goes into accomplishing that goal no matter how long it takes, and as of right now, it's you that he wants."

Holly's heart swelled with excitement. She returned to the dishes praying that he would wait just a little while longer for her.

They rejoined the rest of the family in the den. Lacey found Damien nodding off in the recliner. It had been a long day for him and he needed his rest. She gathered their things; then woke him up. At the door there were hugs and kisses. Eventually she and Damien were able to make their getaway.

Damien stood in the entryway of his home reacquainting himself.

It seemed like ages since he had walked out this very door and had his whole world turned upside down. Moving into the living room, he could tell that someone had been keeping it clean. There wasn't a speck of dust anywhere. And the newspaper that he had left on the coffee table that morning was gone. The one or two houseplants that he owned were healthy and growing. Assaulted by a rush of emotion, he took a seat on the sofa absorbing it all.

Lacey carried Damien's luggage to his bedroom. She had moved some of her things over to his house yesterday. It had been decided that she would stay at his home while he continued to recover. His home was large and housed a home gym which would be important in his recovery process. She returned to the living room to find Damien right where she had left him. From his expression she could tell that his thoughts were miles away.

"Hey, is everything all right?" she asked drawing his attention. She squatted down in front of him. Her eyes searched his.

Damien knew that Lacey was concerned. Her beautiful sherry brown eyes were unable to hide her emotions. "I'm remembering the last morning I was here. I phoned you that morning to say that I loved you." He reached out caressing her face.

"I remember. It was the day I found my wedding dress. I was at the counter when the news of the fire came on the television in the shop." Her voice broke as the pain of that day came racing back. "I was so frightened for you. Then our cell phones started ringing all at once and I knew..." The dam broke on her emotions. All the ups and downs had taken their toll. The tears flowed as she expressed her fears. She crawled into Damien's lap when he pulled her up with his good arm and folded her against his chest while she cried. His soothing words only made her cry harder. She had been so afraid that she would lose him and never share a moment like this again.

Tears tracked down Damien's face as he held Lacey. He also had been filled with fear, but with Lacey's bountiful strength, the love of his

223

family, and the aid of his therapist, he had made it through. He raised Lacey's chin bringing her mouth to his. He kissed her reverently; a simple pressing of the lips, until his control snapped, and the initial fear of dying in that blazing warehouse surged to life. Burying his hand in Lacey's hair, he pulled her closer as his lips parted hers and he took possession of her mouth. His tongue relearned the shape and taste of her. She was sweet in his arms and he had to have more.

"I need to touch you, baby," he rasped out while fighting with the buttons on her silk blouse.

"I'll do it," Lacey whispered.

"No. I can do this." And with determination and the use of both his hands, Damien managed to free each button. He swept the soft fabric off her arms. Sitting back, his deprived eyes took their fill of Lacey's beautiful body. He wanted her. He reached around unsnapping Lacey's bra. Her breasts fell forward in invitation.

"God, you are so beautiful," he managed to say before claiming a dark nipple with his lips. He teased the peak with his tongue, loving the feel of it in his mouth; the taste of it on his tongue.

Lacey cried out with passion as Damien suckled her. It had been so very long since they had made love and the need between them was almost desperate. Lacey held Damien's head against her while his mouth tortured each breast. Then all of sudden it wasn't enough for either of them. Damien tore his mouth away and began removing her pants.

"Stand up," he ordered.

Lacey did as requested and watched through a haze of passion as her love stripped her bare before him. When she was completely nude, Damien sat for several minutes simply looking at her.

She was gorgeous. Her willowy frame possessed just the right curves to make a man's mouth water with desire. And those long beautiful legs of hers inspired erotic thoughts that he couldn't wait to put into action.

"Come here, baby."

Lacey raised her hands to her hips looking at Damien. Liking the raw sexual hunger in his hazel eyes, she turned and walked out of the living room. In the entryway, she glanced over her shoulder and said, "Come get it if you want it." She flashed a taunting smile before giving Damien a good view of what was waiting for him; then disappeared down the hallway.

"You'll pay for that, Lace," Damien groaned with agony. The sexual display and taunt had him swelling with need and hard as steel. He rose from the sofa to follow.

"I'm counting on it," her voice purred from down the hall. She laughed when she heard Damien come up behind her. He palmed her backside as he rushed her down the hall and into the bedroom.

Lacey broke away and turned to face him. She cradled his face between her hands as she kissed him hotly. The dance of her tongue heightened the desire. She freed his belt buckle and lowered the zipper on his pants. She placed her hand into the opening and caressed the hardened length of him.

Damien's legs nearly buckled as her hand covered him. His eyes closed of their own volition. The heat from her hand and the stimulating friction made him painfully hard.

"I need to be inside of you," Damien hissed as the throbbing in his groin increased.

"Well, let's get you undressed." Lacey reached for his shirt and began freeing the buttons.

"Don't!" Damien shouted and backed away. The passion in his eyes extinguished. In its place was haunting fear.

Fully aware of what was happening, Lacey refused to back off, or allow Damien to withdraw from her. She softened her voice as she leaned her nude body into him. "Sweetheart, this is me. You never have to hide yourself from me." She undid a button. "I love you and want to make love with you. Don't you want that?" Two more buttons were released.

"Yes, damn it. I want you so bad I hurt," Damien managed to say over the rising fear.

"Touch me," Lacey ordered. She was pleased when Damien complied by caressing her left breast with his right hand. But needing to convince him that he had nothing to fear by undressing in front of her, Lacey gingerly brought his pressure bandaged hand to her other breast. "You have two hands and I have two breasts. You wouldn't want the other one to feel neglected now would you?" The last button came free.

Damien was surprised when Lacey covered her breast with his bandaged hand. But how would she react when she removed his shirt and saw the less severe scars at the top of his arm and shoulder. He held his breath as she gently peeled away his shirt. She was looking at him, but he couldn't face her. He turned away not wanting to see pity or disgust in the eyes that only a moment ago held passion.

Lacey knew that Damien waited for her reaction. She decided the worst thing that she could do was to behave with indifference. As the shiny discolored skin came into view, she asked whether they were painful. She was pleased when he answered no.

"Those are minor and have healed." Damien inhaled deeply with emotion as he felt Lacey lips against his damaged flesh. She placed loving kisses on each scar. The knowledge that she wasn't afraid to touch him overwhelmed him. Tears blinded his vision.

"Is there a reason we shouldn't make love?" she asked turning his face back to her.

There was no pity or disgust visible in her eyes. None. Only a woman's passion for the man she loved. My arm is still tender so we might have to alter position," Damien informed her with a shy smile.

With his fear unfounded, he was able to enjoy the moment. His hazel eyes had filled with sexual desire and playfulness.

Lacey flashed him a wicked smile. "In that case let me take the lead."

"Anything you want, sweetheart." Damien kissed the side of Lacey's head as she concentrated on removing his slacks. Bending at the waist, she freed him of the constricting fabric, then took his hand and led him to the bed. Damien eased down, then reached for her. He brought her warm scented body into him as he placed kisses from her breasts to her abdomen. His hands caressed the soft flesh of her buttocks. His tongue dipped into her navel while he savored the feel of her hands caressing his back.

"I've missed you," Lacey whispered as she nibbled on his earlobe.

"Not half as much as I've missed you," Damien responded as he caressed the womanly flesh between her thighs.

Lacey climbed on the bed straddling him. She kissed his lips while caressing her body against him. Her lips trailed lower down his neck, then on to his chest, before retaking his lips. A hand slipped to his lap and finding him hard and ready, she eased down on to him, joining their bodies. For a moment neither moved.

Damien clutched Lacey to him as he savored the feel of her enveloping him. Then she began to move and the pleasure was great. Her nails raked across his chest and circled his nipples. Leaning forward he managed to claim one of her own jutting nipples. Her sigh of pleasure was like music to his ears. It wasn't long before they were both racing toward completion and when release came, they were both damp with perspiration and shaken to the depth of their souls. Tonight they had surpassed being lovers and had become soul mates. In this world and the next they would recognize and know each other. Their love was stronger than any challenge placed before them and eternally lasting.

EPILOGUE

Lacey ran a hand over her wedding gown admiring its beauty. The white creation of silk and pearls was a treasure she would always hold dear. She turned in Damien's arms loving him more this day than ever before, because only he had made her dream come true. She was now his wife and as of this morning, the mother of his children. They had been blessed to adopt a set of twins; a boy and girl who now carried their names. They had decided to move into Damien's much larger home. One of the empty bedrooms had been transformed by Damien and Phillip into a beautiful nursery.

"I hope one day Nicolette will want to wear this dress," Lacey said to her husband of two years. "I want to build traditions to be passed on to our children and their children later."

"Our children," Damien repeated. "That's music to my ears."

Lacey smiled, knowing exactly how he felt. It had taken years for their paths to cross and the reality of this moment to be, but they were here, in the nursery with their children. Two identical white cribs were placed to the right of the closet where Lacey's dress hung. She had removed everything from the closet and placed the children's things in it, but the wedding dress remained. She wanted to be able to share it with her daughter as she grew up.

Nicolas was awake and cooing playfully for attention. Damien went to the crib and removed his son. Holding the warm bundle that smelled of baby powder and oil against him, he eased down into the nearby rocking chair. His hand caressed the silky black curls covering his son's head. The arm which held him possessed scars that were no longer of concern. Lacey had shown him that it was he she loved and the physical scars didn't change that love.

"You're going to spoil him," Lacey teased as she sat on the floor beside him.

He caressed her cheek. "I plan on spoiling all of you, sweetheart. It took way too long to bring all of you into my life and I think I deserve to do a little spoiling."

"We both have been through a great deal and you won't get any complaints from me." She smiled up at him with pride.

After months of healing and rehabilitation after the fire, Damien had regained full use of his arm and the once blistering scars had smoothed to less noticeable ones. He had returned to the department in the capacity of fire investigator. In his off-duty time, he had received training to be a counselor to other fire victims. It was a program he believed in wholeheartedly after being a recipient of burn counseling.

Lacey, so impressed by the work that Damien was doing, decided to receive training herself to aid spouses and loved ones of fire victims. Her latest novel depicted the life of a young man injured in a blaze and the woman who loved him. She captured the fear and pain that she and Damien had lived through on the pages. It was receiving rave reviews.

The doorbell announced the arrival of their families. Rising from the floor, Lacey scooped her sleeping daughter up into her arms and followed Damien out of the nursery to the front door. They passed the large mirror in the entryway and were halted by the image reflecting back. There in the mirror, despite the absence of bloodlines, stood a family—father, mother, son, and daughter. Side by side, Damien and Lacey opened the door to their families and proudly introduced them to theirs.

AUTHOR BIOGRAPHY

Giselle Carmichael resides on the beautiful Mississippi Gulf Coast. An Alabama native, she is a graduate of the University of Alabama at Birmingham. Daughter and wife of career airmen, she has traveled extensively throughout the United States and Europe. Her works include *Magnolia Sunset* (2002), *Life Goes On*, a novella (2002), and *I'll Be Your Shelter* (2003) which received Shades of Romance Reader's Choice Award for Best Genesis Press Book of The Year. In March of 2004, *Forever Mine*, a short story was published in Arabella Magazine's Premier Issue.

Visit Giselle at **www.gisellecarmichael.com**.

EXCERPT FROM

FALLING

BY

NATALIE DUNBAR

Publication Date January 2005

PROLOGUE

The beautiful, famous, and wealthy had filled the candle-lit chapel and anxiously awaited the final moments. Imani Celeste, more beautiful than ever, graced the altar in an antique white Cara Sutton gown. A sheer veil streamed out from the silk and lace-accented gold circlet that adorned her long black hair. Her dark, exotic eyes sparkled, her lush lips smiled. At her side in a black tuxedo and antique white shirt with black accents, Perry Bonds, Detroit Pistons basketball star, gazed at his bride with love and adoration.

DeAndra sat midway back in the church, on the bride's side with Judge Damon Kessler. She stole a glance at the man who had loved and lost Imani. His fingers grasped the edge of the pew as if his life depended on it. Knowing that she could never stand to see Damon marry another woman, she understood how he felt. She loved Damon. Had loved him since she was a fifteen-year-old with everything but school on her mind. He'd been a young, very handsome and idealistic lawyer, who'd forced her to participate in her own defense in court for truancy and delinquency. He'd inspired her in the process. What a road they'd traveled.

Focusing on the happy couple, she leaned forward to hear them exchange their vows. It was done. They kissed passionately for several moments, then released each other to face the crowd.

When everyone stood to throw rice and blow bubbles as the couple started down the aisle, DeAndra heard Damon cough, and turned in time to see him swipe at his eyes with a thumb and forefinger.

She stared. Was he was actually crying? She couldn't tell for sure, but even the thought of him crying for Imani hurt her heart. She stiffened, a burning pain in her chest. Then she moved closer and slid her hand in his, silently reminding him that she was with him. When he didn't respond, she fought the sharp sting of rejection.

Outside the church, she stood in the line with him and watched him hug Imani, who told him how glad she was to see him. Damon wished her every happiness, then moved on to shake hands with Perry. When DeAndra extended a hand to Imani, she was enfolded in a hug. "Please take care of him," Imani whispered.

"If he lets me," DeAndra mumbled, aware that it was going to be hard.

"He does love you," Imani whispered back.

DeAndra moved on to congratulate Perry, suddenly aware of how hard it is to hate someone who nudges you towards what you want most and tells you what you want to hear.

Afterward, Damon was silent as he drove her home. Feeling a little low herself, DeAndra didn't push it.

"I'm not up to the reception, so I'm going to skip it," Damon told her as he stood at her front door.

"We could do something else," she suggested, not surprised when he declined, and throwing everything she had into being understanding,

"I just want to go home," he said.

DeAndra drew him into her arms and kissed him. "Take care of yourself."

When he hadn't so much as called two weeks later, DeAndra got her hair done, showered and donned a sexy red dress that clung to every perfumed curve. Then she assembled a care package of his favorite foods: 1993 Dom Perignon Champagne, succulent red strawberries dipped in gourmet chocolate, almonds and cashews, lobster tails and petite filet mignon, and Caesar salad. She knew she'd splurged, but Damon was worth it.

She stood on the porch a good ten minutes before he answered the bell. Usually impeccably dressed, Damon looked battered and depressed in a faded pair of navy blue sweats.

"Come in, DeAndra, we need to talk."

"I brought something for us to eat," she said brightly, letting him take the basket into the kitchen. She followed, noting the dusty tables, and the dirty dishes piled into the sink. .

"I'm not very hungry." His eyes were flat and dull.

In the act of unloading the basket onto his kitchen counter, she stared at him, anger filling her up. Here he was wasting away because Imani hadn't had the good sense to realize that he was the better man. Not that she was sorry. She knew that she was the one he really needed, not Imani. If only he would give her a fourth of the love he'd lavished on the woman who was now Mrs. Perry Bonds. "Damon, she's married now."

His eyes turned towards her, stark and haunted. "Yes, I was there. I had to see it to believe it," he said in a harsh voice. "Now…now I need time to accept that and move on with my life."

DeAndra set the Dom Perignon on the counter, her heart pumping so hard that she struggled to catch her breath. "What are you trying to say?"

He motioned her to a seat beside him at the great room counter. "I'm trying to say that I've never made a secret of my feelings for Imani, and with everything that's happened, I've failed to clarify my feelings for you."

Beside him, her throat was dry as sawdust. She couldn't say a word.

Damon took her hand. "You're a lovely, intelligent, and very giving person, DeAndra, and I care for you very much. I'm not proud of the way I've behaved with you while I was going through my off again, on again engagement."

Standing, she sought to stop the flow of his words. "We *made love*, Damon."

He shook his head. "No. I used you and I'm ashamed. You deserve so much more."

Unadulterated pain seared her heart. Her eyelids stung as she fought tears. She was not going to cry. "Let me be the judge of what I deserve."

He grabbed her hand in frustration. "You don't understand. Things will never be the same. I've never felt so deeply and completely for anyone. I'm a mess. I don't have any more love to give, so you can't hang around hoping I'll grow to love you!"

DeAndra snatched her hand away and her voice rose in cutting fury. "You had to ruin everything, didn't you? I loved you. Do you hear me? I still love you and nothing's going to change that, but you don't have to worry about poor little DeAndra hanging around hoping you'll grow to love her. I'm done! I won't bother you again!"

Running to the other side of the counter, she grabbed her purse and jacket, and bolted from the house.

"DeAndra! DeAndra!" Damon called after her, his voice filled with regret.

She made it all the way to the car before a flood of tears blinded her. Feeling for the lock with shaking fingers, she fitted her key and locked the door. Inside, she blubbered like a baby and mopped vainly at the tears with a Kleenex.

Turning at the sight of movement, she saw that he was coming down the steps. Somehow she managed to start the car and drive away.

LACE

2004 Publication Schedule

January	Cautious Heart Cheris F. Hodges $8.95 1-58571-106-3	Bodyguard Andrea Jackson $8.95 1-58571-114-4
February	Wedding Gown Dyanne Davis $8.95 1-58571-120-9	Erotic Anthology Simone Harlow & Caroline Stone $14.95 1-58571-113-6
March	Crossing Paths, Tempting Memories Dorothy Elizabeth Love $9.95 1-58571-116-0	Office Policy A.C. Arthur $9.95 1-58571-110-8
April-July	No Titles	
August	More Than a Bargain Ann Clay $9.95 1-58571-137-3	Code Name: Diva J. M. Jeffries $9.95 1-58571-144-6
September	Vows of Passion Bella McFarland $9.95 1-58571-118-7 Stories to Excite You Anna Forrest & Ken Divine $14.95 1-58571-103-9	Time Is of the Essence Angie Daniels $9.95 1-58571-132-2
October	Hard to Love Kimberley White $9.95 1-58571-128-4	A Happy Life Charlotte Harris $9.95 1-58571-133-0
November	Caught Up in the Rapture Lisa G. Riley $9.95 1-58571-127-6	Lace Giselle Carmichael $9.95 1-58571-134-9

After February the size of the titles will increase to 5 3/16 x 8 1/2, as will the price to $9.95.

2005 Publication Schedule

January

Echoes of Yesterday	A Love of Her Own	Higher Ground
Beverly Clark	Cheris F. Hodges	Leah Latimer
$9.95	$9.95	$19.95
1-58571-131-4	1-58571-136-5	1-58571-157-8

February

Timeless Devotion	I'll Paint the Sun	Peace Be Still
Bella McFarland	Al Garotto	Colette Haywood
$9.95	$9.95	$12.95
1-58571-148-9	1-58571-165-9	1-58571-129-2

March

Intentional Mistakes	Conquering Dr. Wexler's Heart	Song in the Park
Michele Sudler	Kimberley White	Martin Brant
$9.95	$9.95	$15.95
1-58571-152-7	1-58571-126-8	1-58571-125-X

April

The Color Line	Unconditional	Last Train to Memphis
Lizette Carter	A.C. Arthur	Elsa Cook
$9.95	$9.95	$12.95
1-58571-163-2	1-58571-142-X	1-58571-146-2

May

Angel's Paradise	Suddenly You	Matters of Life and Death
Janice Angelique	Crystal Hubbard	Lesego Malepe, Ph.D.
$9.95	$9.95	$15.95
1-58571-107-1		1-58571-124-1

June

Pleasures All Mine	Wild Ravens	Class Reunion
Belinda O. Steward	Altonya Washington	Irma Jenkins/John Brown
$9.95	$9.95	$12.95
1-58571-112-8	1-58571-164-0	1-58571-123-3

July

Falling	Misconceptions	Life Is Never As It Seems
Natalie Dunbar	Pamela Leigh Starr	June Michael
$9.95	$9.95	$12.95
1-58571-121-7	1-58571-117-9	1-58571-153-5

August

Beyond the Rapture	Taken By You	Rough on Rats and Tough on Cats
Beverly Clark	Dorothy Elizabeth Love	Chris Parker
$9.95	$9.95	$12.95
1-58571-131-4	1-58571-162-4	1-58571-154-3

2005 Publication Schedule (continued)

September

A Will to Love
Angie Daniels
$9.95
1-58571-141-1

Blood Lust
J.M. Jeffries
$9.95
1-58571-138-1

Soul Eyes
Wayne L. Wilson
$12.95
1-58571-147-0

October

Blaze
Barbara Keaton
$9.95

Untitled
Kimberley White
$9.95
1-58571-159-4

Red Polka Dot in a World
  of Plaid
Varian Johnson
$12.95
1-58571-140-3

November

Hand in Glove
Andrea Jackson
$9.95
1-58571-166-7

Untitled
A.C. Arthur
$9.95

Across
Carol Payne
$12.95
1-58571-149-7

December

Bound for Mt. Zion
Chris Parker
$12.95
1-58571-155-1

Other Genesis Press, Inc. Titles

Acquisitions	Kimberley White	$8.95
A Dangerous Deception	J.M. Jeffries	$8.95
A Dangerous Love	J.M. Jeffries	$8.95
A Dangerous Obsession	J.M. Jeffries	$8.95
After the Vows (Summer Anthology)	Leslie Esdaile T.T. Henderson Jacqueline Thomas	$10.95
Again My Love	Kayla Perrin	$10.95
Against the Wind	Gwynne Forster	$8.95
A Lark on the Wing	Phyliss Hamilton	$8.95
A Lighter Shade of Brown	Vicki Andrews	$8.95
All I Ask	Barbara Keaton	$8.95
A Love to Cherish	Beverly Clark	$8.95
Ambrosia	T.T. Henderson	$8.95
And Then Came You	Dorothy Elizabeth Love	$8.95
Angel's Paradise	Janice Angelique	$8.95
A Risk of Rain	Dar Tomlinson	$8.95
At Last	Lisa G. Riley	$8.95
Best of Friends	Natalie Dunbar	$8.95
Bound by Love	Beverly Clark	$8.95
Breeze	Robin Hampton Allen	$10.95
Brown Sugar Diaries & Other Sexy Tales	Delores Bundy & Cole Riley	$10.95
By Design	Barbara Keaton	$8.95
Cajun Heat	Charlene Berry	$8.95
Careless Whispers	Rochelle Alers	$8.95
Caught in a Trap	Andre Michelle	$8.95
Chances	Pamela Leigh Starr	$8.95
Dark Embrace	Crystal Wilson Harris	$8.95
Dark Storm Rising	Chinelu Moore	$10.95
Designer Passion	Dar Tomlinson	$8.95
Ebony Butterfly II	Delilah Dawson	$14.95
Erotic Anthology	Assorted	$8.95
Eve's Prescription	Edwina Martin Arnold	$8.95
Everlastin' Love	Gay G. Gunn	$8.95

Fate	Pamela Leigh Starr	$8.95
Forbidden Quest	Dar Tomlinson	$10.95
Fragment in the Sand	Annetta P. Lee	$8.95
From the Ashes	Kathleen Suzanne	$8.95
	Jeanne Sumerix	
Gentle Yearning	Rochelle Alers	$10.95
Glory of Love	Sinclair LeBeau	$10.95
Hart & Soul	Angie Daniels	$8.95
Heartbeat	Stephanie Bedwell-Grime	$8.95
I'll Be Your Shelter	Giselle Carmichael	$8.95
Illusions	Pamela Leigh Starr	$8.95
Indiscretions	Donna Hill	$8.95
Interlude	Donna Hill	$8.95
Intimate Intentions	Angie Daniels	$8.95
Just an Affair	Eugenia O'Neal	$8.95
Kiss or Keep	Debra Phillips	$8.95
Love Always	Mildred E. Riley	$10.95
Love Unveiled	Gloria Greene	$10.95
Love's Deception	Charlene Berry	$10.95
Mae's Promise	Melody Walcott	$8.95
Meant to Be	Jeanne Sumerix	$8.95
Midnight Clear	Leslie Esdaile	$10.95
(Anthology)	Gwynne Forster	
	Carmen Green	
	Monica Jackson	
Midnight Magic	Gwynne Forster	$8.95
Midnight Peril	Vicki Andrews	$10.95
My Buffalo Soldier	Barbara B. K. Reeves	$8.95
Naked Soul	Gwynne Forster	$8.95
No Regrets	Mildred E. Riley	$8.95
Nowhere to Run	Gay G. Gunn	$10.95
Object of His Desire	A. C. Arthur	$8.95
One Day at a Time	Bella McFarland	$8.95
Passion	T.T. Henderson	$10.95
Past Promises	Jahmel West	$8.95
Path of Fire	T.T. Henderson	$8.95
Picture Perfect	Reon Carter	$8.95

Pride & Joi	Gay G. Gunn	$8.95
Quiet Storm	Donna Hill	$8.95
Reckless Surrender	Rochelle Alers	$8.95
Rendezvous with Fate	Jeanne Sumerix	$8.95
Revelations	Cheris F. Hodges	$8.95
Rivers of the Soul	Leslie Esdaile	$8.95
Rooms of the Heart	Donna Hill	$8.95
Shades of Brown	Denise Becker	$8.95
Shades of Desire	Monica White	$8.95
Sin	Crystal Rhodes	$8.95
So Amazing	Sinclair LeBeau	$8.95
Somebody's Someone	Sinclair LeBeau	$8.95
Someone to Love	Alicia Wiggins	$8.95
Soul to Soul	Donna Hill	$8.95
Still Waters Run Deep	Leslie Esdaile	$8.95
Subtle Secrets	Wanda Y. Thomas	$8.95
Sweet Tomorrows	Kimberly White	$8.95
The Color of Trouble	Dyanne Davis	$8.95
The Price of Love	Sinclair LeBeau	$8.95
The Reluctant Captive	Joyce Jackson	$8.95
The Missing Link	Charlyne Dickerson	$8.95
Three Wishes	Seressia Glass	$8.95
Tomorrow's Promise	Leslie Esdaile	$8.95
Truly Inseperable	Wanda Y. Thomas	$8.95
Twist of Fate	Beverly Clark	$8.95
Unbreak My Heart	Dar Tomlinson	$8.95
Unconditional Love	Alicia Wiggins	$8.95
When Dreams A Float	Dorothy Elizabeth Love	$8.95
Whispers in the Night	Dorothy Elizabeth Love	$8.95
Whispers in the Sand	LaFlorya Gauthier	$10.95
Yesterday is Gone	Beverly Clark	$8.95
Yesterday's Dreams, Tomorrow's Promises	Reon Laudat	$8.95
Your Precious Love	Sinclair LeBeau	$8.95

RULES & REGULATIONS

1. **ELIGIBILITY:** *Sweepstakes open only to legal U.S. residents, who are 21 years of age or older and have Internet access as of 12/17/04.* Void in CA and where prohibited by law. Employees of Genesis Press Inc. USA, and its agencies, parents, subsidiaries, affiliates, vendors, wholesalers or retailers, or members of their immediate families or households are not eligible to participate. Federal, state and local laws and regulations apply. Grand Prize Winner is required to complete and return an Affidavit of Eligibility/Publicity Release and a Travel Release. Travel companion must be 21 years of age or older and must sign a Travel Release/Publicity Release. Affidavit of Eligibility/Publicity Release and Travel Releases must be returned within 2 days of notification or the Grand Prize will be forfeited and an alternate winner will be randomly selected. Must be 18 years old or older.

2. **DRAWINGS:** *Prize Winner* will be selected in a random drawing on or about 1/10/05 from among all valid entries received. Grand Prize winner will be contacted by telephone on or about 1/10/05 at the daytime number listed. If, after two (2) attempts, contact has not been made, prize will be forfeited and an alternate winner will be randomly selected.Winner will be randomly selected before a panel witnesses and judge.

3. **NO PURCHASE NECESSARY. YOU MUST BE 21 YEARS OF AGE OR OLDER, A LEGAL RESIDENT OF THE CONTINENTAL UNITED STATES, AND HAVE INTERNET ACCESS AS OF 12/17/04, TO ENTER. VOID IN CALIFORNIA AND WHERE PROHIBITED.**
   To enter the Tempting Memories Sweepstakes, send above information to by postmark date 12/17/04 to P.O. Box 782, Columbus, MS 39701-0782 beginning at 12:01:01 am ET on 12/10/05 log on to www.genesis-press.com and complete an Official Entry Form. Entries must be received by 11:59:59 pm ET on 12/17/04. Proof of entry submission does not equate to proof of receipt. Limit one entry per person, per IP address per 24-hour period. All other mailed entries will be matched by name and address. If multiple entries are received, only the first entry will be entered into the Sweepstakes and all other entries will be disregarded. In case of a dispute over winner's identity, entry will be deemed to have been submitted by the IP address owner (who must meet eligibility requirements). Sponsor not responsible for entry submissions received after deadline, incomplete information, incomplete transmission defaults, computer server failure and/or delayed, garbled or corrupted data. All entries become the exclusive property of the Sponsor and will not be returned or acknowledged. Any attempts by an individual to access the site via a bot script or other brute-force attack will result in that IP address becoming ineligible. Sponsor reserves the right to suspend or terminate this Sweepstakes without notice if, in Sponsor's sole discretion, the Sweepstakes becomes infected or otherwise corrupted. By entering this Sweepstakes, entrants agree to be bound by these Official Rules and the decisions of the judges which shall be final, binding and conclusive on all matters relating to this Sweepstakes. Sweepstakes starts at 12:01:01 am ET on 1/10/05 and ends at 11:59:59 pm ET on 1/10/05.

4. Winner will be notified by certified mail.

5. Prize is non-transferable, nor redeemable for cash.

6. Once travel dates are selected by winner, they can not be modified. Any changes will forfeit the prize.

7. If winner does not respond within 30 days, prize will be forfeited.

8. One (1) Winner will receive a trip for two (2) adults to the. Trip includes round-trip coach airfare for Winner and Guest to Barbados from the major airport nearest the Winner's residence 4-days/3-night hotel stay (standard room, double occupancy accommodations/hotel to be selected by Sponsor. Prizes provided by Barbados Tourism Authority.

9. **RELEASE OF LIABILITY & PUBLICITY:** Prizewinner consents to the use of his/her name, photograph or likeness for publicity or advertising purposes without further compensation where permitted by law. All entrants release Genesis Press USA, and each of its parents, affiliates, subsidiaries, officers, directors, shareholders, agents, employees and all others associated with the development and execution of this Sweepstakes from any and all liability with respect to, or in any way arising from, this Sweepstakes and/or acceptance or use of the prize, including liability for property damage or personal injury, damages, death or monetary loss.

10. **Genesis Press Inc.,** nor any of its subsidiaries or partners are will be held liable from any and all damages, accidents injuries, negligent actions, breach etc., that might incurred by WINNER during the acceptance of the prize pursuant to the services performed and agreed to herein.

Order Form

Mail to: Genesis Press, Inc.

P.O. Box 101
Columbus, MS 39703

Name _____

Address _____

City/State _____ Zip _____

Telephone _____

Ship to (if different from above)

Name _____

Address _____

City/State _____ Zip _____

Telephone _____

Credit Card Information

Credit Card # _____ ☐ Visa ☐ Mastercard

Expiration Date (mm/yy) _____ ☐ AmEx ☐ Discover

Qty.	Author	Title	Price	Total

Use this order

form, or call

1-888-INDIGO-1

Total for books	_____
Shipping and handling:	
$5 first two books,	
$1 each additional book	_____
Total S & H	_____
Total amount enclosed	_____

Mississippi residents add 7% sales tax

Visit www.genesis-press.com for latest releases and excerpts.